LOVE ALWAYS TRUSTS

LUISA CISTERNA

Cover Design: Benjamin Cesar

Also from the author:

Loves Always Protects

See You Next Christmas

CONTENTS

CHAPTER ONE

The line between omission and lying blurred until Anna could no longer tell the difference. Each anxious breath seemed to erase it a little more.

She dragged a comb through her honey-blonde hair, cut neatly above her shoulders, her fingers trembling just enough to snag a strand. Adjusting the rearview mirror, she studied the reflection of a woman who looked composed: chin firm, gaze steady, every detail in place. To anyone walking by, she might have seemed confident, capable, ready to seize the next opportunity.

But Anna Weber knew better. Beneath the calm surface, her heart thudded in dread. She was about to betray the very honesty she prided herself on—not with a blatant lie, but with a silence heavy enough to tip the scales of truth. And that silence might decide whether she'd walk into Grace Harbor Clinic as their new nurse or drive away in shame.

Trying to steady the tremor running through her, Anna tossed her hairbrush into the leather purse and reached for the lipstick. She outlined her full lips with a soft pink and took a deep breath. Before stepping out of the car, she cleaned her tortoiseshell glasses and slid them back onto her face, where a practiced smile waited.

She deserved a "fraud" sticker on her forehead. But what wouldn't a woman do for love? Or out of desperation?

Anna stepped out of the car, shut the door, and crossed the small parking lot beside the single-story white building with a carved wooden sign that read *Grace Harbor Clinic*. Her black heels clicked against the pavement as she passed the empty space marked *Reserved for Dr. Kevin Miller*. Hopefully, the doctor hadn't been called away on an emergency somewhere in town, leaving her waiting for nothing.

After all, she'd driven the thirty kilometers from Providence just for this interview—the one that could change her life. She'd spoken with Dr. Miller twice on the phone after exchanging emails about her experience as a nurse. And experience she had plenty of. If not for the secret she carried—one that could crush her chance at this job—Anna would have felt certain the position was hers.

She liked Dr. Miller's calm, thoughtful manner and imagined he ran his clinic the same way. Grace Harbor was a small town that relied heavily on the hospital in Providence, so the clinic's pace must have been much gentler than what she'd known in the bustling hospital where she'd worked for three years.

If it hadn't been for the terrible accident that took her husband's life and left her with a bittersweet inheritance, she never would have resigned. And if she had known, just days before signing her resignation papers, what her husband had left behind, she would have clung to that job like a shipwreck survivor clings to a life preserver.

But it was too late for that.

Her shapely, long legs, revealed just above the knee by a fitted skirt, carried her up the three steps to the old white clapboard house with flower boxes beneath the windows. She reached for the door handle, but it swung open before she could touch it.

A large man barreled past her, nearly knocking her aside without a word of apology. Maybe he'd just received bad news, she considered. After years in nursing, Anna was used to stress and to people who didn't handle it well.

Inside the clinic's reception area, Anna straightened her purse strap and buttoned her dark blazer. Her eyes were drawn to the bright smile of a young receptionist behind the counter, a petite woman with a turned-up nose and a head of short, bouncy curls that made her look like a cartoon character, maybe Betty Boop.

Across from the counter, a frazzled mother tried to fill out a form while balancing a fussy, runny-nosed baby on her hip. The child smeared green mucus from one chubby cheek to the other with a tiny arm.

"Can I help you?" the receptionist asked cheerfully. "Are you here for an appointment with Dr. Miller?"

Anna glanced toward the row of waiting chairs. Three men and two women sat reading old magazines—or pretending to. A professional habit made her wonder what might have brought each of them there.

Stepping forward, she handed a card to the young woman whose name tag read Erica.

"I'm Anna Weber. I have an interview with Dr. Kevin Miller."

Erica twirled a curl around her finger. "So glad to meet you. Dr. Miller had to step out for an emergency, but he should be back in—" she glanced at the wall clock—"about twenty minutes."

Twenty minutes. Better than no interview at all. "I'll wait."

Just then the baby began to cough. Erica handed a box of tissues to the mother, who looked pale with worry.

"My son's fever is really high," the woman said. "What should I do?"

Anna looked at Erica, who hesitated, clearly unsure. The baby's cries grew louder, punctuated by coughing fits. Anna's hands itched to help. She was trained, capable—*called*—to care for people in need. But she wasn't part of this clinic. Not yet. She couldn't risk seeming like a pushy outsider before even being hired.

The young mother paced the floor, rocking her child as the others buried themselves in their magazines again. The faint rustle of pages filled the room, the nervous soundtrack of any waiting room.

Anna's own waiting was of another kind. Not for a diagnosis, but for a decision that could determine her future. Just as a test result once had, weeks before. A job interview or a lab report, both could change a life.

She sat with her back straight, eyes fixed on the clock. The hands crept forward. The baby's cries grew sharper. Fifteen more minutes, if Dr. Miller was punctual.

One of the men stood up and left without a word, ignoring Erica's plea for him to stay. The phone rang. As Erica answered it, the baby vomited, splattering the floor and his mother's arm. Still holding the phone, Erica grabbed another box of tissues and gestured helplessly.

That was enough for Anna. She dropped her purse on the chair, hurried to the counter, and grabbed a handful of tissues. Kneeling, she began wiping the yellowish mess as the embarrassed mother apologized.

"It's all right," Anna said gently, glancing up at her. "Let me take care of this." Her mouth filled with thick saliva, the kind that came with nausea, but she forced a steady breath.

The phone rang again. Another patient left, slamming the door behind them. If this was a typical day at Grace Harbor Clinic, peace and quiet might be a lost dream.

Then the door opened. From her position on the floor, Anna saw a man stride in; tall, broad-shouldered, wearing a light blue shirt and black slacks. He moved with the crisp confidence of someone in charge.

"Erica, please prepare exam room two for Lucia and Pedro," he said.

"Thank you, Doctor," the young mother replied.

The man turned and paused when he saw Anna crouched with tissues in her hands. The sour smell of baby vomit filled the air.

"Anna Weber?" he asked.

"That's me."

He started to offer his hand, then thought better of it. Anna could feel the dampness of the tissues seeping into her palms. She needed to spit, or she might gag. Standing up was another challenge; her tight skirt and extra pounds made it nearly acrobatic.

"Can you wait just a few minutes?" he asked kindly. "I need to see this patient first."

"Of course," she said. "I could use a sink anyway."

Dr. Miller gave a warm smile and disappeared into one of the three exam rooms.

Anna pressed her heels into the dry part of the floor and pushed herself upright, hoping no one was watching her graceless performance. Her knees wobbled. She must look like a newborn giraffe learning to stand, all legs and urgency. Thankfully, the other patients kept their eyes on their magazines, and Erica simply pointed her pen toward the restroom sign. So much for the poised professional image she'd practiced in the mirror.

A wave of nausea rolled through her. Panic surged. Abandoning dignity altogether, Anna hurried toward the washroom, hoping she'd make it there before her nerves decided to stage a full rebellion. Anna rinsed her mouth, washed her hands, and took a slow breath. If she could trust the doctor's kind smile, the job might already be hers. But how would she tell him the truth? It didn't seem fair to take a position knowing she might need a leave of absence in a few months.

She dried her hands, smoothed her hair, and looked at her slightly puffy reflection. Then she tugged at her skirt's waistband and straightened her blazer.

Back in the waiting room, she noticed two patients remaining, each flipping through their magazines with exaggerated focus. Erica was mopping the floor where the baby had been sick.

"Thanks for cleaning up," Erica said, grinning as she nudged the mop bucket with her foot. "You wouldn't believe what I deal with around here. I swear, some days I'm the janitor, the therapist and clown." She rolled her eyes dramatically.

Anna smiled. She liked Erica. "Is it always this busy?"

"If by busy you mean babies throwing up, patients walking out, and Dr. Kevin running late," Erica said with a grin, "then yes, at least once a week."

Curiosity stirred in Anna's mind. What exactly made things fall apart here every week? The orderly part of her brain was already forming possible solutions.

Just then the door opened, and the young mother stepped out of the exam room, the baby now calm and drowsy in her arms.

"Dr. Kevin, you always make me feel better," she said.

"You're a wonderful mom," he replied with an encouraging smile.

Another point in his favor, Anna thought. She'd worked with her share of arrogant doctors. Kind ones were a rare blessing.

The mother thanked both women and left. Anna picked up her purse, ready to sit again, but Dr. Miller was already walking toward her, his white coat flaring slightly as he moved, stethoscope swinging from his pocket.

"Just two more patients, then I'll meet with you," he said.

Anna nodded, managing a polite smile. Her pulse quickened, thudding in her ears. The room suddenly felt smaller, the air sharper.

In just a few minutes, she would know if her life was about to change, for better or worse. And there was no lipstick, no practiced smile in the world that could distract her now.

CHAPTER TWO

T he skirt button popped off and skittered across the worn vinyl floor. Seated in the chair, Anna stretched out her leg and pressed her shoe over it. Dr. Kevin Miller was busy rifling through paper files in a side drawer and seemed not to notice the noise. Anna shifted, trying to find a position where the waistband wouldn't dig in so much. Wearing a suit had been a terrible idea. Her bathroom scale had already confessed to two extra pounds. From now on, stretchy fabrics would be her best friends.

Dr. Miller's fingers moved along the files, a wave of blond fair hair falling across his forehead before he tucked it neatly behind his ear. At last he found what he needed and looked up at Anna from the other side of a paper-strewn desk.

"Anna Weber." He tapped the folder. "You have no idea how glad I am that you accepted my invitation to work here."

Invitation to work? Weren't they still interviewing? That meant she would have to tell this kind, earnest doctor her situation. But she needed this job so much. What if he changed his mind?

Anna adjusted her glasses and slipped into a professional posture. "I thought this was an interview."

He tucked a stray lock behind his ear again. "Just a formality. I thought we were settled on our last phone call."

Anna searched her memory and found nothing that sounded like a firm agreement. Maybe the doctor's office—piles of books tossed over two chairs—hid a misfiled note confirming it.

Her hand tightened on her purse strap. She didn't even have a place to live in Grace Harbor yet. Since the accident, she'd been sharing an apartment in

Providence with her cousin—temporary at best—but she wasn't ready to hunt for a new place immediately.

Dr. Kevin, as their patient called him, laced his fingers on the folder and smiled. "I hope the chaos out there didn't scare you off. We're not always like that."

His grin was boyish, the kind of grin that, in old black-and-white films, let a kid get away with mischief. All he needed was a white dog with a black ring around one eye and a soapbox car to race downhill.

"Actually," Anna said, dragging her shoe back with the button under the sole, "I wasn't prepared to move to Grace Harbor right away."

"You're in Providence, right?" There was that smile again.

"I am. It isn't far, but where I'm staying is temporary." She pictured the young mom and her coughing child and imagined herself caring for them.

"I understand," he said with a soft sigh. "How much time do you need?"

That word time was like an electric jolt. She didn't have much. With every passing day, her condition would become more obvious. A tide of doubts washed over her. He seemed so sincere, so ethical. How could she be anything but honest? Deception wasn't in her nature. The tightrope of omission offered no guarantees, and without a safety net beneath, the fall could be disastrous.

She twined her damp fingers together. "I can look this weekend, if you can wait."

His boyish smile widened, and a dimple appeared in his right cheek. "Of course I can. I don't have another candidate. Your résumé was excellent, and our phone calls told me what I needed to know, that your heart's in this. As you saw out there, I need someone who can organize and who truly cares. Some days everything piles up, and you saw the result."

Relief loosened her shoulders, and she let out a quiet breath. "Then I think we have a deal."

Dr. Kevin stood, came around the desk, and offered his hand. "Welcome to the team. Erica's going to be thrilled."

Anna rose, still with the button under her shoe. She hadn't yet come up with a graceful way to bend down and grab it. She shook his warm hand, her own still cold. "I'll let you know as soon as I sort out housing."

"Perfect." He released her hand. "Anything else you wanted to say or ask?"

Yes, she thought. *How do you handle a truth I've been leaving out—one that will cause a headache for you in a few months?*

Saved by the bell, or rather, by the door that flew open. Erica stood there, flustered.

"Kevin, a patient came in with a huge cut on her arm. Huge!" She stretched the word out in alarm.

The doctor's whole posture shifted; physician mode engaged. He headed for the hall, then paused and looked back at Anna. "Come help me."

Anna bent, snatched the button, and slipped it into her purse. She hurried past a wide-eyed Erica, briefly wondering why the young woman called him by his first name. But a cry from the waiting room snapped her back to the moment. She followed Dr. Kevin as he supported a long-haired young woman whose T-shirt was soaked with blood.

"Room one," he called.

Anna rushed ahead, pushed open the door, and darted to the sink to scrub her hands. She dried them with a wad of paper towels while scanning the labels on cabinet doors and drawers for suture supplies. She grabbed two pairs of gloves and handed one to the doctor.

Dr. Kevin settled the weeping patient on the exam table, washed his hands, and pulled on his gloves. With calm efficiency, he asked Anna for what he needed to clean, numb, and close the wound. They worked in easy rhythm, two professionals speaking the same language. Minutes later, the cut was stitched, and the patient had stopped trembling.

"Stay here a bit, Patty," he said gently. "You've lost some blood and you're in shock. You might faint." He tossed the torn packaging and his gloves into the trash.

Anna wiped down the work surface and fluffed the pillow under the patient's head. *He knows his patients by name,* she noted. Another point in his favor.

"Anna, can you stay with her a few minutes?" Dr. Kevin asked. "I've got one more patient to see."

"Of course."

"There are printed care instructions in the left drawer. Would you give one to our brave patient?" He pushed his hair back, smiled at Patty, and slipped out, closing the door.

Anna's hands were busy, opening the drawer and pulling the aftercare sheet, but her mind ran ahead. What had just happened in this exam room told her that working with Dr. Kevin would be deeply satisfying. Looking at Patty—pale, eyes closed, breathing evening out—Anna felt the quiet weight of purpose. The clinic mattered to this town. It was where people came first, where compassion met skill. At the Providence hospital, patients wouldn't get Dr. Kevin's thoughtful, personal touch.

She'd already taken a quick look at rentals and found a small complex near the clinic. The price was reasonable, and though she hadn't discussed salary, she hoped it would cover basic expenses. In recent months she'd learned to live lean, quite a change from the comfortable bubble Dalton had crafted around them. The family accountant had burst that bubble, and Anna had stumbled through the ruins like a woman lost in a maze. Part of the blame was hers because she had rarely checked on their finances, his or hers. After Dalton was laid to rest, she discovered the house was mortgaged to the hilt, and most of the insurance payout had vanished to impatient creditors. At least those weights were gone. No debt, but no savings, either. What she had left was the strength of her own two hands.

"Could I have some water?" Patty murmured, turning her head on the pillow toward Anna.

"Of course. I'll be right back." Anna slipped out.

The waiting room was empty. No patients. No Erica. At the end of the hall, she found a small staff kitchen with older appliances and a simple wooden table with four chairs, enough for quick breathers between appointments.

She opened the yellowish fridge and took a small bottle of water. When she returned, Patty was sitting up on the exam table, talking with the doctor.

"Come back in a week so I can check the stitches," he said. "And if you see any sign of infection, call me." He held out a prescription. "Here are the medications you'll need."

Colour had returned to Patty's cheeks. She thanked both doctor and nurse and headed out.

"Thank you, Anna." Dr. Kevin peeled off the blood-speckled paper from the exam table and tossed it away.

"I'll finish the cleanup." Anna pulled on a fresh pair of latex gloves and opened the cabinet with the disinfectant sprays.

He slipped the stethoscope from his neck into his coat pocket. "I'm convinced our patients are going to benefit from your care."

The crisp ripping sound of fresh table paper echoed in the small room as Anna covered the exam table again. This was the moment to tell him. Either he would take back every kind word, or he would offer grace.

"About your question before Patty came in, I have something to say." Her hands trembled.

He leaned against the Formica counter. "As long as you're not quitting on me, I can handle anything." The boyish grin appeared again.

"I'm pregnant."

His smile faded, inch by inch. Maybe this was the one thing he couldn't handle.

Chapter Three

For a moment—just long enough for Kevin to recover from the punch he felt in his gut—he thought Anna might be joking. She was pregnant?

But when he looked into the honey-brown eyes behind the lenses of her glasses, the conviction he saw there hit him even harder. She was telling the truth.

A flash of memory stirred—a pregnancy, not too long ago—that had thrown his own life off balance.

Kevin hadn't noticed a ring on Anna's finger, but he knew well that expectant mothers came from every kind of story, every kind of situation. What was hers? Not that it was his place to ask. What *was* his concern, however, was the matter of maternity leave. In a few months, he'd have to find another nurse. Judging by the barely noticeable curve of her waist, Anna was still in her first trimester.

The simplest thing would be to let her go now and avoid complications. But experience had a way of softening a man's heart. Over the past year and a half, Kevin had seen more than enough of how messy and sacred a pregnancy could be, especially when life didn't go as planned. During his residency, he'd witnessed both the beauty and the heartbreak of humanity: young women breaking down at the news of an unplanned pregnancy; families dividing over what to do next; and others finding a way to cling to grace in the middle of fear. But when it happened within his own family, Kevin had learned the hard truth, that he could no longer just observe. He had to choose between being part of the problem or part of the solution. As a doctor, he could compartmentalize compassion. One patient left, another arrived, and the ache blurred into the background.

But as a man, he couldn't.

Life was sacred. Responsibility couldn't be shrugged off.

And turning away this capable nurse would only replace one problem with others: guilt, sorrow, and the weight of conscience.

Kevin crossed his arms and paced the small exam room, aware of Anna's gaze following him. She waited for an answer. He wasn't sure how to give it.

Sometimes God had a strange sense of humor. Every day, Kevin saw Erica and battled the quiet guilt that still lived inside him. And now here stood another woman, carrying a precious life within her, a fragile, holy state that didn't require a doctor to recognize. He knew that lesson by heart now.

Wait. The word itself grated on him. Too often, in his twenty-nine years, he'd felt like he was stuck on one of those endless phone calls—*Your call is very important to us. Please hold.*

Anna's situation wasn't really about waiting. It was about delay. His dreams for the clinic would slow down if he chose to let her go.

He stopped in front of her. His doctor's eye caught the faint pallor spreading across her lips and cheeks. Before she could fall, he reached out and steadied her by the arm.

"Lie down," he said gently, helping her onto the exam table. He took her blood pressure, then said, "Your pressure's low. When did you last eat?"

Anna rested her forearm across her forehead, shifting on the paper-covered bed, which tore softly beneath her too-tight skirt. "About four hours ago," she said, unbuttoning her blazer.

"Hold on." Kevin stepped out and went to the small kitchen.

From a cabinet, he grabbed a packet of salted crackers and returned. Anna was sitting up now, blazer folded beside her. He handed her the package, and she ate quickly, a few crumbs scattering over her dark skirt.

"Anna," he said after clearing his throat, "I'll admit, your news caught me off guard."

She brushed her fingers across her lips. "I'm sorry, Dr. Miller. I never should've come. I should've told you in our last conversation."

"I agree," he said honestly.

Anna stood, tossing the empty wrapper into the trash. "I'm sorry for wasting your time." She straightened her shoulders, gripping her purse, and moved toward the door.

"The job's still yours."

She turned, eyes wide. "It is? Really? I don't want to be a burden, and I promise I won't leave anyone stranded."

Kevin ran a hand through his wavy hair. "We'll have one thing to figure out a few months from now, won't we?"

"I'll manage. I won't need much time off, just a few days to recover," she said, clutching her purse strap.

"We'll talk about it later. Right now, I need your help."

And it was true. His plans for the clinic depended on someone reliable and skilled, and few nurses wanted to work in quiet little Grace Harbor, where career growth was slow but hearts ran deep. Anna had experience, warmth, and courage.

He extended his hand. "Once again, let's seal the deal."

She took his hand, her smile trembling with gratitude. "Thank you. You don't know how much this means to me." She touched her stomach lightly. "You won't regret it."

"Now," he said, "about your move to Grace Harbor, what do you need to get settled?"

Kevin knew he was crossing a line, but he couldn't help it. If he could make her transition easier, she could start sooner. And truthfully, neither of them had much time to lose.

Anna set her purse on the counter and gave a shy smile. "Well, it would help to know how much I'll be earning."

He smacked his forehead. "Of course! We started things a little backwards, didn't we? If you're feeling up to it, let's go over the paperwork in my office."

"I'm feeling better," she said, following him back to the office.

He opened a folder on the desk and turned a page toward her. "Here's the contract draft."

Anna read it carefully. "Everything looks good."

Kevin exhaled with quiet relief. "We can revisit the salary in a few months. I've got plans for the clinic and I'd like your input when the time comes."

Anna smiled, this time with genuine enthusiasm. "Whenever you're ready, Doctor."

"I'll send your information to my accountant as soon as you fill out the form I'll email."

"Would you happen to know a place to stay nearby until I find something permanent?"

The question eased a tightness he hadn't realized he was carrying. She truly meant to move here. Kevin opened one drawer, then another, until he found a small brochure. "There's a lovely place called Tranquility-by-the-Sea Inn. The owners treat guests like family. It's not far from here."

Anna took the brochure, scanned the image of a Cape Cod cottage and smiled. "What a charming place. I'll stop by before I drive back to Providence."

Kevin walked her to the door and locked it behind her when she left. The clinic was quiet now, still faintly smelling of the baby's sour milk from earlier. The day's small chaos had reminded him just how urgent change was. Everything around him still bore the stamp of the old Dr. Vincent Miller, his stern father.

The elder Dr. Miller had been a pillar of compassion in Grace Harbor, but also stubborn and frugal to a fault. The clinic had never been properly renovated, only patched together over the years. The aging equipment groaned for replacement, especially the ultrasound machine.

Kevin longed to leave his own mark on the place, not just in décor but in spirit. Anna could help him get there. With her support, he could finally move forward on the renovations and begin inviting more specialists to join the practice. It would be good for him, and for the town.

Anna struck him as a woman of her word, and of quiet action. He admired the way she'd knelt without hesitation to clean up Pedro's mess, and how calmly she'd assisted him with Patty's treatment. She had the gift of soothing people, the kind of gift that couldn't be taught.

Back in his office, Kevin slipped papers into his leather case and grabbed the keys to his Hyundai Tucson. The clinic was closed for the day, but one more person still needed his attention.

He reversed out of the parking lot and steered down Grace Harbor's main street toward home. Erica would be there, waiting with her usual stack of excuses ready on her lips.

Why did she have to be so stubborn?

Chapter Four

Anna set her glasses on the dashboard of the Honda Civic and blinked away the tears clouding her eyes. She wasn't the kind of woman who cried easily, but Dr. Kevin's offer had lifted such a heavy weight from her heart that the relief found its way out as tears. Leaning back against the soft seat, she glanced once more at the sign that read Grace Harbor Clinic. From the light still glowing in Dr. Kevin Miller's office window, she figured she had a few minutes in the darkness of the parking lot to pull herself together before heading to Tranquility-by-the-Sea Inn.

Anna rested her hands on her stomach. It was far too early to feel kicks or hiccups yet, but her baby was there, tiny and alive, with a beating heart. A life she alone was responsible for. She wouldn't allow herself to lose hope or waste her energy resenting Dalton.

The last few months had been an unrelenting storm of emotion. The sudden loss of her husband in a car accident, the accountant's announcement of bankruptcy, and then the unexpected result of the pregnancy test, each had demanded a strength she hadn't known she possessed. It was a miracle the pregnancy had survived all the stress and despair. Just thinking about starting over alone and penniless was enough to make her chest ache. And now, with a child on the way, everything felt bigger, as though a giant magnifying glass had been placed over every flaw and fear she'd tried to ignore.

Her father couldn't help; his Parkinson's disease had advanced quickly after her mother's death. And her brother, well, he was practically a stranger, distant and dismissive for reasons she couldn't fathom.

Anna drew in a deep breath and let it out slowly, stroking her belly. "I'll take care of us," she whispered. "I'll take care of you."

The tears came freely then. Inside her, a life no bigger than a pea was growing, a miracle of divine love. What could be more sacred than that? She carried a picture of the first ultrasound in her purse: a tiny head too large for the body, little arms and legs, and a heartbeat so small and steady it could hold all the love she already felt for her little pea.

Through her blurred vision, Anna saw the light in Dr. Kevin's office go dark. She pulled a tissue from the box on the console, dabbed her face, and blew her nose. Sliding her glasses back on, she started the GPS and pulled out of the lot toward Tranquility-by-the-Sea, the first home that would belong to just her and the tiny life growing inside her body.

Driving slightly under the speed limit along the quiet coastal road, Anna opened her window and breathed in the salty air. Maybe this small, sleepy seaside town would be good for her health and her soul. She prayed the people of Grace Harbor wouldn't ask too many questions once her belly began to show. How could she ever explain the tangle of grief and hurt she felt toward her late husband?

That grief had woven itself together with disappointment, anger, and mourning into one bitter thread. Why had Dalton lied to her? Why had he gotten himself tangled in deceit and gambling? What had been missing at home that made him crave a reckless life of indulgence? Her long hospital shifts had given him too many opportunities to go astray.

The GPS instructed her to turn left. Moments later, Anna saw the warm glow of lights ahead. The inn was even lovelier than the brochure had promised. A tall spruce stood wrapped in tiny white lights, still twinkling with Christmas charm even though summer was barely over. The rustic building looked like something out of a storybook, its sloped roof reminiscent of a gingerbread cottage.

She parked in one of the five spaces beside the inn, smoothed her hair in the dim reflection of the window, and stepped out. Opening the door, she entered a softly lit room decorated in soothing pastels. Gentle background music drifted from a hidden speaker, welcoming her. To the right, glass French doors offered a glimpse of a cozy library with wicker shell chairs and shelves lined with books.

Dr. Kevin had said the owners treated their guests like family. Standing there, Anna could already feel the inviting atmosphere. The place radiated warmth, comfort, and the simple beauty of home.

A door opened at the back of the front desk, and a tall woman with Asian features appeared, her smile bright and kind.

"Welcome to Tranquility-by-the-Sea. I'm Esther." She came around the counter and extended her hand.

"Thank you. I'd like to talk with you about a long-term stay." A sweet scent hung in the air, and Anna's stomach rumbled in response.

"Of course," Esther said with a cheerful nod. "I'd be happy to help." She moved behind the counter, pulled out a laptop, and began typing. "Just one guest?"

"Yes." *Two,* Anna thought tenderly, *but the other is safe and warm in my belly.*

"I have a suite with a garden view," Esther continued. "How long do you plan to stay?"

Anna laced her fingers together. "I'm not sure yet. I'll be starting work at Grace Harbor Clinic on Monday, and I'll need some time to find a permanent place."

Esther's smile widened. "With Dr. Kevin? That's wonderful news! You'll be warmly welcomed in Grace Harbor."

For a moment, Anna wanted nothing more than to lean into this woman's shoulder and rest. "Do I need to give you a check-out date?"

"Not at all. Let's do this: I'll reserve the suite for one month. If you need to extend, just let me know. And if you leave sooner, no problem at all." Esther typed a bit more and pulled a key from the drawer. "Where's your luggage?"

"I don't have it with me. I'll bring everything tomorrow."

"Of course. Would you like to see the suite?"

Anna hugged her purse close. "If it's not too much trouble."

"Not at all. Come with me."

Anna followed Esther up the stairs. The carpeted hallway smelled fresh and clean. When Esther opened the door, Anna sighed softly. The room was just as inviting as the reception area below. The bed looked like a fluffy white cloud, piled high with pillows and a comforter. Pale blue curtains reminded her of gentle waves rolling onto the beach at low tide. The scent of soap and fresh air floated in through the open window. How she longed to sink into that bed and sleep, but she still needed to drive back to Providence for her things. And food. Lots of food.

"This room is beautiful," Anna said, admiring the watercolor paintings on the wall showing shells, the beach, a kite flying in a cloudy sky. "Who painted these?"

"My daughter, Jade," Esther said, resting her hand on the doorframe. The pride in her smile was unmistakable.

"I hope I get to meet her."

"Oh, you will," Esther laughed. "She loves to meet our guests. She's out but will be home soon."

"I'd love to meet this young artist," Anna said, studying the paintings. She imagined herself one day speaking with that same pride about her little one.

Esther locked the door behind them as they left the room. They walked side by side down the stairs. On the last step, Anna hesitated and reached for the railing.

"Are you all right?" Esther asked.

"Just a little dizzy," Anna murmured, touching her cool fingers to her forehead.

Esther looked at her with concern. "You know, my husband is out tonight. Would you like to have dinner with me?"

"Oh, I couldn't impose. I thought the inn only served breakfast," Anna said.

Esther patted her hand lightly. "It does, but this invitation isn't business, it's personal. I live in the cottage behind the main house."

A few minutes later, Anna found herself sitting at a kitchen table with a plate of roast beef and pasta before her. The savory aromas filled the air, teasing her hungry senses. Esther joined her, and they shared the warm, simple meal together.

"Mmm, this is delicious," Anna said, wiping her lips with a paper napkin.

"Eat all you want," Esther encouraged, taking another bite.

When their plates were clean, Esther satisfied Anna's earlier curiosity about the sweet aroma by placing a slice of apple pie before her.

Anna closed her eyes, savoring the flavors of cinnamon and sugar melting on her tongue. "This is wonderful."

By the time they finished their coffee, Anna already felt at home. "I'll be back tomorrow after lunch," she said.

Esther sipped the last of her coffee and set the cup down. "I hope you don't think I'm prying, but do you live far from here?"

"In Providence," Anna said, stirring the remaining coffee with a spoon.

"Then may I make a suggestion?"

"Of course."

"Why not stay here tonight? You can collect your things tomorrow, unless someone's waiting for you."

Heat rose up Anna's neck. No one was waiting. Not even her cousin. "To be honest, I'm exhausted. That bed upstairs looks irresistible." She wondered if Esther could see the weariness in her eyes.

Esther stood. "I keep a welcome pack for guests who arrive unprepared." She disappeared down the hall and returned with a small bag bearing the inn's logo. "There's a T-shirt, toothbrush, toothpaste, and a few toiletries inside." She handed the bag to Anna.

"Oh, thank you. Just the thought of a warm shower and that soft bed is making me sleepy already," Anna said with a tired laugh.

"I'll walk you back to the inn," Esther offered.

Anna followed her through the garden that separated the cottage from the main building.

Under the warm water of the shower that night, Anna imagined herself caring for people like Esther and for her own baby in this small, peaceful community.

After almost four months of heartbreak and uncertainty, the future finally held a flicker of hope.

CHAPTER FIVE

The baby's cry could easily have been mistaken for colic, pained and uneven, with tiny hiccups breaking through. Kevin closed the front door and dropped his work case onto the leather armchair. He slipped off his shoes and set them neatly beside a pair of flat sandals. On his way to the kitchen, he scooped up a stuffed blue elephant and a rubber ball from the floor. His ultimate destination was the master bathroom after finding something to eat though he doubted Erica had made dinner.

Kevin didn't mind cooking, but the day had wrung every ounce of energy out of him and whatever creativity he usually had in the kitchen had evaporated somewhere between the last patient and the drive home.

The baby gave a small cry that was quickly muffled, probably by a pacifier. Eight months ago, Kevin had come home to silence. Now, silence and order were rare commodities, as evidenced by the dish rack filled with baby bottles.

He opened the refrigerator and, to his relief, found a tray of store-bought lasagna. He cut a piece, set it on a plate, and took a generous forkful of the cold meal. Who had the energy to warm anything up after a day like this?

Balancing the plate in one hand, he stopped by the wooden box on the kitchen counter to collect the mail. He dragged his feet to the living room. Dropping into the leather chair, he stretched his feet out onto the soft rug. He flipped through the envelopes, making two piles: one for the trash, one that actually mattered.

By the time the last bite of cold lasagna disappeared, Kevin set the plate beside the mail and pulled his phone from the pocket of his pants. Scrolling through his messages, he found the thread of texts he'd exchanged with Anna over the past few weeks. He wanted to reread them now that he'd met her in person.

She'd been a nurse in the cardiology wing at Providence Hospital but had also worked in the ER. One of Kevin's plans was to extend clinic hours to handle minor emergencies. His father's philosophy had always been work to live, though the man's well-padded bank account had suggested that maybe it was more of a slogan than a creed.

Still, Kevin believed that giving Grace Harbor residents a real healthcare option was a good step forward. Not that he wanted to swing to the other extreme—living to work. Self-help books liked to preach about life-work balance. Nice idea for book sales, not so easy to live by when life's board game kept tossing you back two spaces for every one you advanced.

Not that going backward was all bad. Some lessons had to be repeated. Still, "balance" was a work in progress for him. With Anna's help, maybe he could aim for something close to it or at least a more manageable version of chaos.

He had other ideas he wanted to discuss with her, but he'd wait to see how she handled the new job during the pregnancy. Go back one space.

Small hands began to knead his shoulders. Kevin looked up into the mischievous face and upturned nose of his sister.

"Theo finally fell asleep," Erica announced, flopping onto the sofa and stretching out her petite frame to face him.

"Colic again? Did you give him the drops I bought?" Kevin propped his feet on the coffee table and nudged his empty plate aside with his leg.

"I did, but I think the formula's upsetting his stomach." She rubbed her chest with a sigh. "It's a shame my milk dried up so early."

Kevin leaned back, resting his arms on the wide chair. "We tried everything, but it just didn't work."

Erica gave him a crooked smile. "So, tell me—what do you think of Anna?"

"She's competent. After you left, Patty came in with a nasty cut. Anna helped me stitch her up." He could read the glint in his sister's eyes; he'd known that look all his life.

"She's pretty, isn't she? Long, long legs," Erica teased, raising one of her own in mock comparison and tugging at her gray sweatpants. "Unlike mine, short and stubbly. I haven't shaved in days."

Kevin grabbed a pillow off the floor and tossed it at her. "You'll never outgrow your matchmaking habit. After a day like mine, do you really think I have time for romance?"

"Not romance," she said with mock offense, lifting her arms dramatically. "One reckless love story is enough in this family." She patted her stomach meaningfully.

Kevin didn't laugh. She liked to make light of things, but he knew better. Her rushed, careless relationship with Bob had cost her dearly. Kevin loved little Theo with all his heart, but he and Erica both knew this wasn't the life she'd planned. She'd had to drop out of her final year of nursing school and leave the dorms. Bob had walked away from both her and the baby, muttering something pathetic about not having time to change diapers.

Moving in with Kevin had been the most practical solution. Her receptionist job barely covered her expenses as a single mother.

Kevin found himself thinking about Anna again. What was *her* situation? She'd be staying with Esther at the inn for a while before finding a place to rent. What would be next for her? And child care?

Erica had been lucky to find Daphne, a stay-at-home mom of twin girls and writer of cozy mysteries, to care for Theo during the day. It was a perfect arrangement for now, though it, too, was temporary.

Erica sat up cross-legged, her eyes sharp. "Anna seems like a serious, focused person. When I watched her at the clinic today, I got the sense she'd take charge of the chaos." She narrowed her eyes playfully. "She was watching everything—thinking. So serious looking." She threw her head back in laughter, quickly covering her mouth to muffle the sound.

Kevin tapped his fingers against the armrest. "I noticed that too."

What he didn't tell his sister was that Anna's seriousness came, in part, from the weight of her pregnancy and her uncertainty about the job.

Erica stretched her arms overhead. "I wonder what her story is."

"You're not going to start snooping again," Kevin warned. There was only one thing worse than a matchmaking sister—a nosy one.

"*Investigating*, thank you very much. And for the record, my *investigating skills* are the only reason you dodged Genise." She lifted her chin proudly.

"Oh, Lord. That woman practically lived at the clinic, always with a new complaint."

"Her real diagnosis was a bad case of Kevinitis," Erica said dryly.

"By her sixth visit, I was starting to suspect those symptoms were imaginary."

"Please. I could smell the seduction a mile away. Once I dug a little, it wasn't hard to find the husband."

Kevin raised his hands like he was typing on an invisible keyboard. "Imagine the headline: *Grace Harbor Doctor Caught in Affair with Married Patient!* That kind of scandal would destroy a career."

"You're welcome," Erica said, flopping back onto the sofa. "Try showing a little gratitude, big brother."

"Thank you, little sister."

"Now, back to Anna," she said, undeterred. "She's quite pretty. Usually I can't read people with glasses—the glare hides their eyes—but she's got this innocent look about her. I'd love to know if it's real or just an act."

Kevin tickled his sister's stomach. "I don't have the energy for your chatter tonight. Good night." He stood and yawned, stretching as he untucked his shirt.

Still laughing, Erica sat up. "Are you taking the three a.m. feeding or the six?"

"Hmm. I'll wait until Theo's old enough for a burger at the pub," he joked.

Erica tossed the pillow back at him. "Three or six?"

"Six."

She blew him a kiss. "Best big brother in the world."

"Your *only* brother," he said, setting the pillow back on the chair.

"Still the best."

Kevin smiled, running a hand through his messy hair. "Good night."

He walked down the hallway, already half-dreaming of the shower he'd take with his eyes closed, one less step before collapsing into bed. That was, if his mind would stop spinning.

What kind of trouble had he gotten himself into, hiring a pregnant nurse? If her condition took a bad turn, she might need bed rest—and then what?

A foolish doctor, indeed.

Kevin sighed and ran his fingers through his hair as he turned on the tap of the shower, eyes closed.

CHAPTER SIX

How good it felt to float on clouds! Anna let her tired body sink into the soft, clean-scented bed. The long, draining day had ended well. The result? A job and a friend. At least that's how she liked to think of Esther. She was safe, but most importantly, her baby was safe.

The next day, Anna would pick up her things in Providence, settle into the inn, and stop by the clinic. After the long shower, a message arrived from Dr. Kevin asking if she could see him the next afternoon. *I have a few ideas I'd like to share with you,* he'd written. That was a good sign. Anna wouldn't just work at the clinic; she'd help shape the plans. Long-term goals felt impossible for now, but short-term plans were essential.

Rolling onto her side, Anna watched the parade of shadows outside the windowpane. A light wind stirred the branches and leaves, making a humming sound. She pulled the comforter up to her chin when loneliness threatened to creep in with the eerie smile of a horror-movie clown. How hard it was to absorb the enormity of Dalton's reckless choices, the late-night "step out for some air," as he'd called it. That step had cost him his life. She later learned he'd taken the car to meet his bar friends for a card game. When the phone call came from Dalton's stepfather, Anna thought she was dreaming. There were no softeners, no gentle lead-in: "Dalton crashed the car and died. I'm sorry. If you need anything, let me know." The announcement began with a punch and ended with empty words. The whirl of emotions, like a giant washing machine tossing water, soap, clothes, and Anna herself from side to side, left her in a daze for days. A missed period hadn't scared her: stress, she'd thought. When nausea started, she tried to find another medical explanation. But when her cousin brought home a pregnancy test, there was no more escaping. Her little "pea" was already growing.

Anna wiped her nose with the back of her hand. How was she supposed to put her life in order alone? Correction: the lives of two people, one utterly vulnerable and innocent of the parents' sins. Yes, her sins, too, because Anna cursed Dalton every day. She had so much work ahead at the clinic and in her heart. Her baby must not enter the world burdened by her bitterness. The child would not have a father figure, but Anna knew she couldn't destroy Dalton's image entirely. It would be up to her to plant in this new little mind the idea of a father who *would* have loved his child if he were alive, even if he hadn't loved Anna the way she'd believed.

A long sigh cleared her thoughts, and they turned toward her own father. The Parkinson's patient demanded care she could no longer provide. *What will become of him when I leave Providence?* Even though Grace Harbor wasn't far, his current nursing home was out of the way.

Propping herself on an elbow, she grabbed her phone from the nightstand and typed: *nursing home, Grace Harbor*. Two options appeared; one near the clinic: Sunflower Retirement Home. Anna bookmarked the page, determined to call the next day. If the price was similar to the current one, it would be worth bringing her father closer. "Big Serge," as his friends used to say, most of whom had drifted away after the Parkinson's diagnosis, had a decent pension that covered his medical expenses. The decision to move into assisted living had been his. "I can't even button my shirt anymore," he'd argued. Anna respected his decision and agreed. The Providence facility had spacious rooms with 24-hour medical support. If Sunflower Retirement Home offered the same, moving would make sense. Another advantage was Grace Harbor's size. Smaller than Providence, it would let her father stroll the streets safely with her or a caregiver. Perfect.

Big Serge had been delighted about the coming grandchild, though he had condemned his son-in-law's behavior in no uncertain terms. "I wish I could help you both," he'd said. And he *would* help by staying well and walking alongside Anna in this new season of motherhood.

The comforter wrapped Anna's expectant body, but anxiety, ever opportunistic, slipped into the bed alongside her. And it was in that uneasy company that Anna spent her first night in Grace Harbor.

When dawn came, doubt rose with the sun. How would she make it five more months without any certainty about what life would look like after her little one arrived?

Choosing silence, Anna got ready and slipped out of the inn without telling Esther. The sunrise was timid, bringing more questions as she climbed into her white Honda Civic. The faster she collected her things from Nadia's apartment, the better. She hoped her cousin had already left for work. Nadia never missed a chance to prod Anna and stoke her fears. But as Anna arrived in their neighborhood, Nadia's car, parked in front of the building, warned her what was coming.

Anna opened the door to the second-floor apartment and heard a man's laughter from the hallway. One more reason to leave quickly and respect Nadia's privacy. On tiptoe, she headed for the small bedroom she used. A door slammed; the shower came on; more laughter.

Anna opened drawers and pulled out her clothes. She dragged her suitcase from the closet and started packing. The material sum of her life was split between Nadia's apartment and the storage unit in the garage. She'd fetch the rest another day. In a rush, she pulled more clothes from hangers that seesawed as each piece came free. In minutes, the suitcase was packed. Maybe she could slip out unnoticed. She'd text her cousin later to say she'd taken the bedroom things and would come back for the boxes in storage.

Choosing to carry the suitcase rather than roll it, Anna passed the closed bathroom door. But when she reached the living room, she ran right into her cousin standing there in a sheer nightgown, sipping coffee. Dark hair wound into a topknot made Nadia look taller than she was. Her athletic frame broadcast her love of exercise.

"Nadia, good morning."

Her cousin turned, hand to her chest. "Good grief, I thought you'd stayed out."

"I did. I came for some of my things. I'll come back for the storage boxes another day," Anna said. "Thank you for letting me stay."

Nadia set her mug beside a row of self-help books on the shelf. "Did the job work out?"

From the hallway came the man's off-key singing in the shower.

"It did. And I found a temporary place to stay."

"That's great." Nadia glanced toward the music. "I met Titus last month. He's a good guy."

Anna bobbed her head as if agreeing. "I hope it works out." What else could she say? Her cousin didn't listen to advice; she called it judgment. Besides, what authority did Anna have to speak about relationships? She looked from her suitcase back to Nadia. "Well, I'd better go. Thank you again for everything."

Nadia gave her a brief hug. "Take care. And remember what I told you." She nodded toward Anna's belly. "There are ways to handle that."

Heat flashed up Anna's neck like someone had poured boiling water down it. "We've already talked about this."

"You're going to work with a doctor. How convenient," Nadia said, leaning against the window, the lace of her nightgown revealing her full curves.

Anna tugged her suitcase toward the door. "Thank you for helping me through a hard time. I'm going to do what's best for me and my baby." She opened the door, stepped through, and pulled it shut with a damp palm.

The man's singing grew louder. On the other side of the door, Anna could hear muffled conversation and laughter.

Back in the car, she lifted a disposable cup from the holder and sipped the now lukewarm tea. She thought about her cousin's words. Why did people insist on speaking fear and death over a pregnant woman, instead of courage and life? Wasn't the world already brimming with injustice, violence, and lack of love? How could it possibly hold more darkness and despair without collapsing when what it needed was hope?

With a deep breath, Anna set the car in motion, the road unfolding toward Grace Harbor.

CHAPTER SEVEN

"My mom said you're going to live with us." The brown-haired, almond-eyed girl stepped out from behind the inn's front desk and glanced at Anna's suitcase. "You brought just that?"

"Jaaade," Esther called, typing a few things on the laptop.

"I know, Mom—I'm not supposed to ask nosy questions." The girl winked at their guest.

"Oh, it's fine," Anna said, letting go of the suitcase handle. "I have more things, but this is all I need for now." She loved how the girl with Down Syndrome handled things professionally.

"If you need anything, let me know. I'd be glad to help," Esther said, closing the laptop.

"Or tell me," Jade added, swishing her ponytail tied with colorful ribbons.

"If you could help me take the suitcase upstairs, I'd appreciate it." Anna adjusted her purse strap on her shoulder.

"I can carry it myself." Jade grabbed the handle and hauled the suitcase toward the stairs while looking at her mom.

Anna looked to Esther, who gave a little nod to let her daughter help. She followed Jade up the stairs, hoping Esther didn't find it odd Anna hadn't carried the suitcase herself.

In the bedroom, Jade set the suitcase on a chair. "I hope you have a great stay." She smiled. "My mom says I'm supposed to say that to the guests."

Anna's heart felt gently stroked by Jade's words. "Thank you. I'm sure I will."

Jade said goodbye, and the new guest closed the door. The girl's sweetness had lifted a small weight from Anna's shoulders. Nadia, on the other hand, had added another weight. Anna didn't want to be ungrateful—her cousin had taken her in when her world collapsed—but she already had more than enough doubts. Not about her baby; "taking care of it," as Nadia had suggested, meant by Anna's definition, loving and protecting the child. It was her responsibility to handle things the best way she could.

With her clothes neatly put away in the white dresser and wardrobe, Anna checked her phone for Dr. Kevin's last message. Their meeting was in two hours. Then she confirmed the address for Sunflower Retirement Home and headed to the car. The button on her jeans scraped her navel as she sat, reminding her she'd soon need new clothes.

She adjusted her glasses, tapped her phone screen, and started the GPS. Ten minutes later, she parked in front of Sunflower Retirement Home. First impressions were good: a well-kept two-story building shaded by large trees. Her father loved to read, and the benches scattered across the lawn looked perfect for losing oneself in a book.

Anna followed the sign toward the front door. An orderly pushed a wheelchair for a white-haired woman who was sleeping. A nurse passed by with a tray of medications. At the front desk, a young woman with straight black hair greeted Anna.

"Good morning, how can I help you?"

"I called earlier and was told you have an opening. It's for my father." Anna ran a finger along the tight waistband of her jeans.

"We do. I'll call our manager." The receptionist spoke briefly on the phone, then hung up. "Samara will be right with you."

The manager, a woman with thick dark hair pulled into a perfect ponytail, came out from a back door and extended her hand to greet Anna.

After introductions, Samara invited Anna to her office. Half an hour later, Anna left the facility convinced it would be a good place for her dad. The first floor housed more independent residents; each apartment had a small living room, a bedroom, and private bathroom. The unit her father would occupy had excellent natural light and a view of the garden. Anna thanked Samara for her time and said she would call the next day after speaking with her father.

Relief washed over her, and with that lightness she stepped into Grace Harbor Clinic.

Erica waved from the front desk as the nurse walked in. On the phone, the bubbly receptionist was scheduling an appointment.

"Tomorrow, three-thirty," she said.

Glancing around the waiting room, Anna felt the urge to speak to the elderly man flipping through a magazine and the woman with curly hair and a leg cast. But the door to Exam Room 1 opened. Dr. Kevin followed a woman and her little girl out, then smiled at Anna and headed to the front desk. He handed Erica a form and said goodbye to his patient.

"Good morning, Anna. Can you give me a few more minutes?" He nodded toward the woman in the cast.

"Of course, but can I help with anything?" she asked.

He slipped his pen into his coat pocket. "There are some boxes in the kitchen. Could you open them and stock Exam Room 2?"

Anna walked to the end of the hallway and stepped into the kitchen. She hung her purse on a wall hook and washed her hands. From the boxes she pulled out gauze packs, syringes, and other supplies, then arranged everything in the proper drawers and cabinets in Room 2. It was shaping up to be a good day after all.

When she finally sat across from Dr. Kevin in his office, anticipation ran high. He explained his idea to extend clinic hours.

"With your help, I'll have the support I need. We can create a fair schedule that won't overload you," he said, twirling the pen between his fingers.

"I'm used to shifts." Anna rested her hands on the chair arms.

They discussed options and agreed to adjust hours as needed.

"Settled, then. And if you want to start right away, the gentleman in the waiting room needs a tetanus shot."

After giving the injection and reviewing instructions with the patient, Anna saw him out and took a slow lap around the exam room. This was her element. Better yet, Grace Harbor Clinic might be the perfect place to restart her career and her new life as a single mom.

By week's end, Anna had already found her rhythm. She liked Dr. Kevin's approach to care; he made a point of knowing his patients and their life situations. As for Erica, she sometimes lost track of tasks, so Anna began helping her get organized.

On Friday at five, Erica locked up and joined Anna in tidying the exam rooms. Dr. Kevin had left early to check on a post-surgery patient at the hospital in Providence.

Anna rolled fresh paper over the exam table. "Have you worked here long?"

"Eight months," Erica said, tying off the trash bag.

"Were you in healthcare before this?" Anna wiped down the wall-mounted equipment with disinfectant.

"I was in nursing school. Then Theo arrived, and I needed steady work." Erica set the trash in the hallway.

"Theo?"

"My son. He's almost nine months." She smiled the unmistakable smile of a proud mom.

Anna's hand went to her own belly. Erica looked very young. Was she married? She had called the doctor by his first name. What was their relationship?

Erica pulled out her phone. "Here. Theo and Kevin."

Dr. Kevin is the baby's father? Anna wondered, seeing the doctor in the photo, bottle-feeding the baby. "Your husband is very involved, isn't he?"

"Husband?" Erica slipped the phone back into her pocket. "Theo's father doesn't care about him."

Then what about the photo? "What do you mean?"

"We had a messy relationship. It didn't last." Erica turned on the faucet to rinse the sink.

"Dr. Kevin seems to support you." Anna stared at Erica.

The young woman laughed. "Sometimes I think he wishes I'd get out of his hair." She turned off the tap.

Anna tried to make sense of their complicated dynamic. "Why wouldn't he take care of you and the baby?"

Erica stepped closer and lowered her voice, as if someone else might overhear. "Because the minute Kevin falls in love and gets married, he won't want me around." She lifted her hands in a *Isn't it obvious?* gesture and walked out.

Anna's jaw dropped. *What kind of man is the doctor, anyway?* She followed Erica to the open front door. On the sidewalk, she turned and said, "I don't understand why Dr. Kevin wouldn't support his own child."

Erica slipped the clinic key into her bag and frowned. "Child? What child?"

Anna adjusted her glasses. "Yours and Dr. Kevin's."

Erica burst out laughing. "You thought my Theo was Kevin's?"

"He's not?"

Erica patted Anna's shoulder. "Kevin is my brother. He just hates introducing me as his sister. Says it feels more professional, but I think he does it to scare off the ladies." With a wave, the receptionist headed down the sidewalk, still laughing.

In one moment, Anna had decided the doctor was a monster who'd abandoned his supposed son. A split second later, her opinion of Dr. Kevin shot skyward like a rocket. Whether for professional reasons or convenience, it didn't matter why he didn't introduce Erica as his sister. What mattered was his generous heart in supporting her as a single mother.

Anna's own brother would have received news of her pregnancy with cold indifference. Her father had surely told Victor about the baby by now. She didn't expect her brother to reach out and congratulate her.

Was it too much to hope that someday, Anna and her child might know the kind of supportive love Erica found in her brother?

Chapter Eight

"But she understood that you're my sister, right?" Kevin wiped a paper napkin across Theo's highchair tray, soaking up the spilled water.

Erica came from the stove with a plate piled high with pasta and sat down beside her son. "Don't worry. I made it very clear we share the same DNA."

Theo banged his little plastic spoon on the soup and splattered yellow broth across an already messy bib. Erica swiped her index finger along his cheeks and dabbed the extra mess into the napkin.

"You women talk in so many circles, it's no wonder you misunderstand each other." Kevin twirled his fork in the pasta and took a generous bite. If he'd understood Erica's explanation about her conversation with Anna, the new nurse's first impression of him had been terrible. He pictured himself as the kind of man who would abandon a pregnant woman and his own child. When Erica first told him she was expecting, his gut reaction had been to confront the boyfriend. But his sense of responsibility told him that what she needed most was his arms, not a lecture or a fight. Time would tell, and Erica's conscience would agree, that the mistake carried consequences far deeper than "just a baby." The little life forming in Erica's womb was the innocent part of the story and therefore needed to be surrounded with protection and love. So Kevin took the responsibility on himself. Theo needed a father figure, and his uncle gladly stepped into that role.

"I wasn't talking in circles," Erica said, taking a sip of water and leaning toward her brother. "You're the one who puts us in this position, using me as a shield to keep women away."

"You have a point. This shield saved my life." He laughed. "While Genise thought you were my wife, things were easier."

Erica shrugged, dismissing the comment. "I thought Anna looked unwell."

"Why do you say that?"

Erica stood with her plate, streaked with sauce. "Not sure. Something about her didn't seem right."

"You don't even know her yet." What had Erica noticed? Anna's pregnancy wasn't obvious.

Erica set the plate in the sink and lifted Theo from the highchair. "I'll find out. Right now I've got to take care of this little guy." She hoisted her son, kissed his soup-smeared tummy, and Theo giggled, showing four tiny teeth.

She left the kitchen, chatting to him that it was bath time. Kevin took a few more bites and stood. As usual, Erica had left the kitchen looking like a war zone: pots, plates, pans, and spoons crowding the sink, tomato splatters freckling the stove. Rolling up the sleeves of his white shirt, Kevin mapped out the best strategy to restore order. From the hallway came the sound of the bathtub tap, laughter, then a brief wail.

Soon the house would be quiet until the three a.m. feeding, which no longer seemed necessary, but Erica insisted Theo was always hungry. He was the doctor, but Erica was the mom. From the first days with Theo at home, they'd agreed she would make the calls about her baby.

He attacked the dishes first, rinsing plates, cups, and cutlery and loading the dishwasher. Then he moved on to the oversized pots, absurdly large for the amount of food they held. As he scrubbed a pan, Kevin glanced out the window to the starry night. The sky was clear, perfect for his favorite ride. Erica teased him, calling him a werewolf for his love of the night. But what in nature was calmer than a sky strewn with stars? What better displayed God's majesty than the lights Kevin could see from Earth? It was inspiring to count the stars, trace the constellations, and imagine a stroll on the moon.

Hurrying through the cleanup, Kevin checked the microwave clock and decided the night was too perfect to waste. The week had been so busy he'd postponed his date with the moon four times.

He turned off the tap and set the last pan in the rack. He wiped the stove and the floor, then jogged to his room. Theo's soft fussing floated down the hallway. Soon he'd be asleep, and Erica would curl up to another episode of her favorite true-crime show. Since her dating misadventure, she hadn't joined Kevin on his nighttime outings, a tradition they have shared since childhood when they'd lived on a small farm on the edge of Grace Harbor. Back then they'd spread a blanket on the grass, lie on their backs, and talk about the stars. For a while, Kevin had told his sister he was from another planet. She'd been wide-eyed over tales of zero gravity and his green friends. Eventually she caught on, and astronomy took a more realistic turn.

Kevin couldn't wait to introduce his nephew to the starry sky and tell him stories, true ones, this time. That day would come soon.

In jeans, a T-shirt, and a navy-blue jacket, Kevin passed through the living room, snatching a rattle and a rubber teether off the floor. He dropped them into the basket by the sofa and stepped outside. He clicked the garage remote and watched the door rise slowly. Inside sat his passion: Lola. The sky-blue '60s Chevy pickup seemed to smile at him. Her rounded hood and big headlights like friendly eyes welcomed him. He'd found her at a junkyard and adopted her. Through his college years he'd worked hard to restore her to her former glory. Now Lola repaid the care with gentle drives along the back roads.

"Lola, did you think I'd forgotten you?" Kevin ran a hand over her waxed hood. From the neatly organized tool bench, laid out like surgical instruments, Kevin grabbed a bit of polishing cloth and ran it slowly along the fender. "I never forget you. It's just been a busy week." He moved to the truck bed and opened the tailgate. His special gear was stored in a big blue metal box: a plaid blanket, a flashlight, a pirate-style telescope, and a vintage yellow radio. He shut the tailgate with a grin.

"Let's take a spin and watch the heavenly show." He climbed into the cab. At the turn of the key, Lola answered at once, purring, thanks to Dr. Kevin's care.

They rolled down a street lit by ornate iron lampposts, heading away from the sea. Most folks in Grace Harbor flocked to the pier, the candy shop, and the attractions along the waterfront. Kevin sought the opposite—a dark place where the stars and moon smiled down.

He switched on the old radio in the dash, and soft instrumental *bossa nova* filled the cab. He drummed his thumbs on the wheel in sync with the percussion. "Pa-pa-pa-ra-pa," he hummed.

The headlights washed over worn asphalt as Lola purred along.

"Ta-ta-ra-ta-ta..."

Fifteen minutes later, Kevin signaled and turned onto a dirt road lined with scrub. He stopped in a clearing, his favorite spot. He cut the engine but left the headlights on a moment. Jumping into the truck bed, he opened the metal box and unpacked his gear. He spread the thick plaid blanket over the rubber mat and snapped the two parts of the little pirate telescope together. Then he hopped down to switch off the headlights, returned to the bed, and stretched out on his back. He crossed his ankles and laced his fingers behind his head. What could be more perfect than a sky spattered with stars and a soft breeze scented with sea and lemongrass?

For a while he simply admired the cosmic show. Then he pulled the radio from the box, turned the music down low, and lifted the telescope to the sky. It was an amateur's tool, but Kevin didn't mind. What mattered was the quiet, lying in Lola's bed, listening to good music, counting stars. In moments like these, he felt as if he were riding a magic carpet, crossing constellations, visiting planets, chasing shooting stars. He wasn't an astronomer; he was a stargazer, an amateur observer. He knew the names of constellations, planets, and their moons. This was his refuge when life on the Blue Planet got complicated.

"Tan-tan-ta-ta..."

His eyes scanned the heavens until they settled on the moon. For a moment, his thoughts drifted to the new nurse. Anna. What had happened to her baby's father? She wore no ring. Maybe her story wasn't so different from Erica's. The difference was that Anna had a profession. Still, from his experience with Erica and Theo, he knew it wasn't easy for any woman to raise a child alone, not because they weren't capable. Erica amazed him every day. But even with his help, he could see his sister's quiet fear of the future. As she liked to put it, half joking, half poetic, "The day my big brother gets married, I'm toast."

Truthfully, she didn't mind being the shield that diverted women's attention from him. Even so, he was relieved Anna now knew the blood tie between him and Erica. It wasn't good to begin a partnership with misunderstandings.

Anna seemed confident and well prepared. With a baby on the way, how would she balance work and motherhood? It wasn't Kevin's place to tell her how to juggle home and clinic. But that didn't erase a certain responsibility on his part.

He was her employer; the job would support her and the baby. Whether he liked it or not, he had a stake in her well-being.

Kevin set the telescope beside him and folded his hands behind his head again. He smiled at the quiet irony: the single doctor with two babies. Unless Anna was carrying twins who would grow up around him. "What are You saying with this, God?"

One blessing of stargazing was that prayers came more easily. Kevin could almost see the Father smiling down at His son stretched out in the Chevy's bed, but withholding an easy answer. This was something Kevin would have to discover in time.

God never handed him explanations on a silver platter.

CHAPTER NINE

The man's hands trembled as he held the disposable cup of water. Anna had noticed the tremor worsening over the past few weeks. It was so hard to watch her father, the great Serge, lose control of his arms and legs. For a while now, he hadn't been able to pivot on his heels. Walking in a straight line, he could still manage, but for how long? Falls had become more frequent. The faint scar on his left forearm told the story of a tumble into the glass-top table in his old apartment, before the move to assisted living. Shards had scattered across the living room floor, and Serge had gone down with his elbow taking the full impact. Anna had arrived for dinner minutes later. She left the pieces where they lay; the cut needed stitches. When they returned home, Anna cleaned the floor while her father studied the bandage over the sutures. After dinner, he'd declared it was time to find a place where help was close at hand. Anna had hugged him and agreed, knowing how much courage the decision had cost him. To dismantle the life he'd built with his wife, to part with the memories of Anna and her brother, to sell the house and close a chapter, that was a new season entirely, one marked by hardship and change. Parkinson's offered no return path, even with all of the therapies. Even so, he remained optimistic about the future.

Anna tucked her father's clean clothes into the dresser drawers, watching him from the corner of her eye as he tried to steady the cup. He bristled at what he called her "excessive fussing." If Anna's mother were still alive, she would have cared for him, fussing or no fussing. The young nurse had inherited her mother's passion to tend and to heal, even though Vanya had been a homemaker all her life, and the best Anna had ever known.

"I like it here, but if my moving to Grace Harbor will make things easier for you..." Serge Weber held the cup in both hands, the water making waves.

Anna closed the drawer and noticed the damp ring on his white shirt. "You've been to Grace Harbor before. I know. I fell in love with it."

Serge shuffled from the dresser, where he'd been bracing himself, to the window, his sneakered feet sliding over the floor. "If you liked the view from my new apartment, so much the better."

Anna sank onto the sofa and stretched out her long legs. She'd spent all Saturday morning running from one exam room to another at the clinic. It seemed the townsfolk had saved their appointments with Dr. Kevin for the last possible moment. According to him, summer Saturdays were usually quiet. Yet despite the heat and the beach calling, patients had shown up with everything from sore throats to sprains.

"The manager's name is Samara," Anna said. "She told me she took over about a year ago and it changed a lot. Fresh paint on the walls, new furnishings in the rooms." Anna arched her back and rested a hand on her belly. On her walk from the inn to the clinic, she'd stopped at a charming little shop and bought a light blue scrub set. The elastic waistband had sealed the deal. Her belly was round and tight now.

"I'll get everything in order, and you can come for me next weekend," Serge said, running a trembling hand through his straight gray hair. "I need a haircut."

"We can take care of that in Grace Harbor," Anna answered.

Climbing into the car after saying goodbye, she felt even more certain about moving him. Her child would need a grandfather nearby. Yes, she had to provide material things for her little pea, but she also had to nurture bonds of love. Without a father in the picture, the baby would depend doubly on her to meet those needs.

Later that Saturday, Anna headed to her cousin's home to collect the boxes from the storage unit. Mustering her courage, she texted Nadia before getting on the highway. She prayed her cousin wouldn't be home to pile more weight on her shoulders and more fear in her heart. But the prayer went unanswered. Nadia replied that she'd be waiting.

Merging onto highway toward Providence, Anna turned on her playlist. Through the car speakers, *bossa nova* set a pocket of calm around her, keeping the traffic at bay. She asked God for peace for the meeting with Nadia. Her cousin would surely prod again about "taking care of the pregnancy." Anna thought of the many women she'd cared for at the hospital who had miscarriages. One of them, Julia, had come in at her doctor's direction. The baby hadn't moved in two days. Anna had searched for a heartbeat and found none; the on-call physician confirmed the loss with an ultrasound. What followed were hours of anguish as labor was induced. In the end, Anna and the doctor delivered the baby while the young mother wept. Nineteen weeks, fully formed. That image had never left Anna's mind.

Even Tom Jobim's gentle voice and the pure, sweet notes of the song couldn't strip that picture from her thoughts. It had been her first truly shattering case, the one that taught her the deep weight of her calling and the absolute need for compassion. The worst thing for a patient was to be met with harshness and pride.

The sign for Providence appeared. Just a few more miles to go. Anna shifted her slightly swollen body in the soft seat. She needed to drink more water.

Pulling up in front of Nadia's building, Anna sighed. Let this be the last time she visited; better yet, the last time she depended on her cousin.

Nadia met her at the door, strapless black satin dress, makeup done to perfection.

After a brief greeting, Nadia jingled the storage key. "Let's go downstairs. I've got somewhere to be."

Anna followed her down the steps, nearly overwhelmed by Nadia's perfume. Her stomach warned her. Strong scents were getting harder to handle. *Last time,* she told herself.

In the underground garage that smell of fuel, Nadia pointed to a shopping cart. "Use that to haul your things to the car." She checked her phone and tapped an impatient heel against the concrete floor.

Anna hurried. Dalton had left her in this humiliating position. Her life had been boiled down to a few boxes that needed to be out of the unit quickly because Nadia had a party to attend.

Her cousin unlocked the storage door and stepped away to take a call. Anna hoisted the first box and wondered why it felt heavier than she remembered.

"I'm on my way, I'm on my way. As soon as I get rid of my cousin," Nadia said, making no effort to lower her voice.

Anna stacked another box into the cart. When she bent for the last one, a sharp tug in her lower back told her she'd be paying for this in days to come.

Nadia locked the unit. "When you've loaded the car, leave the cart by the stairs. I have to go." With a wave of a hand with long, red-polished nails, she jogged toward the garage gate, wobbling on silver heels, and disappeared.

Anna pushed the cart, trying to ignore the ache in her back. One hand steadied the top box so the stack wouldn't topple; the other steered through the parking area.

Transferring the boxes from the cart to the trunk demanded every bit of arm strength she had so she could spare her lower back. She glanced around, silently asking God for an angel to help. But headlights slid by on the avenue, each car intent on its own destination. Angels, it seemed, were off-duty.

At last, she shut the trunk, returned the cart, and slipped into the Honda Civic. She closed the door and, removing her glasses, rested her forehead on the steering wheel while she kneaded the sore muscles at the base of her spine. For the first time since Dalton's death, Anna cried without holding back. She cried for her grief, for the discovery of her husband's gambling, for the loss of material things, for the shock of her pregnancy, for her father.

The tears felt endless, like a waterfall fed by a bottomless spring. In Anna's case, the spring was pain—pain for what had been lost, pain in her back, pain for what would never be.

Chapter Ten

U nder the dim glow of the lamppost, Anna spotted Jade playing hopscotch in the inn's parking lot with a younger girl. She parked the Honda between two cars and was immediately greeted by her young hostess, who tugged the little friend by the hand. Anna climbed out carefully, a sharp pull in her lower back cutting through her like a blade. The boxes would stay in the trunk until further notice; until an angel offered to help her.

"Hi, Anna! This is Vicki. She lives next door." Jade pointed to a house partly hidden among the trees. The little girl smiled, revealing a gap where her central incisor should be.

Anna shut the car door. "Hi, Jade. Hi, Vicki." She pointed to the chalk squares on the ground. "I love hopscotch."

Jade swished her ponytail. "Wanna play with us?"

Anna rested her hand on her belly. In a few weeks, she wouldn't be able to hide it anymore, not even under her blue scrubs. "Not right now. Maybe another day."

Jade's phone rang, and she pulled it from the front pocket of her pink overalls. "Hi, Mom." Pause. "I know, Mom. Anna's here. Okay." She hung up. "My mom wants to know if you'll have dinner with us. Roberto, my heart dad, made lasagna. It's my favorite!"

Anna considered the invitation. From the bit she'd overheard, Esther had called just for that reason. Her empty stomach decided for her. "I'd love to. What time?"

"Mom said seven." Jade checked the time on her phone. "That's in fifteen minutes."

"Perfect. I'll just get changed." Anna's stomach rumbled in agreement.

Jade and Vicki went back to their game, hopping all the way to the chalk-drawn heaven.

Inside the inn, Anna greeted the receptionist with a nose piercing, the same girl she'd met that morning. The young woman was on the phone and waved as Anna passed.

In her room, Anna was met by the crisp scent of clean sheets. She dropped her bag on the chair, slipped off her sneakers, and undressed on her way to the bathroom. The warm water would ease some of the pain. In the shower, she washed her face, probably streaked with mascara. The soothing water slid down her tired, swollen body. Her soaked hair clung to her face and shoulders as she massaged her scalp with peach shampoo and closed her eyes. The steady sound of falling water was a balm.

Then her stomach growled again, but this time, it wasn't hunger. She pressed a hand to her belly. The faint flutter was lower, just below her navel. She rinsed the shampoo off and waited. There it was again, a soft movement, like a butterfly's wings brushing inside her. Anna bit her lip and squeezed her eyes shut as her heart swelled.. It wasn't her stomach; it wasn't hunger. It was life. Her little pea, her miracle, was growing, stretching, saying hello for the first time.

Anna wanted to shout, to tell someone, to share the news. But who would rejoice with her? Her father would, certainly. Dalton never would. And her late mother couldn't share in her daughter's joy.

Leaning against the wet tile, Anna laughed. The ache in her back suddenly didn't matter.

At first, the laugh was soft. Then it grew. She laughed until her tears mingled with the shower water. *Life is so perfect,* her heart prayed in gratitude. How could she ever let her baby down? How could she give in to weakness? Never.

"Mommy's here, sweetheart," she whispered, caressing her belly. "I promise to take care of you, no matter what it takes."

Ignoring the pain, she toweled off and slipped into a loose navy-blue dress. She brushed her hair and, still damp, let it cool her back. Sitting on the bed, Anna imagined her baby swimming in her belly, a miracle of God's own design. Her love for this tiny creature was so immense that it felt like an explosion in her chest. Was that what the Bible called agape, unconditional love? Because Anna would die for this life any time.

She finally blow-dried her hair, put on a light cardigan and walked to the cottage behind the inn. She rang the doorbell, and Jade opened the door, fresh from her own bath, hair wet and fragrant. "Come in! My parents are in the kitchen."

Anna followed her through the cozy living room, with leather sofas and an unlit fireplace. The air smelled of cheese and basil so heavenly it made Anna's stomach twist with ravenous appetite. She could eat a whole pan of lasagna by herself.

By the kitchen island, Esther stirred a pitcher of something that looked like lemonade. A tall man in an apron came toward Anna with his hand extended.

"Hope you don't mind the smell of onions," he said, flashing a bright smile against his dark skin. "I'm Roberto, Esther's husband."

Jade jumped between them. "And my heart dad! Did you know my real dad left when I was a baby? My Uncle Parker took care of me until Roberto came along, but I was already big and mature by then."

"Jadeee." Esther groaned, rolling her eyes at Anna and setting down the long-handled spoon on the marble counter. "Don't mind her. My girl's full of stories."

Anna shook Roberto's hand, and he returned to the stove to check the oven.

"Precious Pebble, why don't you show Anna where she'll sit?"

"Right next to me, so we can talk!" Jade tugged her to the round table by the big kitchen window.

Roberto brought the lasagna, and everyone sat down. In the middle of Jade's prayer, Anna's stomach rumbled again—and her baby fluttered once more.

"Amen," Jade said, then turned to Anna. "You're hungry. Your tummy went brooooo!" She giggled at her own joke before focusing on the gooey slice of lasagna her dad set before her.

Esther scratched her neck, shaking her head. "Sorry for my daughter's too-honest ways."

Jade just smiled, pulling a long string of mozzarella from her mouth.

"No need to apologize," Anna said. "I like honesty."

And oh, how true that was. *Better someone who talks too much than someone who hides terrible secrets,* she thought, Dalton's shadow flickering through her mind.

Anna relaxed as she listened to Esther and Roberto's easy conversation. She noticed the tenderness in the way he looked at his wife, and the quiet respect in how she looked back. The connection between them was obvious. Jade was safe, loved by her mother and by her heart dad, even if he'd come into her life when she was already "mature."

Halfway through her second serving of lasagna, Anna shifted in her seat and winced.

"Something wrong?" Esther asked.

Roberto helped Jade to seconds.

"I lifted too much weight today and pulled a muscle," Anna admitted, pressing her hand to her lower back.

"I can give you a massage later," Esther offered.

"Oh, I don't want to trouble you."

"My wife's massages cure anything," Roberto said. "Trust me. I pull muscles all the time when I run."

"In that case," Anna smiled, "I'll take you up on it."

Supper ended with coffee and red velvet cake in the living room. Jade was assigned to clear the table and load the dishwasher.

"Are you enjoying your new job?" Roberto asked, sitting beside his wife.

"Very much. It's only been a week, but I already know some of the patients by name, and sometimes I even run into them in town." Anna lifted her cup to her lips.

"Dr. Kevin has won over all of Grace Harbor," Esther said. "His father was the community doctor for over thirty years. He retired last year, and now the son's running the clinic."

"A man with drive and responsibility," Roberto added.

Esther smiled, her eyes soft with memory. "He reminds me of my brother Parker. He helped me raise Jade. Not every man would do that, raise his own niece." She patted Roberto's leg. "I'm blessed to have two such men in my life."

A comment like that might have stung a pregnant widow, but instead, Anna felt peace. Knowing Esther and Jade's story, she was simply grateful that such selfless love still existed in the world. Love that sacrifices. Agape. Just because Dalton had failed her and their baby didn't mean all men were irresponsible. Her own father had always been a pillar—at home, in church, and in their community. Even trembling and weak in body, he was still a giant in spirit.

"It's easy to see how happy Jade is," Anna said softly.

Esther sighed. "She's been through so much: misunderstanding, prejudice, hurt."

Roberto squeezed his wife's hand. "Our precious Pebble is strong. She teaches us every day. I'm the proudest dad in the world."

Anna's eyes filled with tears. Could her child, however unlikely, one day have a dad from the heart, too?

Later, with her soul light and her back eased by Esther's massage, Anna slipped into the cool sheets and closed her eyes. She rested a hand on her belly.

"I don't know what will become of us, my baby," she whispered. "But I promise you'll have all my love and protection."

CHAPTER ELEVEN

"All alive and happy." Erica performed a happy dance and locked the door of the clinic.

Anna collapsed into one of the waiting-room chairs. "Halfway through the day, I thought I was back at the hospital: dog bite, fever, coughs, and abdominal pain."

Erica dropped into the chair beside her. "End of summer break. A lot of our patients disappear in the fall and they'll pack the clinics where they actually live." She grabbed a magazine and fanned herself, her short curls fluttering back and forth in the breeze.

Anna turned to her. "How's Theo?"

The young mom shot upright. "Oh my goodness!"

"What is it?" Anna frowned and glanced around, searching for whatever had alarmed Erica.

"You've been here forever and you haven't met Theo." She smacked her palm against her forehead.

Dr. Kevin came out of his office with his leather briefcase. "We survived. Well done, both of you."

Erica sprang up and latched onto her brother's arm, ignoring the compliment. "Anna still hasn't met Theo."

He looked from his sister to the nurse. "A serious oversight on your part, Erica."

The cute receptionist pivoted to Ana. "Come have dinner with us."

Anna looked from Erica to Dr. Kevin, whose face clearly showed the fatigue of the day. "I don't know. It's been a long one."

"Nonsense. Nothing like a home-cooked meal to shake off a day like this," Erica said. She checked the wall clock. "Kevin, text Anna our address. I've got to run to Daphne's and pick up Theo." She hurried out, the door thudding shut behind her.

Anna stood and adjusted her glasses. The exhaustion on Dr. Kevin's face was proof enough he probably wanted to unwind, not host company midweek. "Maybe another time." She started down the hallway toward the kitchen where her purse was.

"Anna," Dr. Kevin called after her.

She looked back, hating to be included out of obligation. "I'm just grabbing my purse."

"Come have supper with us."

"It really has been a full day."

"Erica's right. A home-cooked meal helps. I insist." He pulled his phone from the pocket of his khaki slacks and tapped quickly. "There. Sent you our address."

Anna heard the ping in her scrub pocket. "Dr. Kevin, I'm grateful, truly, but you don't have to feel pressured because of Erica."

He smiled. "Erica blindsides me like a runaway truck barreling downhill. Once the shock passes, I decide whether she has a point." He pushed his hair behind his ears. "In this case, she does. Come. You and I have already crossed the formality line. If you don't mind an omelet and yesterday's rice, you're more than welcome. That's Erica's idea of a home-cooked meal."

Crossed the formality line? Given their awkward first meeting, followed by her confession about the pregnancy, that sounded...good. "An omelet with expired rice sounds delicious."

He held up a hand. "Whoa—*not* expired. Leftover." He chuckled.

Anna relaxed at the sight of the dimple in his right cheek. "My apologies. Leftover."

He pointed toward the door and started out, turning back with his hand on the knob. "One more thing, Anna. Call me Kevin."

She arched a brow. "And the patients?"

He tilted his head. "Okay—at the clinic, 'Doctor' is fine." He twirled his hand in the air like he was greeting royalty. "Outside of it, I'm Kevin."

Anna laughed at the theatrical flourish. She liked his humor and lightness. Erica had quite a brother to help with Theo while Anna's own stayed as far away as possible for reasons unknown. "All right, *Doctor* Kevin." She grinned at his mock scowl. "We're still in the clinic, remember?"

"Touché." He stepped onto the porch and looked back. "We'll be waiting."

"I'll be there as soon as I lock up."

Anna made one last round, closing the doors to the exam rooms. Since last week, she'd taken over the end-of-day checklist, much to Erica's delight, since the receptionist bolted at five on the dot to pick up Theo. She called herself the *Afternoon Cinderella*. Erica had nicknames for everything; it had to be a Miller family trait.

When the GPS announced the destination, Anna let out a long sigh. She'd half expected the doctor to live in one of the new developments on the edge of Grace Harbor, those houses that looked like imaging clinics, square-shaped with steel and glass everywhere. Instead, she parked along a street arched with old trees and lined with Craftsman homes, her favorite style. She stepped from the Honda and opened a white picket gate set into a neat hedge. A navy-blue door stood out against the freshly painted white siding and matching shutters. A small dormer jutted from the cedar-shingled roof—maybe a study or reading nook. The place was irresistibly charming and unassuming.

Anna rang the bell and was greeted by Erica, Theo clinging to her hip and chewing a piece of bread. A pinch caught at Anna's heart. Soon she'd be holding a baby too. Where would she live? What would the nursery look like? So many questions; so many unknowns.

"Hi, Anna. This is my Theo."

"Ta-ta-ta, ma-ma-ma," the little boy babbled, scattering damp crumbs.

"Hi, Theo, I'm Anna."

"Na-na-na," he answered.

"Come in," Erica said, stepping over a few toys on the floor and leading the way.

Anna shut the door and followed her into the open-concept kitchen. A stack of containers crowded the counter. "Need a hand?" She set her purse on a dining chair.

Erica deposited Theo into Anna's arms as if passing a sack of flour. "Here, pop him in the highchair."

Theo smelled of baby soap with a hint of sour milk. His rosy cheeks were dotted with chewed bread. Anna buckled him in and took the seat beside him. At the stove, Erica stirred a pot, sending occasional splatters of brown sauce across the burners.

Kevin strode in, running his fingers through damp hair. In jeans and a white T-shirt, he looked different from the crisp professional she knew. "Anna, looks like Theo's already won you over."

"At first sight," she said.

"What can I get you to drink?" he asked.

"Wine in the fridge," Erica called over her shoulder.

Kevin glanced at Anna. "Water? Juice?"

Grateful for the rescue, Anna smiled at him. Erica didn't know about the pregnancy, even though the scale had tattled an extra pound that week. "Water, please."

The twister that was Erica-in-the-kitchen somehow produced a delicious beef stew with potatoes and a pot of fresh rice. "No expired rice," she told her brother as she set the bowls on the table.

Anna savored not only the meal, which truly did dissolve some of the day's stress, but the company of Kevin, Erica, and Theo. The doctor was easy to talk to and carefully steered conversation away from work and world disasters.

"It's a full moon." He glanced out the window.

Erica wiped Theo's mouth and leaned toward Anna. "My brother has a terrible secret."

Anna looked at Kevin, who rolled his eyes. "Here we go, little sister."

Erica shrugged. "He's a werewolf." She scooped up Theo. "He loves full moon and rides with Lola." She swayed down the hallway, humming.

Who on earth is Lola? Anna turned to Kevin just as he pulled his phone from his pocket. He gestured for Anna to wait and stepped out the back door into the dim backyard.

Anna looked around, shrugged, and started clearing the table. She'd do her part and wash up. Maybe Dr. Kevin had a date with Lola. She wouldn't be in the way.

Through the kitchen window she saw him pacing the yard, talking seriously.

She soaped the sponge and attacked the mess Erica had left. Household noises ebbed and flowed around her: baby cry, running water, a thud, Erica's voice.

When Kevin came back in, Anna was loading the last plates into the dishwasher. Pots and serving bowls were draining in the rack.

"Anna, I'm so sorry. You didn't need to do the dishes—that's my job." He tucked his phone into his back pocket and stepped closer.

"It was the least I could do after such a good meal." She dried her hands and hung the towel on its ring.

"Please, come sit. I'll make some tea." He guided her to the living room.

She sat down, feeling the warmth of the leather sofa. The bustle in the hallway quieted. The kettle began to sing and Kevin returned to the kitchen. Anna rubbed her lower back, remembering the boxes still in her trunk. No angel had shown up yet; maybe she'd ask Roberto tomorrow.

She leaned her head back and closed her eyes. The clink of mugs and the whispering kettle lulled her. *Just a minute. I'll close my eyes for just a minute.*

Her phone startled her awake. She pushed her glasses up, now halfway down her nose, and wiped the corner of her mouth with the back of her hand. Seated across from her, Kevin sipped from a mug and smiled.

"Oh, did I fall asleep?" She fished out her phone. "Hello, Dad." Pause. "Yes, all good. I'll pick you up the day after tomorrow." He told her everything was ready. "Perfect. Love you. See you soon." She slipped the phone back into her pocket. "That was my dad," she said pointlessly.

Kevin passed her the other mug from the coffee table. "Does he live in Providence?"

She took a sip of the warm peppermint tea. "In a retirement home. He has Parkinson's. I thought it best to bring him closer to me. My mom passed away. It's just the two of us." She lifted a shoulder. "I mean, I have a brother, but he keeps his distance. He rarely visits. So technically, it's me and my dad." She set a hand on her belly. "For now."

"I'm so sorry about your dad, Anna. If there's anything I can do, say the word." He studied her face and took another sip.

"He'll be your patient, I'm sure. I'm glad for that." She scooted to the edge of the sofa.

"It's my pleasure," he said gently—and there was the dimple again.

Maybe it was fatigue. Maybe it was the phone call. Tears pressed behind her eyes, and the pregnancy hormones certainly weren't helping. "Thank you, Doctor—uh, Kevin."

Later, when Anna laid her head on her pillow, Theo's face drifted through her mind. She tried to hold on to the peace she'd felt in Kevin and Erica's home. It was a household of mother, child, and uncle—different, but warm and safe. Erica and Theo were cared for and protected. Anna would do her part and work hard to give Dr. Kevin some rest so he could keep being the uncle and caregiver they needed. And if Lola was the doctor's girlfriend, she was a lucky woman.

A warm tear slipped down Anna's cheek. She turned toward the window and watched the play of shadows on the glass.

CHAPTER TWELVE

The room's darkness was softened by the faint blue glow of a nightlight plugged into the corner outlet. A mobile of stars and planets spun softly above the crib, playing a gentle lullaby. Kevin rocked in the chair, shifting the bottle in his hand. The warm weight of his nephew in his lap stirred every kind of feeling in him. Theo wasn't his son, but his heart told a different story. He would die for this chubby little boy. When Erica finally dropped the middle-of-the-night feeding, Kevin knew he would miss these quiet hours. This was when the doctor could think about his own life and what direction it would take once Erica moved out.

Medicine had been his only faithful companion through college and residency. Paola had finally given up competing with his growing responsibilities. He hadn't been surprised to get her wedding invitation six months after they broke up. Erica kept trying to find him a girlfriend, but Kevin had other priorities: improving his clinic and stepping out of his father's shadow. He didn't want to be "Dr. Kevin, son of Dr. Vincent Miller." He wanted his own name, his own reputation. The people of Grace Harbor remembered him as a boy and a teen, but when he left for the big-city university, he'd cut those ties. Now he needed to use that distance to establish himself as a competent, independent physician. It was hard to earn trust when folks remembered him mainly as the rebellious kid of the prestigious family. His recklessness was in the past, but it still lived on in his father's memory.

Theo finished the last of the milk, and Kevin set the empty bottle on the dresser. He stood and put his nephew up on his shoulder to burp, padding barefoot across the soft rug. When Theo finally burped, Kevin laid him in the crib. The baby fussed a little, then drifted to sleep.

Back in his room, Kevin leaned against the pillows and switched off the lamp. In the next room, Erica slept soundly. It was inevitable that his thoughts turned to Anna and her situation. She was still at the inn. Why hadn't she moved into a place of her own? Her salary matched Grace Harbor's cost of living just fine. Her father was in assisted living. Was Anna covering his expenses? Questions popped like popcorn in his mind. No matter how often he told himself it wasn't his problem, he still thought about it. The experience with Erica had taught him a lot about the serious things of life, including motherhood and fatherhood.

In spite of his concern for the new nurse, sleep won out. But by dawn the thoughts returned as he dressed for another day.

As he pulled into the clinic parking lot, he spotted Anna half-buried in the trunk of her white Honda. He parked and hurried over.

"Everything okay?" He hitched the leather satchel higher on his shoulder.

Anna straightened and pulled a plastic bag from one of the boxes. "Just looking for a few things."

"Moving into your new place?"

She shut the trunk and hugged the bag. "Not yet. I'm still at the inn."

He searched her eyes behind the lenses. "Anna, do you need help?"

She rubbed her lower back. "I haven't been able to get the boxes up to my room at the inn. I hurt my back."

"Why didn't you ask me?" The question was out before he could stop it, and he saw her eyes widen.

"Because you're my boss, Dr. Kevin. You aren't responsible for my personal life." She clicked the lock on the key fob.

"Anna, I didn't mean to offend you." *Anna is not Erica,* he scolded himself.

She shook her head. "You didn't. I'm sorry for snapping." She exhaled. "I have to learn to manage on my own. The back's better. I'll take the boxes up later."

Kevin walked with her to the clinic door. She pulled out the key and unlocked it, then turned back to him. "Dr. Kevin, you've already done far more for me than I ever expected. You took a chance on a pregnant nurse. You trusted me. You even gave me a key to the clinic." She lifted it. "I'll be grateful forever for all of it. I didn't mean to be rude, but I do have to learn to take care of myself and my child, who will never know his or her father."

Kevin's feet went cold, the chill rising up his legs. In so many ways, Anna's story echoed Erica's. He wanted to ask where the baby's father had gone, if he'd run like Bob. "I understand," he said softly. "For what it's worth, I did what I believed was right in hiring you. And as far as I'm concerned, you'll be here a long time. I have plans, you know that." He forced a smile to cover the worry tugging at him.

"Thank you. You don't know how much that means."

Their first patient arrived to find the doctor and nurse talking at the door. Right behind him came Erica, breathless and smoothing her hair.

Kevin's day settled into the usual rhythm of appointments, stitches, prescriptions. All the while, he kept a discreet eye on Anna. She was steady and skilled; the pregnancy hadn't dimmed her energy. He noticed the small swell beginning to show under the blue scrub top. He was almost surprised Erica hadn't blurted something indiscreet by now.

Late in the day, Kevin got a call to see an elderly patient who lived near the clinic. He didn't usually make house calls, but this was better for the patient. At ninety-seven and a widower with no children, Mr. Paco could no longer get out. Dr. Vincent Miller would have scolded his son for "wasting time," but Kevin was determined to chart his own course.

In the old house downtown, Kevin examined him. Paco was strong for his age, but his diabetes kept slipping out of control.

Afterward, Kevin called Erica, who told him Anna had seen the last patient, just a suture removal. Relieved, he headed for home. Lola was waiting, and a drive under the stars would clear his head; the thoughts of Anna and the baby wouldn't let him go.

He turned onto Main Street. A few blocks later, he passed in front of Tranquility-by-the-Sea Inn. And there it was, a surreal repeat of that morning at the clinic: Anna, half inside the trunk of her white Honda. He braked, backed up, and parked beside her car. Climbing out, he walked over.

"I swear I'm not following you," he said.

"If I didn't know your schedule, I might think you were," she teased, smiling back. "Looks like I won't be able to turn down your help this time." She nodded toward the boxes.

"Looks like fate had a hand in this." Relief washed through him. Kevin locked his SUV, hefted one box from her trunk, then stacked a second on top and lifted them both. "You lead. I'll grab the last one after."

Anna opened the inn's door. Esther looked up from her laptop at the desk, then hurried over and flung the door wide. "Need a hand?" She held out her arms.

"I've got it," Kevin grinned over the top of the boxes.

"Dr. Kevin! Now I can see you back there," Esther said, smiling in recognition.

"How's Jade?" he asked, steadying the load.

"Stubborn as ever. It's incurable." Esther shut the door behind them.

Anna waved to her host. "I'll go ahead." She started up the stairs.

Kevin excused himself and followed. In the room, he set the boxes beside the wardrobe. The place was as cozy as he'd imagined. No wonder Anna was content to stay; maybe she liked having people close by. Esther seemed exactly the kind of person who would look out for her.

"I'll grab the last one." He dusted his palms on his khakis and stepped back into the hallway.

When he returned, he set the final box with the others. "All set."

"I don't know how to thank you," Anna said, clasping her hands.

"It was nothing. I'm glad you're settled in."

She laced her fingers, following his gaze around the room. "This place is so cozy that I haven't even started looking for a house."

He let out another quiet breath of relief. "Esther, Roberto, and Jade know how to care for people."

"They sure do. I feel cared for."

On the way home, Kevin felt the weight on his shoulders slowly lift. Esther and her family were watching out for Anna and the baby, even if, as far as he knew, they didn't yet know about the pregnancy.

He ended the night with a drive in Lola. The ride on his magic carpet brought rest to his heart.

And all along that starry path, Anna's face stayed with him.

CHAPTER THIRTEEN

"Whenever he goes out with Lola, he comes back all cheerful," Erica whispered to Anna.

The nurse slid a clipboard across the counter to the young receptionist. Dr. Kevin had arrived at the clinic as if he were walking on summer-morning clouds. He was whistling a tune—bossa nova, Anna recognized the soft Brazilian jazz melody—and greeted both his sister and the nurse with a broad smile and that deep dimple.

This Lola must be very special. Anna forced a polite smile for Erica. It wasn't in her nature to chat about coworkers' personal lives, least of all her boss's.

She turned and called the next patient. "Mario, Exam Room Two."

The man with stitches in his hand nodded to Anna and followed her in. She settled him on the exam table.

"No redness around the stitches?" she asked, washing her hands at the sink.

"No. Just a little itch."

Anna stepped closer to inspect. "Looks good. Dr. Kevin will take a look."

He came in still whistling, still floating. Anna moved back and waited for instructions.

"All set. Anna will remove the stitches." He smiled at her, then peeled off his gloves and tossed them in the trash.

Through the remaining appointments, Dr. Kevin kept up that soft whistle. Anna realized she'd never made Dalton whistle. There had been very little music in her marriage, but plenty of complaints about her shifts, though. Looking back, she was convinced the hospital years had been worth it. Without that experience, how would she be prepared now to find a solid job and provide for her baby? No one married planning for the worst, but the worst, in Anna's view, deserved a moment's sober thought. Anyone could fail a spouse. Dalton might have blamed her long hours, but their lack of real conversation had been a warning sign all along. The worst came, and it came hard.

That was then. This new season pointed toward opportunity.

At day's end, Anna and Erica stayed to close the clinic.

"With my brother in such a good mood, I thought he'd let me duck out early," Erica said, wiping down the wall-mounted instruments. "I've got to pick up Theo. I don't want to overuse Daphne's kindness."

"Go ahead. I'll finish up." Anna closed the cabinet in the exam room.

"Really? Thank you!" Erica washed her hands, then paused at the door and turned back. "What do you do on weekends?"

"I visit my dad. He's in a retirement home. He has Parkinson's." She explained that he was moving to Grace Harbor the next day.

"And besides that?"

Anna pulled the paper off the exam table. "I don't have friends here yet to go out with."

Erica clapped once. "I've got an idea. I'll ask Kevin to take you out with Lola."

Anna's eyes nearly popped. Since when would Kevin take her along as a third wheel with his girlfriend? "That's...a little odd, don't you think?"

"Why odd?" Erica frowned.

"Me, your brother, and his girlfriend, or friend, whoever she is."

"What girlfriend? Did Kevin say anything like that to you?"

They stared at each other for a beat. Then Erica doubled over laughing, laughing so hard she had to catch her breath. "Oh wow," she said, still trying to steady her breath. "No wonder Kevin says women don't know how to talk."

Anna rubbed her forehead and nudged up her glasses. "I'm not following."

"You think Lola is a person, don't you?"

"Isn't she?"

Erica took Anna by the arms. "We really do need to learn to communicate. No. Lola is not a person. Not flesh and blood. She's made of metal."

"Metal?" Anna echoed.

"And you know what? I'll let you discover exactly what Lola is. Kevin would love to explain." Erica waved goodbye and slipped out.

Anna could hear her laughter down the hallway until the front door clicked shut. Finally, Anna laughed too. *Are my hormones playing tricks on me? I need to be more careful about assumptions. I've misjudged Kevin more than once already.*

Back at the inn, she could barely stand the curiosity. What metal treasure deserved such a charming name?

***

"Nonsense," Esther said, pouring coffee for Anna. "Jade and Roberto went out. Once a month they have a daddy–daughter date. I don't like eating alone."

"Thank you, again. Supper was wonderful." Anna lifted the mug and took a sip.

"Too strong? Roberto is a better barista." Esther sat across from Anna.

"No, it's just that I'm avoiding coffee at night because…" She stopped mid-sentence.

"It's all right. You don't have to explain." Esther offered her a gentle smile.

"I'm pregnant," Anna said, fixing her eyes on the mug.

"Oh, congratulations," Esther said softly.

Anna glanced up at the woman's almond-shaped eyes. "My husband died in a car accident."

"I'm so sorry, Anna."

"And he left me in debt and alone with a baby to raise." There. If that complicated things too much for Esther, their friendship would end here.

Esther nodded, understanding. "That's a hard road."

"It was a miracle Dr. Kevin hired me."

"I'm not surprised," Esther said. "He stepped in for Erica without a second thought."

"I'm a little scared," Anna admitted, tracing an imaginary pattern on the white tablecloth.

"Who wouldn't be? But please know you can count on me and Roberto. And I'm sure you'll be able to count on many people here in Grace Harbor."

What could strangers possibly do for her and her child? Anna already felt blessed just to have a job and a peaceful room to rest in. Still, Esther's empathy was unmistakable; perhaps this friendship could grow.

"I'm grateful for your kindness, truly, but I know I need to stand on my own two feet."

"I understand," Esther said. "Just leave the door open a crack."

"Do you think I'm being proud?" Anna stilled her finger and laced her hands.

Esther stood to fill a kettle and set it on the stove. Anna angled her chair toward her and waited. Esther leaned against the granite island.

"Motherhood taught me that each of us knows the weight of our own story," she said. "You have your reasons for closing doors or for doubting people's intentions. Pain makes us skeptical. It's a natural, self-protective instinct."

The kettle whistled. Esther poured hot water into a mug, set it beside a box of teabags, and sat again.

Anna chose chai and dipped the teabag into the steaming water. "I still feel like I fell off a cliff. Dalton gambled while I worked. It was like trying to fill a bucket full of holes. And I had no idea. I learned it all from the accountant. My sense of self shook. I was sleeping next to my adversary and didn't know it."

"I know what it is to sleep next to an adversary," Esther said quietly. "If it hadn't been for my brother, Parker, I don't know what would've become of me and Jade. Maybe I would've made it on my own, but it would have been so much harder."

Anna took in Esther's words, the mother of a special girl, a woman with stature that went beyond height. It was easy to glance around this warm kitchen, at Esther's calm face as she waited for her husband and daughter to return from their date, and forget the storms she must have weathered to reach this shore. "I want to open the doors," Anna said. "I'm just so afraid."

Esther squeezed Anna's hand. "It's scary, but your baby will gain so much if you do. Believe it."

The back door opened and Jade burst in with a small bouquet of daisies. She raced to Esther, breathless. "Mom, Dad gave me flowers!"

Roberto followed in a suit and tie. Jade, in a twirly yellow dress, was a ray of sunshine. Heat pricked Anna's eyes at the sight of such restoration. Who was she to doubt God's power to open a new path through hard ground? It was so easy to see someone's healing and assume the way there was smooth with gentle hills and lovely vistas. We praised their cure or even envied it without asking how they arrived there. What stories, what obstacles, what wounds? No one was exempt from adversity. God never promised smooth sailing; storms were inevitable. But someone did command them to be still. Esther was living proof. Anna didn't know what tempests mother and daughter had survived, but with Jade and Roberto in the boat, the waters had calmed. *When will I find calm?* Bitterness clouded the vision like cataracts—distorting, blurring, draining hope. All Anna could see was storm.

"What beautiful flowers, sweetheart," Esther said, breathing them in. "Did you say hello to Anna?"

Jade turned to her. "Look at my flowers!"

"They're lovely," Anna said, sniffing back tears.

"Good evening, ladies." Roberto filled his mug with coffee before joining them.

Anna returned the greeting and stood, smoothing her scrub top. "Thank you for supper, Esther. I'm going to head up."

Jade stepped close and peered at Anna's belly. "You ate a lot, huh? Your tummy's big."

Esther stood and gently drew her daughter aside, but Roberto intervened.

"Pebble, remember what we talked about? What kinds of things we say to people?"

Jade stuck out her lower lip. "Say nice things."

"That's right," he said.

Jade looked at Anna, and a chill ran up the nurse's legs. If the girl had noticed her belly, others soon would too.

"Anna, your hair is very pretty. I can loan you some clips," Jade offered, glancing at Roberto for approval. He gave her a thumbs-up.

Anna touched her hair. "I'd love a clip."

Half an hour later, Anna stretched under the covers, a pink barrette in her hair. She laid a hand over her belly. Her little one was lively, somersaulting in the warm dark.

Anna wondered if it was time to tell Erica about the pregnancy.

Chapter Fourteen

With the house to himself, Kevin did a quick tidy-up, gathering Theo's toys into the living room basket and putting away the clean dishes. Erica had left early with her son, taking advantage of her day off to walk on the beach with Daphne and the twins.

Kevin turned on his *bossa nova* playlist, and the sound of piano and drums filled every corner of the living room and kitchen. In jeans and a T-shirt, he whistled along to the melody between replies to a message on his phone. The ultrasound machine would arrive in an hour, just enough time to enjoy a quiet morning and give Lola a good polish.

In the garage, Kevin grabbed a rag and ran it lovingly over the blue body of his car. Everything in his life was going well. Theo's routine was well established. Erica was growing more confident as a mother.

Anna. She had finally accepted Kevin's help carrying the boxes. That had made him happy. *Move forward one square this week,* he thought, picturing the board game of his life. Kevin had hired a contractor to renovate the clinic. He'd need to discuss the stages with Anna to make sure the work didn't interfere with appointments. On Monday, he would call her in to talk. With the new ultrasound equipment, he'd have more tasks for her, maybe even a raise, since patients would be coming in more often for scans. In the last years before retirement, his father had let the clinic run down, sending more and more patients to Providence for tests and consultations. Kevin wanted to bring them back.

With circular motions, he polished Lola's hood. "Ready for our ride tonight?"

Leaving the garage, Kevin entered the house, still flooded with *bossa nova,* and took a quick shower. He tossed his jeans into the laundry basket and pulled a pair of khakis from the closet. Grabbing the first T-shirt he found, he headed to the clinic.

The technicians arrived right on time, carrying the new ultrasound machine to the designated room and removing the old, obsolete one. Kevin left them to their work and went to his office. He had just installed new software to store patient information and had begun transferring data when the door opened. His heart sank.

"Dad, what a surprise." Kevin stood up.

Dr. Vincent Miller looked around the room, then craned his neck toward the waiting room. "What's all that noise?"

"The technicians are installing the new ultrasound equipment." Kevin studied his father's long, lined face. The loose trousers and vest gave him the look of a weary university professor tired of grading mediocre papers.

"I'm making a few improvements to the clinic," Kevin said, already knowing the look of distrust he'd receive. Sure enough.

"Improvements? What for? What matters is our knowledge."

Kevin sighed inwardly. "Knowledge is essential, but nowadays we also have technology."

"Bah."

Kevin hated that expression of disdain, his father's favorite, the same one he'd used when he learned about Erica's pregnancy and that his son intended to take her in, even though the family home was three times larger.

"Any special reason for this visit?" Kevin asked as a faint electronic sound came from the hallway.

"I came to tell you I'll be traveling for a golf tournament. If you could check on the house for me, I'd appreciate it."

To his father, Kevin was more of a caretaker and errand boy than a doctor. Dr. Vincent Miller pulled a ring of keys from his pocket and set it on his son's paper-cluttered desk.

"Sure. I'll do that. Have a good trip."

Dr. Vincent Miller gave the office another critical once-over. "You should organize these folders."

"I'm transferring patient files to the computer."

"Bah."

The man left with a curt wave. Kevin dropped into his rolling chair, making a mental note to replace every piece of furniture in that office.

After listening to the technicians' explanations and instructions about the ultrasound machine, Kevin returned to the tedious job of entering patient records. He reviewed their cases as he went—symptoms, treatments, and his father's notes. There were new approaches to some conditions he planned to discuss with the patients.

Two hours had passed when the doorbell rang. Anna and Erica had keys to the clinic, and the sign outside clearly showed the hours of operation. Maybe it was an emergency—a new patient in the area.

Kevin stood, tucked his hair behind his ears, and walked quickly through the waiting room. When he opened the door, his heart sank even further. The day had started with *bossa nova* and Lola, continued on with his father's visit, and now, the reappearance of Genise. He braced himself for the traps she was bound to set, just as she had until Erica discovered she was married and had been inventing symptoms.

"Good afternoon, Genise. We're closed." Kevin pointed to the sign beside the door.

The curvy woman, face sculpted by some greedy plastic surgeon, smiled. Her artificially plump lips curled like the grin of Alice's terrifying Cheshire Cat. "Dr. Kevin, I came to ask forgiveness for the misunderstanding."

"You're forgiven," Kevin said flatly, keeping a firm grip on the door, leaving only a narrow crack open. Her perfume hit him like blades, a sharp pain radiating through his head.

She stepped closer, her white dress clinging to her body, trapping her chest like two melons desperate for freedom. "Is Erica here? I wanted to apologize to her too." She craned her neck to peer past Kevin into the reception area.

For a moment, Kevin considered lying, saying Erica was busy in the back. With a woman like Genise, witnesses were always useful. The game on his life's board had just gotten more complicated. One wrong move and his reputation would be in ruins.

"She's not here," he said curtly.

"Then, Dr. Kevin, could we talk? I'd like to explain the misunderstanding and tell you that my husband and I have separated." She pressed her lips together in feigned sorrow and blinked her long false lashes that, to Kevin, looked like spider legs. And he had arachnophobia.

"As I said, there's nothing to explain. Everything's perfectly clear."

Kevin glanced past her, and a wave of relief washed over him. He opened the door wide and smiled. "Anna, thanks for coming so quickly. I wanted to show you something."

Anna, in a loose floral dress and with damp, freshly washed hair, looked at him with a faint frown. "Of course, Dr. Kevin." She passed the woman and stepped inside.

This nurse never lets me down, Kevin thought, feeling his earlier good mood return.

"I heard you have a new nurse. I didn't know she worked weekends," Genise said with a sneer.

"Anna Weber is an excellent professional. And if you'll excuse us, we have work to do." Kevin began closing the door. The reception phone rang.

"Dr. Kevin, I—" the woman tried, pushing the door with the tip of her high heel.

"Dr. Kevin, an urgent call," Anna said, waving the receiver.

Kevin glanced between the nurse and Genise. "Duty calls." He pushed the door shut as the woman clicked away across the porch in her stilettos. Locking it as though against invaders, he turned toward the phone, but Anna hung it up.

"But—" he started.

Anna smiled, lifting her cell phone with the screen still lit. "I was the one who called."

Kevin burst out laughing, throwing his arms up like a runner crossing the finish line, though he restrained the sudden urge to hug her in gratitude. "You have no idea how you just saved me from a trap."

"I imagined as much. I told you I'd find a way to repay your help with the boxes." Anna dropped her phone into her bag, biting back a laugh.

"Repayment or not, you saved my skin, and maybe my reputation."

Anna smiled. "Then I'm glad."

Yes, the mood of *bossa* and Lola had returned. Kevin looked at the woman before him, in her floral dress and without makeup, and his admiration growing by the second. Her damp hair framed a face both strong and gentle, the firmness of her chin balanced by her clear eyes. Even her glasses seemed part of a perfect harmony. How he longed to know more about her, what made her smile beyond caring for patients, what she read, where she liked to walk, what music she loved.

What kind of man had left her in such circumstance? What kind of man could abandon a woman like this—and pregnant, at that? Kevin swallowed the anger bubbling inside him. "The ultrasound machine arrived," he said at last. The questions bombarded his mind.

"Oh, I'd love to see it. Actually, after dropping my father off at his new retirement home, I drove past and saw the technicians' van. I noticed your car and decided to stop by," she said.

"Is your father doing well? Does he like the new place?" Admirable woman—her scent as soft as wildflowers, her voice clear as a mountain stream. *Foolish man that I am,* Kevin thought, scratching his head.

"Yes, and he's found a friend who lives there now. I'm relieved."

Anna told him about her father's move and how much calmer she felt having him nearby. Kevin felt calmer too, knowing her father was close.

In the exam room, Kevin showed her the new equipment and explained some of its features. Then he said,

"I'm not your doctor, but I feel I should ask—how's your prenatal care?" He covered the machine with a plastic sheet.

Sitting on the padded exam table, Anna smiled. "I have a doctor at Providence Hospital. The baby and I are fine—both gaining weight." She laughed, running a hand over her belly.

"You know you can count on me," Kevin said, feeling a strange warmth creep from his neck down through his chest and into his tingling fingers.

"I know, Dr. Kevin, but I'm being well looked after," she replied.

He caught her playful tone as she called him Dr. Kevin—they were, after all, in the clinic.

"But I do have a question," she added. "What's Lola?"

"Ah, Lola! My companion on moonlit, starry-night rides."

"A motorcycle?"

Kevin grinned. "No. Want to see her?"

"Now you've made me curious." Anna slid off the exam table.

"You know what? I'd love to take Theo on his first ride with Lola. How about we all go together? I'll talk to Erica."

"Deal. What time?"

"Seven."

That evening, Kevin left the clinic whistling, feet light as he made his way to the car. He got home still whistling his Tom Jobim tunes.

Dr. Miller Senior and Genise seemed determined to ruin his life, to sour his days, but his conversations with Anna were pure *bossa*.

Chapter Fifteen

T he navy-blue door stood wide open when Anna climbed the steps of the cheerful porch. Piano, drums, and a baby's cry drifted to her as she paused in the doorway.

"Come in, Anna," Kevin's voice called from the living room.

She stepped inside and waited, taking in the built-in shelves lined with books and seaside décor: a bronze lighthouse, two rope-wrapped vases, and an ivory seahorse on a bronze pedestal. Though there were clear signs a child lived here, the room still smelled distinctly masculine—of leather and wood. Anna breathed in, held it as if diving beneath a wave, and let it out. Her stomach didn't rebel like it had at Genise's ultra-sweet perfume.

Kevin appeared with a bottle in one hand and Theo slung over his arm. The boy wore only a diaper and T-shirt, sucking down milk with gusto. "Total disaster. I had to wash Theo, the bedding, and scrub the mattress. This kid eats like a champ. What goes in, comes out just as fast. He's a cannon."

Anna took in the sight of the tousle-haired doctor juggling baby and bottle. A suspicious brown blotch stained his white T-shirt. She held out her arms. "Want me to hold him so you can clean up?"

"I am a little messy, huh?" He wrinkled his nose.

"A little," she teased, taking Theo and the bottle and settling on the edge of the sofa.

"And to think Erica was just 'popping out' to the bakery. She must be waiting for the baker to knead the dough." Kevin excused himself and disappeared down the hallway.

Theo nursed and grunted with pleasure. Anna bent and breathed in his damp hair. Babies smelled so good. She hummed along with the instrumental music.

Her own little one seemed to catch the cue and fluttered inside. In a perfect world, she wouldn't have to worry for two; there would be a husband to share the load. Dalton had lived like a tourist on planet Earth. She shouldered responsibility; he chased whatever pleased him, and the cost had been Anna's peace and her child's security. The signs had been there when she first met him; she'd looked away, chalking it up to a phase. She wanted marriage and children. The marriage ended in ruin, and the child would have no father. If someone had told the first lie in that relationship, it was Anna, lying to herself that Dalton was ready to commit, that a wedding ring would change everything. That didn't excuse his choices. But now it was all too late. She hadn't waited to truly know him before marrying. He hadn't waited to run wild.

Kevin returned with damp hair and a clean shirt. "Brand-new man. Erica owes me." He laughed and sat beside her. "And thank you again for saving my hide today."

Anna set the empty bottle on the coffee table and lifted Theo to burp him, patting his back. "If we're partners, I have to keep you safe."

"Generous of you," he said, leaning back.

She grinned. "Self-interest. I need the job."

"I don't see selfish motives fitting you. It's not who you are."

He thinks I'm generous? She hardly felt worthy of the word. "I'm not sure I'm what you think."

He turned toward her. "Then who are you?"

Theo burped, and Anna settled him on her knee. "A widow to a man who came into the world to party." *And I ignored the signs—so many signs.*

Kevin straightened, eyes widening. "I'm sorry, Anna. When—?"

"Dalton died right before I found out I was pregnant. He was addicted to gambling. I learned the rest after the crash." If she was going to work with Kevin for a long time as she hoped, better to open a door, as Esther would say.

Theo whined. Anna stood and swayed him in her arms. The front door was still open, letting in the late-summer cool. Night had fallen, but the darkness didn't invade this bright room. With the soft music and warm light, Kevin's living room felt like an antidote to the bitterness that usually slithered in when she spoke of Dalton. How could she give in to resentment with a baby in her arms? Soon she would hold her own, hers and Dalton's. Oh, it was hard to swallow all that had happened and all that was still happening.

Kevin rose and gently took the drowsy boy. "I'll put him down."

Anna stayed in the living room with her thoughts. Had she gone too far, opening her past to Kevin? He hadn't said much, only looked at her, pale.

He returned minutes later. "Anna, I'm so sorry for all of it." He shook his head. "I don't know how to help. Tell me, please, anything."

She pushed up her glasses and rubbed her eyes, then looked at him standing there. "I've told you. You've already helped more than you know."

Erica breezed through the open door with two grocery bags. "Would you believe the baker burned the brioche and I had to wait? Who can live without brioche?"

She greeted Anna, oblivious to the gravity that had hung in the room, and headed for the kitchen. "Kevin, what's that smell?"

Without taking his eyes off Anna, he answered, "Situation contained. Theo's napping."

Dishes clinked in the kitchen. Anna glanced away. "I'll go help Erica," she said, and hurried out.

Erica set brioche in a basket lined with a checked tea towel. "Anna, would you grab the cream cheese and butter from the fridge?"

They set the table together. Kevin came in and started the coffee. "Tea for you, Anna?"

"Tea, please."

Erica froze in the middle of the kitchen, hands on hips. "So, did you figure out Lola?"

Anna shook her head. "Not a motorcycle, but we're all going for a ride on or with her. I'm curious." She looked to Kevin.

"Can you believe Anna thought Lola was your girlfriend?" Erica laughed, dropping into a chair.

Kevin smirked. "A tin-can girlfriend. She takes me on great dates."

Anna sat as well, smoothing her dress. "So?"

"You'll find out after the meal," he said, pulling out a chair and snagging a brioche.

Anna was grateful he'd steered things toward Theo. He recounted the baby's earlier "explosion" and the ensuing cleanup.

"I greeted Anna wearing a splattered T-shirt," he confessed.

"Good training for when you're a dad," Erica said around a bite of brioche slathered in cream cheese.

"Did the training have to be so intensive? So explosive?" Kevin teased, pinching her nose.

Anna watched the siblings with interest. Their playful banter continued as they tidied the kitchen. At last, Erica disappeared down the hallway and returned with Theo dressed in jeans and a light sweater.

"Theo's ready for Lola," she announced.

"Let's go." Kevin opened a drawer and grabbed his keys.

The garage door rose like a theater curtain, and Anna smiled. "I expected a car big enough for all of us but not this one." She stepped inside and circled the Chevy. "It looks brand-new." She glanced at Kevin's proud face, the way a father beams when someone praises his child.

"It's my brother's true love," Erica said, shifting Theo to her other hip. "Just one problem."

"What's that?" Kevin asked.

"We're rookies at this parenting thing. There's no car seat for Theo. And Lola only has two seats." Erica gestured toward Lola.

Kevin scratched his head. "Strike one."

"Okay, here's the plan—you two go. I'll stay with Theo," Anna offered.

"No way. We're all going to see the stars," Kevin insisted.

"I'll follow in my car with Theo," Erica decided.

After much back-and-forth, Anna accepted the plan: she'd ride in Lola with Kevin, and Erica would follow.

Lola sliced into the night, headlights lighting Kevin's path. Anna smoothed a hand over the cool vinyl seat.

"Ta-ta-ra-ta-ta," Kevin hummed along with the music.

"No whistling now?" Anna adjusted the seat belt across her belly.

"You noticed I like to whistle?"

"Even the patients notice." She smiled.

He twirled his index finger in the air. "There's always a record player spinning in my head."

"Good for stress, Dr. Kevin." She bobbed her head to the rhythm, then glanced back at him. "What do you learn stargazing?"

He tapped the steering wheel. "That I'm finite. I am not here on this planet long, so I'd better use what I have well."

Anna rested her temple against the cool window and looked up. "Funny to think we're spinning and spinning without stopping."

He turned onto a dirt lane. "And what do you learn, thinking about all that spinning?"

She laughed. "Philosophical, aren't we?"

"You started it." He eased Lola to a stop in a small clearing.

Erica's compact car pulled in beside them. Anna turned to Kevin. "My life's been spinning too, but like a washing machine. I'm still dizzy."

Kevin studied her face in the dim light. "Stargazing doesn't solve our problems, but I promise it brings peace. God's bigger than all of that, isn't He?" He tipped his chin toward the heavens.

"I believe it, even if I'm still spinning."

Sharp taps on her window made Anna jump. It was Erica, with a sleepy Theo. Kevin hopped out and climbed into the truck bed. "Give me one minute."

Anna stepped down and breathed in grass and sea.

"Come on up," Kevin said, jumping down to help his sister climb in with Theo already nodding off.

Anna moved closer, hand drifting to her belly. Her baby answered with another set of joyful flips. Oh, how she longed to share that joy out loud.

"Need a hand?" Kevin offered.

"I've got it." She caught Erica's curious glance flick from her to Kevin.

"Sit over here," Erica said softly, pointing to the corner beside her perch, Theo cradled against her.

Anna scooted across the spread blanket and reclined against the rear window. "So this is how you gaze at the stars?"

Cross-legged, Kevin lifted things from a metal box. "Or like this." He passed her the vintage telescope. "The early sky-watchers didn't even have these; it was all by eye." Then he lay back with his hands folded beneath his head.

Anna pressed the scope to her glasses and tried to focus. "I'm not sure what I'm seeing, but it's beautiful."

"Now's the moment to pry secrets out of my brother," Erica said, rocking Theo.

Kevin chuckled under his breath. Anna looked over. "What do you mean?"

"When we were kids, we'd lie on the grass and watch the sky. That's when Kevin's mouth opened and the secrets tumbled out."

"What kind of secrets?" Anna asked, curious where this was going.

"Don't tell her about Penelope," he pleaded in mock despair.

Erica pointed at him. "She cut her hair because of you."

Kevin sat up. "I should explain." He glanced at Anna. "I was nine, she was eight. I made the dumb mistake of saying her hair looked like corn silk. The next day she found scissors and chopped it all off. Her mother nearly nailed me with a shoe. I was grounded a whole week of spring break."

Anna laughed. "What did you learn?"

"Never comment on a woman's hair."

"Too bad." Anna tugged a strand of her own. "I was about to ask your opinion for my new cut."

All three laughed, and Theo jolted in his mother's arms.

Anna startled too, then pressed a hand to her belly. "My baby jumped as well." She clapped a hand over her mouth, and saw Erica's eyes go wide.

"Baby? You're pregnant?"

Chapter Sixteen

Kevin's destination was bed. But he was intercepted by his sister, waiting just outside the en-suite bathroom door. He scrubbed his face with the towel and tossed it onto the sink.

"Since when did you know Anna was pregnant?" Erica hopped onto the queen bed and folded her legs, her polka-dot pajamas making her look like a girl.

Kevin tugged the navy-blue quilt, nearly dumping Erica onto the floor. "Since the beginning. And now I want to sleep. It's been a long day." He bit his tongue to keep from mentioning their father's visit to the clinic that morning. He'd save that for a time when he wasn't so exhausted from constantly moving backward and forward on the board game of his life.

"Why didn't you tell me?" Erica scooted back to the middle of the bed.

"Confidentiality, remember?"

"She's not your patient."

"That's why I don't tell you things." He pointed a finger at her. "You want all the details."

Theo fussed. Erica slid off the bed. "Lucky for you I've got mom duties. Good night." She slipped out and closed the door.

Kevin turned off the light, his eyes drifting to the open window. The night sky was the same as an hour earlier when peace had ruled in Lola's truck bed. He, Anna, Erica, and Theo had felt no worries aside from a pesky mosquito or two. All was well, a gentle night. Then Anna's jubilant announcement ended the quiet. It wasn't the new mom's fault; she'd been amazed by the antics of the life growing inside her. But Erica's quick tongue had peppered Anna with indiscreet questions, the very ones Kevin wondered himself but refused to ask. "What happened to the baby's father?" Erica could hardly have chosen worse words. Kevin had seen Anna's wounded face in the moonlight. He'd nudged his sister, and she'd realized her blunder and clamped her mouth shut. The ride back in Lola was silent. Erica drove ahead with Theo, leaving Kevin to apologize, something he only managed when Anna climbed into her Honda in front of his house. He held her door and said,

"You've noticed my sister can be indiscreet."

Anna had offered a half smile. "There's not much point hiding the pregnancy anymore. My belly's making the announcement for me."

Kevin had sighed as her car rolled down the street.

He sighed again now, staring at the stars from his bed, though his relief was only partial. Things with his father were worse than ever. The man wouldn't stop indicting him for his wild teenage years. Couldn't he see Kevin was a man now, not a ragged-jeans kid hanging out with the wrong crowd? Since the day Kevin chose medicine, his life had changed. Maybe his hair still ran a bit long for Dr. Vincent Miller's taste, but the rest was in the past. Kevin knew he still had ground to gain. But the worst was behind him. How much more did he have to prove that he was responsible, that the clinic was thriving, that his relationship with Erica and Theo was built on love, and that he was at peace with God? His mother's death had shaken his world to the core. It was still hard not to see her smile. She had been his greatest cheerleader and the lightning rod for his father's gripes. A routine surgery that turned into a nightmare had taken her life and fueled Kevin's drive to study medicine.

***

Monday's responsibilities buried Kevin's personal worries and brought Anna's smile back. The first appointments and scans with the new ultrasound gave the young doctor and his nurse fresh reasons to feel hopeful about the clinic's future.

Kevin handed a prescription to a patient with an ear infection. The man thanked him and left. Kevin peeled off his latex gloves and washed up.

Anna stepped in with a clipboard. "That was our last patient. Erica's already locked the front door."

He dried his hands with paper towels. "Still up for our meeting?"

"Always," she said, nudging her glasses.

They headed to the office after saying goodbye to Erica, who hurried off to pick up Theo from Daphne's.

Anna sat opposite the desk. "The paper piles are shrinking."

Kevin chuckled and pulled out his chair. "I'm finally getting the charts into the computer."

"I can help too. I'm free on weekends," she offered.

He studied her a moment. The strong, square line of her chin had softened; her left hand rested over the gentle swell beneath her blue scrub top. He wanted to promise that everything would be all right, but what could he offer beyond her job?

Stacking a few folders, he said, "Let's table that. I actually hoped we could revisit the clinic hours."

"What are you thinking?"

"Opening earlier. If it goes well, maybe staying open later, too." He woke the monitor with the mouse. "This week's schedule is tight. Erica says some patients have complained ."

"How would we make it work?"

"If you're willing, you could open and start triage early. I'll be here, but we can't count on Erica first thing."

Anna smiled. "I can start tomorrow, if you like."

"That's determination."

"For someone who's worked night shifts, getting up an hour earlier is nothing."

They set the plan. Kevin gave her the computer password and a few pointers on the new records system.

Half an hour later, they locked up and walked to the parking lot.

"How's the inn?" Kevin asked, the streetlamp washing his face with gold.

Anna clicked her key fob and the Honda chirped. "Good. I'll stay there for now. I like having Esther, Jade, and Roberto nearby."

Kevin remembered Erica's fear of being alone late in pregnancy. How could he tell Anna he'd help if she needed it?

"Good," he said, swinging his leather satchel like a schoolboy.

"I know I'll need to get a crib, baby things, everything, pretty soon."

He noticed the slight pinch at the corner of her mouth—worry, unmistakably. "Erica has lots of Theo's things she's not using." *Sorry, little sister—I'm volunteering you. You owe me.*

"I'll talk to her."

As Anna's Honda pulled out, Kevin swung his satchel again, feeling like a goofy teenager too shy to ask a friend out for ice cream. But in Anna's case, ice cream wouldn't be enough.

How could he help—really help—without overstepping?

CHAPTER SEVENTEEN

T he neon sign flickered *Open*.

Anna parked her Honda, determined to solve the problem of her tightening waistline. The few clothes she'd salvaged from the wreckage of her life after Dalton no longer fit. Grateful that her finances were in order after her first month in Grace Harbor, she stepped into *Love at Second Sight* with a quiet mission—to explore baby items. The last doctor's visit had brought reassuring news: her baby was healthy, growing just as expected.

When Anna opened the glass door, the little bell chimed and her heart gave a leap. Every day, the reality of motherhood became more tangible. Her gaze fell on a white crib in the corner, and she could almost picture her little bundle of warmth and sweetness nestled into the soft mattress. What would she name the baby? To her disappointment, the last ultrasound hadn't revealed the gender. Still, her list of names was ready, though she hadn't shared it with anyone, not even her father. None of the names felt quite right yet. She wanted something different, something special.

"Good afternoon," said the woman with curly hair, walking toward her. "Anna, right? I try to remember all my customers' names."

Anna smiled, glancing from Nina back to the crib. "That's right."

"How's the uniform working out?" the shop owner asked, motioning toward Anna's light blue scrubs.

"Very practical and comfortable." She smiled and she ran her hand on the not-so-soft fabric of the uniform.

On her first week in Grace Harbor, Anna had stopped by the store to buy the scrubs. She was surprised Nina remembered her name.

The bell rang again. Anna turned, startled as though she'd been caught doing something she shouldn't. A plump woman with uneven gray bangs walked in and gave Nina a hug. Then her eyes landed on Anna, and she smiled brightly.

"Anna? Anna Weber?" The older woman widened her eyes.

Anna instinctively reached for her chest, searching for the metal name tag she'd forgotten to wear. How did this woman know her name? She didn't recall seeing her at the clinic.

"Yes, that's me," Anna said cautiously, keeping her tone polite but reserved.

Nina moved back behind the counter to help a customer.

"My name's Grace. I knew your mother, Beatrice. We last spoke on the phone a while ago. She talked about you the whole time." Grace adjusted the large patterned bag on her shoulder. "You're the young version of Beatrice! It's been, a guess, about three years since we talked, with my Abel being sick and all. We never spoke again. How is she?"

Anna's smile faltered. "My mother passed away two years ago."

Grace's hand came to rest gently on Anna's shoulder. "Oh, honey, I'm so sorry. Truly. And your father?"

Anna didn't have good news there either, though at least he was alive. "He lives here in Grace Harbor now. At the Sunflower Retirement Home."
She watched Grace's expression turn concerned, but if the woman had another probing question, she wisely let it go.

"What a coincidence! I volunteer there. After Abel died, the house just felt too empty. Staying busy helps. Serge, right?"

"Yes, that's him."

Grace let the strap of her bag slide down her arm and caught it in her hand. "I'll visit him tomorrow, then." She nodded toward the counter. "I need to chat with Nina here. Enjoy your shopping."

Grace struck up a lively conversation with Nina and another middle-aged woman who had just entered, carrying a stack of books. Anna noticed how naturally the three women spoke, like old friends. Grace Harbor truly was the kind of place where connections bloomed.

Listening to their laughter, Anna wandered among the racks of clothing, trying to shake off the uneasy feeling that she was doing something wrong. After all, she didn't owe anyone in Grace Harbor an explanation for her pregnancy.

She brushed through the hangers of maternity wear, pulling out a white dress trimmed with lace on the sleeves and hem, and loose-fit navy-blue overalls. She chuckled, remembering Kevin's navy-blue front door and several other details in the same color.

Nina came over, leaving the women talking near a corner lined with bookshelves. "Let me open a fitting room for you." She glanced at the clothes in Anna's arms, opened a small changing room, and moved a few hanging items aside. "If you need anything, let me know."

Anna nodded and stepped inside. The dress fit her new curves beautifully, stretching just enough to last through the second trimester. She turned from side to side in front of the mirror, hands resting over her belly. The baby seemed to approve by giving several little kicks.

The soft overalls hugged her rounded figure comfortably. Pleased, Anna left the fitting room and glanced again at the crib. She hoped it wouldn't sell too soon. She could already imagine it in a cozy nursery. *If only I had a home to put it in.* The inn was so warm and convenient, but it wasn't hers.

Drawn to a nearby shelf, Anna passed by the crib and began browsing the baby items: tiny shoes, hats, neatly folded onesies, plush animals. She picked up a soft elephant in shades of pink, blue, and yellow and gave it a gentle squeeze.

"Turn the key underneath," Nina said.

Anna turned to her, then followed the instruction. A sweet lullaby floated through the air. Tears filled her eyes. Her baby's first song. How she longed to share this moment with someone, to talk about it, to be proud with someone.

A gentle touch on her arm made her look up. Nina held out a packet of tissues from her shirt pocket. Anna took one and dabbed her eyes.

"It gets to you, doesn't it?" Nina said kindly.

"Do you have children?" Anna asked, sniffling.

"Yes, my little David will be two soon."

Anna glanced toward the crib again, and Nina followed her gaze.

"I can hold it for you," Nina offered softly.

"I'm only five months along. I don't even have a place to put it yet." Anna looked back at the white crib longingly.

"Then I'll keep it here and mark it *sold*," Nina replied.

"I wouldn't want to take advantage of your kindness."

Nina smiled and gestured toward Grace, who was now reading on a chair across the shop. "In Grace Harbor, we learn that those who receive much, give much in return."

Anna followed her gaze, intrigued. What stories did these two women carry? She only knew that Grace had lost her Abel, likely her husband. What other losses had shaped their lives?

Holding the little elephant and the clothes over her arm, Anna said quietly, "All right then. I appreciate it."

Back at the inn, she placed the toy on her dresser. It would be a daily reminder that her life was about to change completely.

The rest of the week fell into a comfortable rhythm. Anna's arrangement with Kevin was working perfectly. She arrived an hour early, handled patient intake, and guided them to the exam rooms. Working with Dr. Kevin felt like dancing with a partner who knew every step. He was organized, capable, and kind. Patients left the clinic with confidence, and that made Anna listen even more carefully to each story that came through the door.

Friday afternoon, Erica dashed off as usual, leaving Anna to finish cleaning the exam rooms and lock up. Dr. Kevin had gone an hour earlier to check on an elderly patient.

When everything was tidy and ready, Anna stepped into the kitchen, grabbed a bottle of water from the new fridge, and sat down to rest her feet. Her ankles were swollen, and she promised herself a long rest on the weekend. The baby gave a little kick, and Anna smiled. A peaceful evening drive in Lola with Kevin, Erica, and Theo sounded lovely. Ever since their first and only ride together, the calm of that night still lingered despite Erica's shock at learning of the pregnancy. Thankfully, Kevin's sister hadn't asked a single inappropriate question all week, though her eyes often sparkled with curiosity.

The clinic doorbell rang. Anna glanced at the clock; it was half an hour past closing. Had Erica forgotten to flip the sign? Anna finished her water, dropped the bottle in the recycling bin, adjusted her glasses, and hurried to the door. When she opened it, she froze.

Standing there was the same scarlet-lipped woman who'd shown up the day the new ultrasound machine arrived. Her smile faded the instant she saw Anna.

"We're closed," Anna said evenly. "Is this an emergency?"

The woman didn't look ill. She peered past Anna's shoulder. "Is Kevin—Dr. Kevin—still here?"

"No. Would you like to book an appointment? You can call Monday if it's not urgent." Anna didn't care for the way the woman's eyes swept her face and body.

"Have you worked here long?" The woman raised a perfect eyebrow.

Anna straightened and lifted her chin. "If you need an appointment, please call Monday."

Color crept up the woman's face. "I don't need an appointment to talk to Kevin."

"In that case, you know where to find him." Anna began to close the door. The woman wedged the pointed toe of her high heel in the gap. "Was there something else?"

"Kevin won't like hearing how his nurse treated me."

Anna raised an eyebrow. "You're not my patient."

The woman huffed and spun on her heels, clattering away across the wooden porch.

Anna shook her head and shut the door firmly. No wonder Kevin had been so grateful the day she'd rescued him from that "trap," as he'd called it. The woman was trouble through and through. *Look who's talking,* Anna thought. *Could anyone bring more trouble than Dalton left behind?* She smiled wryly. She wasn't exactly in a position to judge. Still, one thing was clear: Dr. Kevin wanted nothing to do with that woman, and Anna could only imagine why. Not that it was any of her business.

She only hoped the woman wouldn't cause problems out of jealousy. Anna had once heard about a male nurse who poisoned a patient just to get close to his wealthy wife. It had even become a TV crime drama episode.

Anna laughed softly to herself. Her imagination was running wild.

What harm could that pushy woman really cause, anyway?

CHAPTER EIGHTEEN

D r. Vincent Miller let his seasoned gaze sweep the room and come to rest on Kevin. The young doctor nearly suggested his father run a finger across the furniture to check for dust. He decided sarcasm would only draw more disdain. Lately, Kevin compared visits with his father to lancing a boil: only pus and a bad smell came out.

"I imagined a different kind of place." The older man sat on the leather sofa.

Kevin tapped his phone to stop the music. His father didn't go with *bossa nova*. Maybe operetta, but Kevin didn't have the patience for drama. "What kind did you expect?"

"Something more... alternative." He crossed his legs and smoothed a crease in his golf khakis.

Even Kevin's wet hair, dripping onto his neck, couldn't cool the heat climbing up his nape. "I don't know what you mean."

"Your hippie life. Now that your sister is here, living among the minimalists, a pile of floor cushions and a few incense sticks would suit."

Honoring his father felt harder than understanding any biochemistry exam. Kevin sat in the armchair facing him. He remembered the big, lifeless house where his father lived, so unlike the home it had been while his mother was alive. During the golf trip, Kevin had gone there twice, watered the plants, aired out the bedroom, just as he knew his father preferred, and fought hard not to be buried under the avalanche of emotion. "This house works fine for me. I'm glad Erica and Theo have plenty of space."

"Are you trying to jab me?" Dr. Miller uncrossed his legs.

Kevin pressed his fingers to his forehead. "Dad, I know you disapprove of my life, my ideas, my decisions. I'm just asking for a little respect. I'm not that rebellious kid anymore. I grew up. It wasn't easy, but I've got different priorities now, different values, the ones you and Mom taught me. Because of those, I found my footing again."

The older man's eyes traveled the room once more. Resting an arm along the back of the sofa, he fixed his gaze on Kevin. "You condoned your sister's sin."

Kevin glanced at the wall clock. Erica wouldn't be back for at least an hour. She'd texted that she was having supper with Daphne and her husband, Andrei. "I didn't condone anything. I welcomed my sister."

"By taking her in, you stamped approval on her mistake."

"I held out a hand. She did wrong, Dad, but what else was I supposed to do—leave her to fall? Mom would have helped her." *Bingo.* His father's expression softened.

"If your mother were alive, Erica wouldn't have fallen into that trap."

Father and son, two doctors, one young and one much older, let silence settle between them, as if honoring the memory of the Miller family's matriarch.

"If Mom were alive, a lot of things would be different," Kevin said at last.

Dr. Vincent Miller stood. "I need to go. I came to see your house, invited or not."

What good would it do for Kevin to remind him that he had invited him? Maybe not formally, but he'd said his door was open anytime. And still, the conversation always came loaded with accusations, never a drop of grace.

Kevin walked him to the door and shut it once the older man slid into his black Mercedes. He thought of Lola in the garage—his Lola—so much more fitting for Grace Harbor life. So much more him.

In the kitchen, he poured a glass of lemonade and sat on a stool at the island, watching condensation bead and slide like tears on the glass. Was a friendly relationship with his father even possible? Not while the man kept seeing him as a long-haired delinquent.

The doorbell rang. Kevin finished the lemonade and set the glass down. He hoped it wasn't his father back for round two.

To his surprise, Anna stood on the porch. "What a surprise! Come in. Is something wrong at the clinic?"

She stepped inside and let her purse slip down her arm. "No, the clinic's fine. But that woman from the other day came by asking for you."

"Genise." Kevin frowned. "Come have some lemonade with me."

Anna followed him to the kitchen and took a seat at the island. The last thing she needed was more relational trouble.

He filled two glasses and handed her one. "Just use good judgment with her." He told Anna about the woman's repeated visits. "I'm not sure I believe she's separated, and it isn't my job to find out."

"I kept our conversation short. I came because I was worried. She left pretty riled up." Anna took several swallows.

"You did the right thing. With Genise, caution's the rule."

Anna stood. "May I use your bathroom?"

"Of course." He pointed down the hallway. "Second door. No promises on its condition."

When she disappeared, Kevin pulled a box of breaded fish fillets from the freezer, preheated the oven, and laid them out on a baking sheet.

Anna returned and sat again. Kevin turned toward her—her face looked a touch fuller, her eyes heavy.

"Would you split some fish fillets with me?" He slid the tray into the oven. "Not exactly home-cooked, but cooked at home." His dimple made an appearance as he smiled.

"My mouth just watered." She traced a fingertip along her glass, returning his smile.

Kevin clapped once. "Your enthusiasm is contagious. I'll throw together a salad."

"Careful, you're making a pregnant woman dangerously hungry."

He grabbed lettuce, tomatoes, a jar of olives, and a carrot. "I'd never tease you, pregnant or not." He tapped his phone, and soft piano notes drifted into the kitchen as the salad came together.

"I feel like I'm mooching off everyone's cooking. I eat with Esther and her family most nights. And now, here I am."

"I'm no chef, but I manage. And I love having company. Gives me a chance to practice." He laid tomato slices into a bowl. "Ta-ta ta-rah-ta..."

"Do you always sing when you cook?" Anna leaned an elbow on the cool granite countertop.

"I sing when I cook, when I work, when I drive around with Lola. It's how I unwind."

The fillets finished baking, and he set them on the table beside the salad. They enjoyed the simple meal to the mellow tune.

"Sometimes I forget how much my appetite's grown. Once I start eating, I can't stop." She took another bite of fish.

"Enjoy it." Kevin smiled. Anna's presence felt like *bossa nova* itself—easy, warm, relaxing. Watching her instinctively stroke her belly, no one would ever guess how hard a season she'd lived through. She was remarkable. Strong. Kevin's prayer rose without effort: that God would shelter her and the baby in Grace Harbor. *If only I could do more without overstepping,* he thought, as he searched for wise ways to help.

"And how's Lola?" Anna asked, spearing a tomato.

"Fresh coat of wax yesterday." Kevin hummed the chorus of the song *Garota de Ipanema*.

"And the stars? Still in the same place?" Anna hiccupped and covered her mouth.

"Right where we left them, always ready for the show." Kevin finished his lemonade, feeling lightheaded. Like a teenage boy, giddy for no good reason.

"Tell me a pretty star name," Anna said, leaning back and setting her fork on an empty plate.

He drummed his fingers. "I like Maia. One of the brightest in the Pleiades. Blue—deep blue."

"Maia. What a lovely name! What does it mean?" Her hands brushed over her belly.

"No one's quite sure. Some say 'water,' others 'mother,' or even 'illusion.'" He watched her slip off her glasses and rub her eyes. When she looked up at him without her glasses, Kevin took the chance (and his sister's advice) to read what might be there. Maybe it was the lemonade, but he saw a tenderness laced with sorrow in her caramel eyes. He had so many questions, too many, but asking them wouldn't be wise or kind. Their relationship was professional, though he wished for more, at least the easy ground of friendship.

She put her glasses back on. "They're all beautiful meanings."

His phone buzzed in his jeans pocket. Kevin read the message and felt the blood drain from his head. With surprising self-control, he switched the phone off and slipped it away.

"Is something wrong?" Anna's brow furrowed.

He stood with his empty plate. "A personal matter I need to take care of."

The door opened and Erica breezed in, a giant diaper bag on her shoulder and a sleeping Theo in her arms. Kevin felt a rush of relief and a prickle of irritation. Relief, because her arrival spared him from a conversation he didn't want to have with Anna about that message. Irritation, because no one had the right to burden Anna with more worry, and that message would bring not only worry, but indignation.

Anna helped Erica with the bag. The two women disappeared down the hall, leaving Kevin standing in the middle of the kitchen, plate in hand, stunned.

Chapter Nineteen

T he music on Kevin's lips had vanished along with his smile. The little
dimple in his cheek was gone, replaced by a crease between his brows. That
image resurfaced in Anna's mind when she woke the next morning and stayed
with her through breakfast at the inn. The night before, Erica's arrival with Theo
had kept Anna from asking Kevin what was wrong, what message he'd received. If
it had been about the clinic, he would have said so. Personal matters weren't part
of their conversations, unless they touched the work of doctor and nurse. That's
why Anna had brought up Genise. Kevin hadn't seemed particularly worried
about her. His whole expression had only changed when he saw that message on
his phone.

Anna wiped buttery fingertips on a paper napkin and finished her latte. The
inn's dining room had grown so familiar that unfamiliar faces at breakfast felt
like intruders in her home. Much of that came from Esther's warm hospitality.
When Anna didn't eat with Esther's family, she stopped by Beth's Bistro, the most
popular spot in Grace Harbor. Beth and her partner, Martha, cooked homestyle
food that always agreed with Anna's stomach, which felt like a bottomless pit
these days.

"Good morning, Anna." Jade approached the table carrying a tray. "I'm helping in the kitchen today 'cause it's PD day and the teachers don't work, you
know."

Anna smiled at the girl in denim overalls and an apron. "That's great. Work is
important."

"It is. My mom taught me that. I could be on my phone scrolling and typing
and talking nonsense, Mom's words, but I'm being useful." Jade picked up

Anna's empty mug. "'Talking nonsense' is gossip, Dad says. I just don't know why grown-ups whisper."

Anna set her plate on the tray. "I think adults sometimes discuss important things other people don't need to hear."

"Do you have important things to discuss?" Jade's almond eyes sparkled.

"A few."

"And I can't know them?"

Anna smiled to herself. "Not all of them, but I can tell you one thing."

Jade grinned. "And that's not gossip?"

Anna shook her head. "No. My dad lives at the Sunflower Rest Home. Do you know it?"

"Oh, yes. Uncle Abel lived there and died." Jade's face scrunched with the start of a cry. "Do people go there to die?"

Anna's first impulse was to laugh at the bluntness. Still, the comment wasn't far from many people's euphemisms, tragic and comic at once. Nursing home. As if it were the last station before the end. Anxiety pricked her. Was it really best for her father to live there, or would it be better for him to live with his daughter and grandchild? Something to consider.

She stood and added the rest of her dishes to Jade's tray. "A nursing home is for older people who need help. It doesn't mean they'll die soon."

"Is your dad very old?" Jade sniffled.

"He isn't."

"Then why does he live there?"

"Jaaade," Esther called, coming closer.

"Mom, Anna was telling me about her dad. It isn't gossip." Jade steadied the tray as the dishes rattled.

"Sorry about my daughter, Anna," Esther said.

"Actually, Jade helped me think through something important," Anna replied.

"I did?" The girl beamed.

"You did."

Esther guided her daughter toward the kitchen. A woman in workout clothes waved to Esther and said she was heading out for a beach run.

"What are your plans today?" Esther asked Ana.

"I'm taking my dad for a haircut, then we're going to stroll somewhere." Anna rose.

After Esther suggested a few local spots to visit, Anna went upstairs to brush her teeth. She checked the mirror once more, approving the new, or gently used, overalls. She slipped a small crossbody bag over her shoulder, kissed the velvety elephant, and headed out. On the drive to the nursing home, her thoughts drifted to the night before. She worried about Kevin more than a nurse should worry about her boss. It was impossible not to compare him to Dalton. How many times had she forced herself to overlook Dalton's questionable behavior while they were dating? She'd tried to believe he would change. But time doesn't change anyone, except physically. The man she'd met at church had worn a Venetian carnival mask: bright and handsome on the outside, but hollow inside. Kevin, on the other hand, never made her suspicious in any way. Aside from Anna's early misunderstanding that he was Theo's father, day by day she found more to admire.

She turned down the street to the nursing home. What was she thinking, admiring her boss as a man? They had a professional relationship. That was all. She was a pregnant woman, newly widowed. A merry widow, she scolded herself.

Her father was ready, waiting in the lobby and chatting with the older woman Anna had met in Nina's shop.

"Grace told me you two ran into each other, and she recognized you because you favor your mother," Serge said, kissing his daughter's cheek.

Anna noticed his freshly cut hair. "Quite a coincidence." She greeted Grace.

"My husband, Abel, spent time here. Now he's resting in heaven." The woman pointed upward.

"Do you volunteer here often?" Anna asked.

Grace lifted a shoulder. "After I sold the shop to Nina, I cared for Abel full time. Now that I'm alone, I like helping out the families."

"'Love at Second Sight'—why that name for the shop?" Anna took her father's arm and they moved toward the glass doors.

Grace walked with them. "Love at first sight isn't always trustworthy. It's good to take a second look. Seemed fitting for a shop of treasures that once belonged to someone else. I don't say 'used.' People around here call it the Broken Hearts Shop."

Then Anna had gone to the right place, because that was exactly the state of her heart. "Do broken hearts stay broken forever?"

They reached the parking lot where Anna's car was waiting.

"We have to let God mend them," Grace said.

Anna nodded. How long did mending take? Grace said goodbye and went inside. Anna helped her father into the car and fastened his seatbelt, then got behind the wheel.

"Looks like we won't need the barber after all." She eased the Honda out and headed toward the beach, per Esther's directions.

Serge lifted a trembling hand to his hair. "Grace cut it."

Anna took a closer look and remembered Grace's slightly crooked bangs. Her signature was on the back of her father's neck. "There are a few uneven bits."

He shrugged. "Where to now?"

"There's a pier just ahead. Esther says it's perfect for a stroll and to watch the fishermen." She parked by the curb and helped him out. Arm in arm, they walked to the boardwalk. The beach wasn't as crowded as she'd imagined; with summer ending, the tourists were heading back to work and school. Father and daughter passed a few fishermen and paused to peer at the fish flopping in wicker baskets. Gulls circled overhead, hoping for lunch.

At the end of the pier, a wide platform held a rustic pergola, good for a bit of wind and sun protection. Anna and her father sat on a bench and watched the sea. A sailboat skimmed the horizon. An airplane passed, trailing a white ribbon across the blue.

"How are things at the clinic?" her father asked.

"Very well. I love the job." Anna found herself telling him about Kevin's plans for the practice, about Erica, Theo, and the siblings' arrangement. She told him about the ride in Lola and Kevin's home.

"So you're all quite close," Serge said, twining trembling fingers—a sign his medicine was wearing off and the tremors growing worse.

"That's the advantage of a small town, where everyone gets to know each other. Like that *Cheers* show." She sang the chorus of intro song for the sitcom, where everybody knows your name. Same with Esther and Roberto and Jade."

"That's about right. This has been my impression since your mom and I first came here. They never forget your name." He smiled, trembling fingers still intertwined.

Father and daughter talked some more about the good, old days when Mom was living. She was such a good mother. Anna desired to be the same kind of mother to her baby.

Back at the boardwalk, Anna ducked into a candy shop and returned with ice cream cones for them both. The little spoon would be a challenge for her father, but he had never been one to turn down a sweet. They returned to the car and repeated the routine: help him in, buckle him up. As she did that, Anna continued talking about Mom, trying to distract him from the humiliation of being cared for like a child, always needing help with something that required fine motor skills. Parkinson's was a slow betrayal of the body. It stole the steadiness of the patients, one small motion at a time. A faint tremor years before when he held his coffee cup had turned into stiffness and shaking, making even walking a struggle. That slowness trapped him inside his own body. His mind was still sharp, but the body no longer obeyed.

Anna noticed his jaw tightening, the familiar sign of frustration. But, she kept talking about Mom.

Soon, Anna rounded the Honda and stopped when she heard her name. Erica was coming down the sidewalk with Theo in the stroller. Anna waved, and Erica came over. She introduced her father.

"What a smiley baby," Serge said.

Erica let him play peekaboo with Theo, then tugged Anna a step aside. "Have you heard the latest?"

"What happened?" Something at the clinic? Or with Kevin?

"Genise is going around saying Kevin is the father of the baby." Erica tilted her chin toward Anna's belly.

"What baby?" Anna's hands flew to her abdomen, as if to shield her child.

"Yours."

The blood drained from Anna's head. Dizzy, she grabbed the car for support. Nausea surged, and she coughed. A hiccup sent a hint of strawberry ice cream back up, bringing the stomach's acid burn with it. Erica pulled a water bottle from the stroller's bag.

"Dear, are you all right?" Serge craned his neck, trying to see her better.

"I think her blood pressure dipped," Erica said. "Here, sit." She opened the back door and helped Anna down. "Drink."

Theo cried. Erica's attention split between friend and son. "He needs a change. I've got to go."

Anna lifted a shaky hand in a weak wave and let her head rest against the seat. She drew a deep breath. Was that what the phone message had been about?

"Anna, are you okay? What did that young woman say to you?" Serge tried to twist around in his seat.

Anna laid a hand on her father's shoulder. She swallowed her tears along with the acid burn. A revolt of feelings raged in her chest. Her baby fluttered. Her father's trembling hand covered hers.

She had to hold it together—for him, and for her child.

CHAPTER TWENTY

K evin paced the living room with a hand on his head. "Are you crazy? Why did you tell Anna that?"

Erica bounced Theo in her arms. "I thought she had a right to know. You're going to let that nutcase talk behind Anna's back? No, sir."

Theo started crying. Erica left the room, leaving Kevin planted on the rug, steadying himself against the unlit fireplace. The house seemed to spin like the Earth on its axis. Just as Anna had said her world was spinning. What should he do now? Going after Genise to set her straight would be like throwing gasoline on a brushfire. A jealous woman was capable of anything. It wasn't only in movies that they put live rabbits in pots of boiling water.

Where would Anna be? Still at the beach? Erica had said she and her father were getting into the car. Maybe she'd gone back to the inn. Yes. He'd stop by the inn. If she wasn't there, he'd wait. He wouldn't intrude on her time with her father at the nursing home. He'd wait all night if he had to.

Kevin did a few more laps around the room, ran to the kitchen, grabbed the SUV keys, and flew to the inn. Esther told him Anna hadn't returned.

"Is something wrong?" she asked.

"I need to have a few words with her."

"Don't you have her phone number?" Esther opened the laptop. "I've got it here."

"No need. I have it. I wanted to talk to her in person." Kevin thanked her and left. He got in the car and took a spin around Grace Harbor, down Main Street with its charming shops, past the train station, and along Seaside Avenue. No sign of the white Honda.

He went back to the inn and waited in the car, staring at the gigantic spruce in the front yard. He needed to talk to Anna. He wouldn't leave it for the next day. He jumped at a knock on the window.

He opened the door. "Jade, everything okay?"

"My mom told me to bring you this bottle of water. It's really hot. Are you waiting for Anna?"

"I am." He took the bottle and opened the cap.

"I like her. Anna," Jade said, ponytail swishing.

"So do I." Much more than he should.

"I'm going back in. My mom said not to bother you."

"You're not bothering me, but do as your mom says."

Jade skipped back into the inn, and Kevin gulped the water down his dry throat, closing the door. An hour later, the Honda pulled into the lot. He flung the door open and got out, following the moving car until it stopped.

"Anna," he called.

She looked through the window and ran her fingers across her forehead. "Why is this happening?"

Anna was so pale. Kevin wished he could take her somewhere safe, away from gossip and added weight. Lola could take her to see the stars. "I don't understand. Jealousy, maybe."

She got out and slammed the door. "I didn't do anything to her. We exchanged a few words at the clinic."

"It's my fault. I should have taken more drastic action when she started pestering me."

Anna shook her head. "It's not your fault."

"I'll take care of it, clear everything up." He reached a hand toward Anna, but thought better of what he was about to do.

"I've spent all this time keeping my pregnancy a secret. People need to know my baby had a father. It's time I swallowed my bitterness toward Dalton for my child's sake."

"Anna, I didn't want to be one more burden on you." He shoved his hands into his jeans pockets so he wouldn't risk any inappropriate gesture.

"You're not a burden. On the contrary. Where would I be if it weren't for your understanding?" Anna pushed up her glasses and pressed her fingers to her eyes.

"I'll admit I don't know what to do. Talking to Genise means kicking a hornet's nest. She's dangerous and vindictive." Anna, let me take care of you. Seeing Anna's pale, sad face was torture. Think, Kevin, think. "Let's take a drive in Lola. I'll call Erica. Jupiter's really visible tonight."

"Jupiter?" She frowned.

Kevin, what kind of idea is that? Anna's upset. "Yeah."

"You and me together? That'll just give Genise more to gossip about. Your reputation."

"I want you to feel okay, to get your mind off things." He pointed at her belly. "Doctor's orders."

She gave a faint smile. "I can't disobey orders, I guess."

"Seven o'clock at my place?"

"Seven. Jupiter."

Kevin walked her to the inn. He left relieved to see her through the window talking with Esther. She could open up to her friend, ask for advice. He felt inadequate dealing with this slander involving Anna, since he was part of the problem. Oh, if only he could force Genise to shut up, to apologize! But Kevin was seasoned enough to know apologies don't always come. The real challenge was handling injustice without growing bitter. Without wanting to wring someone's neck. He slammed the car door and backed out. He laughed at his own immature thought.

At home, he sighed in relief that Erica had gone out. Of course, he would need her for the ride in Lola. He wouldn't dare go out alone with Anna in a climate like that. It would just add fuel to Genise's fire. Still, Kevin needed to calm down. His hands were still trembling with anger. His legs felt weak after walking beside Anna to the inn. Without meaning to, her arm had brushed his, sending sparks across his skin.

"Kevin, you really are out of your mind," he muttered, pressing his hands to his head with a groan. He opened the fridge, grabbed a bottle of water, and took big gulps.

He was sinking deeper and deeper into feelings he'd never experienced before Anna appeared at the clinic. Kevin had arrived late from the hospital that day. His clients had already lost patience waiting. But he'd walked into the clinic and seen that honey-haired woman, in a skirt and heels, crouched, cleaning a small patient's vomit. A wad of dirty tissues filled her hand. She'd looked up at him through the lenses of her glasses with very clear eyes. Right then, Kevin knew he was a goner, that there was no turning back. The shock of her announcing a pregnancy was second only to his disappointment. Pregnant and married. In a few minutes, he'd thought he'd found a woman worth getting to know, only for his little dream to collapse. Then came the revelation that Anna was a widow, and Kevin felt like the worst man in the world for the relief he felt. What a mad, utterly senseless man he was.

Move back two spaces. Forward one. Several back. At this rate, Kevin's game would never end.

He tossed the plastic bottle into the recycling bin. His phone buzzed in his jeans pocket. The name on the screen deflated him even more.

"Hey, Dad. Everything okay?"

"Kevin, what's this pregnancy business?"

Genise was fast. Wildfire fast. Kevin frowned and pressed his forehead to his palm. "Pregnancy?"

"Blah. Don't play dumb. Your nurse. Is it true she's pregnant?"

"Who told you?" Kevin hoped it was just Erica's loose tongue.

"I heard you two already knew each other, and that she's expecting your child. Kevin, when are you going to man up and stop fooling around?" His father huffed.

Kevin stared at the screen in disbelief. For a second, he thought about hanging up. That would be a thousand times worse. His father would take it as Kevin being afraid. "Anna is a widow. We never met each other before she came to Grace Harbor." He would never tell his father he only learned about the pregnancy after hiring her. He'd rather take the criticism. For Anna. For the baby.

"And what got into you to hire a nurse who'll soon be on leave? Can't you see that's an extra expense? What are you going to do? Go without a nurse, get another one? I can see you don't know how to run your own business. The Miller family has a name to uphold."

Kevin sat on the kitchen island stool. His legs trembled, like he was still the boy afraid of getting time out and spanking. And he'd gotten plenty. Honor your father and mother. It was a lot easier to honor his mother. Sweet. Gentle. How had she endured such an intolerant husband?

"Dad." Kevin took a deep breath. He had no hope of earning his father's respect, but he wouldn't add fuel to the fire. "Today, when I hold Theo in my arms, feed him in the middle of the night, I know I'm doing my part." His father tried to interrupt, but Kevin hardened his voice. "When Theo gave me his first smile on a rainy night, I knew nothing mattered more than his wellbeing. For him, Dad, I'd die. I'd make any sacrifice. I'm not a father, but being an uncle is the second-best thing in the world. Erica is happy. If she's happy, Theo's fine. If I can help my sister, I will."

"What does that have to do with the knocked-up nurse, blah?"

"Anna. Her name is Anna, and she's an incredible person. She's going through something similar to Erica. She's on her own. And more: she's competent. I know I can count on her to implement the improvements I'm planning for the clinic. She works hard, never complains, gives me ideas. Why shouldn't I give her a hand?"

"Looks like you want to give her more than a hand, blah."

Kevin clenched his teeth. "I won't let you talk about her like that. You can think I'm irresponsible, a good-for-nothing, a hippie, but don't speak that way about Anna. And if you don't have anything constructive to say, I need to hang up."

"Suit yourself." His father hung up.

Kevin slammed a fist on the granite countertop. Anna's face flashed in his mind. She didn't deserve to be treated like that, like some lowlife. What would she think of Grace Harbor? Some welcome.

No. Kevin wouldn't let more gossip reach her. They'd go out in Lola. Count the stars. Kevin would swallow the fireball burning down his throat for Anna. He'd take the flaming arrows in her place. Theo had taught his uncle the value of sacrifice.

When Erica got home with her sleeping son in her arms, Kevin greeted her as if he'd never heard his father's insults. He helped her lay Theo in the crib and told her about his plan to go out later to look at the stars. Erica agreed without question.

He went to his room, sat on the bed, and opened the nightstand drawer. He ran a hand over the worn Bible cover. He opened to the first page and read his mother's dedication.

Son,

When it feels like the world is collapsing, remember: the same God who sustains and names the stars sustains you too. He knows you by name.

Your mother.

Kevin rested his forehead on the Bible and wept. He prayed. His mother had been wise. She was the only one who knew how to rein in her husband's sour moods. She was gone, and Dr. Miller was out of control. How could he have lived more than three decades with her and learned nothing?

An hour before meeting Anna, Kevin showered, shaved, and combed his hair. He put on navy slacks and a white shirt. Clean, neat. He wasn't a hippie. He was the new doctor in the town of Grace Harbor, respected by his patients.

Determined to protect Erica, Theo, Anna, and her baby.

Chapter Twenty-One

The navy-blue door was half open, an invitation for Anna to step into a house that overflowed with hospitality. That's how she felt there. Perhaps it was the story the house told, of a child without a father who found safety and unconditional love. Anna pushed the door gently with her fingertips. With her other hand, she caressed her rounded belly. She would give anything for her baby to leave the comfort of the womb for the comfort of a home. A sudden urgency rose in her to find a place, even though she felt at home in Esther and Roberto's inn. With her baby kicking, hiccupping, and floating like an astronaut in outer space, the need to prepare a nest grew every day.

Kevin appeared in the living room, barefoot, buttoning a light shirt. "Anna, come in. Another accident with Theo. This time out the mouth: mashed banana. He thinks he can eat a whole bunch without getting sick."

Anna unbuttoned her denim jacket, which was already tight across her chest. The loose white dress had been her latest purchase from the Little Shop of Broken hearts. She looked at Kevin, so calm, and wished her own heart were at peace. Genise's gossip had left her more vulnerable than she already felt. How would she defend her baby against slander? But before arriving at Kevin's house, Anna had promised herself she'd behave in a way that wouldn't ruin the stargazing event. Kevin had been shaken by the news of the gossip and had blamed himself. Anna needed to make an extra effort so he would see her doing well and not reproach himself even more.

"Would you like some water, anything? Erica will be right here."

"No, thank you. Just had supper with Esther and family, and Jade made me drink pink lemonade." She ran a hand over her belly.

"How rude of me. Please, take a seat." Kevin combed his damp hair with his fingers. He pointed to the couch. "How's your father?"

Anna settled in. "He's enjoying the nursing home. He's made a few friends, met up again with a friend, Grace."

"I know. She used to own the little shop." Kevin bent his knees to sit, then stood back up. "Are you sure you don't want anything?"

Kevin's restless. Did he hear something else? Anna scratched an imaginary itch on her arm. "Dr. Kevin... Kevin, do you want to leave the ride for another day?"

"No. Why do you say that?"

Anna's hands went cold. He wasn't as calm as she'd imagined. But she wouldn't tell her boss he was acting oddly, jiggling his legs and wavering between sitting and standing. "It's been a long day."

Kevin finally sat down. "Lola would be disappointed."

Anna smiled. "Then I won't cross her."

Erica came into the room, carrying Theo on one arm and a stuffed quilted bag. "We're ready."

"Where are you going with all that?" Kevin hurried over and took the bag.

"I don't want to be caught off guard. Besides, Theo's sleepy. I'm bringing the sleeping sack."

Kevin helped his sister load her son and the gear into her car, then got into Lola. Anna was already waiting inside. The two cars hit the road, Lola leading the way, quite proud to be heading out for another starry-night drive.

At the clearing, Kevin set up the truck bed. Erica made a little nest for Theo, who was already asleep, covering him with a yellow blanket like a tent. She pulled two pillows from the bag.

"These are for Anna. If we're going to make these stargazing events a thing, she needs to be comfy." Erica tucked the pillows between Anna's back and Lola's side.

"Special treatment," Anna said. Part of the weight in her heart lifted.

Kevin took his telescope from the metal box and peered at the sky. He pointed out Jupiter to Anna, then directed her elsewhere. "That cluster of stars is called the Pleiades, part of the Taurusconstellation ." He handed her the telescope and helped her find the stars. He went on, "You asked me for a pretty star name. I said I like Maia. Maia is one of the seven sisters of the Pleiades."

"Stars have sisters? What are their names?" The infinite sky captured all of Anna's attention.

"Electra, Taygeta, Alcyone, Celaeno, Sterope, and Merope. Maia is the eldest."

Theo whimpered, and Erica lay down beside him.

"Maia," Anna whispered. She gave the telescope back to Kevin and rested against the pillows, still gazing upward. "Creation is perfect."

"The Bible mentions the Pleiades three times," Kevin said, leaning against the truck's side.

"Really? I never noticed," Anna replied.

"Twice in Job and once in Amos, saying that God made the Pleiades."

Anna couldn't help placing a hand on her belly. The same God who created the constellations had created her baby—so small, so fragile, so dependent on the mother. Anna looked at Erica, sleeping with an arm over Theo. Even in sleep, a mother didn't leave her child unprotected.

"Where can I find an apartment in Grace Harbor?" The question slipped out before Anna could stop it. What responsibility did her boss have to help her find housing? She looked at him and, despite the darkness, could see a crease between his eyes.

"A friend of mine, Alex, a lawyer, has some rental houses. New development. His mother-in-law manages it. I'll ask." Kevin pulled his phone from his pocket.

Anna touched his arm, then quickly withdrew her hand. "No need right now. What will Lola think?"

"Lola doesn't butt in, but I'll talk to Alex later." He set the phone aside. Then he laced his fingers behind his head, lay back, and looked at the sky.

Anna picked up the telescope. "Where's Maia again?"

Kevin pointed out the star. "That one to the right."

She took off her glasses and looked through the lens of the telescope. "Maia."

Theo fussed. Erica rubbed her eyes and popped the pacifier into his mouth. Anna returned the telescope to the box. Oh, if only she could stay and count the stars, forget her problems, erase the past! But the night's tranquility wouldn't last forever. Morning would come, bringing responsibilities and hard reality back with it. Anna needed to calm herself and find her own place where she could welcome her child. It was daunting to think of setting up a home from scratch:

plates, pans, towels, sheets, a can opener. After work, she always arrived at the inn exhausted, feet swollen. Imagining herself buying furniture, going from store to store, left her reeling. Her father couldn't help. She didn't even know where the furniture and housewares stores were. She'd have to look online, compare prices, go out in the evening before the shops closed. What time did stores close in Grace Harbor? "Aaah."

Kevin sat upright, turning to her. "What is it? Pain?"

"It just slipped out. A sigh. I was thinking."

"Worried?"

"Sure. It's so hard not knowing what's ahead, how to plan." She tried to close her jacket, but could only fasten one button.

"Anna, I can..." He nodded toward Erica. "We can help."

"Kevin, you're my boss. You're not obligated." She felt silly with that comment. She was stargazing with her boss!

He lowered his head, tucked a strand of hair behind his ear, and looked back at Anna. He tapped lightly on Lola's truck bed. "I think we're a little more than boss and employee. After all, Lola doesn't take just anyone for a ride."

Anna gave a wistful smile. She'd like to think Kevin was more than her boss. What category would he fit into? Friend? Too soon to say what they had was friendship. What comes before friendship? Acquaintanceship? What an old-fashioned word. Companionship? Maybe not yet. In truth, there on Lola, staring at the stars, he was more than her boss. Still, the last thing she wanted was to rush the relationship and put her job at risk.

Anna was about to welcome a child. She couldn't risk the child's wellbeing by overstepping boundaries.

CHAPTER TWENTY-TWO

Why had Anna returned from Alex's office looking so discouraged? Kevin watched her change the dressing on a patient who had been bitten by the neighbor's dog. A week had passed since their last outing with Lola, and Anna had been quieter ever since. She'd gone out at lunchtime to sign the lease for her new home with Alex and had come back more subdued. The busy flow of patients at the clinic left no room for personal conversation.

"Here's some more gauze," she said, handing a pack to the patient. "Dr. Kevin will give you a prescription for the medication."

Kevin typed a few notes about the patient into the laptop. "Cecil, stop by the front desk to pick up your prescription from Erica."

"Thanks, doc." The patient nodded at both of them and left.

Anna stripped the used sheet from the exam table and unrolled fresh paper to cover it.

"How's Alex?" Kevin asked, though he was finding it harder and harder to know how far to go in conversations with her. She had pulled back a little since their last talk. After all, she had made it clear she saw him as her boss.

"Everything's fine." Anna crumpled the paper and tossed it into the bin. "I signed the lease. I'll be moving this weekend."

Kevin closed the laptop on the counter. "Do you need help?" Did she even have furniture? From the boxes he'd carried from her car into the inn, it didn't seem like she owned much. Her father was in a nursing home, so he wouldn't have any to spare. A chill ran up Kevin's spine. What if she had to furnish the entire house? How would she manage on a modest salary?

He thought of his own home, how many things he took for granted there: rolls of toilet paper, a table, chairs, a microwave. What could he do to help without embarrassing her? Give her a raise? The clinic wasn't making enough for that yet. Give her some of his furniture? Buy something as a gift?

"I'll manage, thank you," she said, washing her hands and heading for the door.

"Anna." Think, Kevin, think.

"Yes? I'll call the next patient."

"I've got some furniture my mother stored at my father's house. It used to be mine and Erica's. My father redecorated a while ago." How would he get the furniture without stirring up trouble with his father? But it was true—Dr. Miller had cleared out both his children's rooms to turn them into guest rooms. Guests he never had. Kevin and Erica had long since realized their father didn't want anything around that reminded him of his "rebellious" kids. Kevin would find a way to get those pieces, especially when he saw the tension easing from Anna's brow.

"And your father really doesn't want them? All I need is a bed, a table, and a few chairs. I can manage the rest later." She adjusted her stethoscope around her neck.

"I'll stop by today and see what's in good shape." And I'll see what kind of shape my father's in. Kevin was certain it would turn into an argument. His father would find some excuse, some jab, if he knew who the furniture was for. Ever since Genise's gossip, their relationship had grown even more strained. With Anna nearby, Dr. Miller would seize every chance to needle his son. And still, Kevin wanted Anna close. He would never leave a woman in that situation—whether sister, friend, or acquaintance.

"Thank you." She sighed and left the room.

Kevin shut the door and rested his head against the freshly painted white wood. His insides churned, twisting as if something alive inside him was trying to take over his body. Why couldn't his father see that Kevin wasn't the reckless boy he once was? That he was a man now, one striving to build a life of integrity?

He could accept that God was giving him tougher challenges. That was what he had prayed for, wasn't it? That he would never disappoint people again as he had disappointed his parents. Erica had been his first great challenge, and he believed he was doing well because his sister and nephew were thriving. But according to his father, Kevin was merely "condoning Erica's sin."

What did the old man expect? That he throw his sister and her baby out on the street? That Erica move into a women's shelter? No. His father would just have to live with it. Kevin knew he was doing what was right. His conscience said so.

He began setting up the ultrasound machine for the next patient. What was Anna feeling bringing in an expectant mother for her exam?

The door opened, and Anna stepped aside to let the young couple in. Kevin greeted them and sat on the stool, typing the patient's information into the computer. Out of the corner of his eye, he saw Anna helping the woman lie down and get ready for the scan. The husband sat close, holding his wife's hand. He whispered something to her and brushed a loose curl from her face.

Anna dimmed the lights, leaving the room in soft shadow. Kevin gave the patient a few instructions about how to position her body, then spread gel on her belly and moved the transducer slowly, watching the screen. Soon, the quick, whooshing rhythm of the baby's heartbeat filled the room. It was soft and steady like rushing water through a narrow stream.

Kevin remembered the first time he'd heard Theo's heartbeat. It was impossible not to be amazed by life in the womb.

The steady sound continued, pulsing through the air like music.

"Our baby," the woman said, turning to her husband, who squeezed her hand.

Kevin glanced from the monitor to Anna. The dim light hid her expression. Maybe he should've assigned her a different task outside the room. But she had asked to observe the new equipment in use. There'd been no problem during the liver scan, or the shoulder exam. This was the first prenatal ultrasound she'd assisted with.

"Would you like to know the gender?" Kevin asked as he adjusted the transducer.

"Yes," the woman said, her voice trembling.

"It's a boy," Kevin announced.

The husband kissed her forehead. "Enzo is on his way."

The young mother wiped the tears with her fingers. Anna handed her a box of tissues.

Kevin had never wanted a scan to end faster. He was torn—glad to deliver good news about a healthy baby, yet uneasy thinking about how Anna must be feeling. She was a professional and a mother.

When the exam ended, Kevin and Anna stepped out to let the patient get dressed. Anna excused herself to use the restroom. Kevin stayed in the hallway, hands buried in the pockets of his white coat, waiting for her to close the door.

Then he hurried to the reception desk. Without glancing at the waiting patients, he leaned toward Erica, who was typing.

"I'm going to Dad's tonight to get some furniture for Anna."

Erica froze, her fingers suspended midair. She looked up at him, eyes wide. "Ready for a showdown?"

"Ready. Anna needs it."

"I'm coming too and I'll bring Theo as backup." She gave him a crooked smile.

"Are you ready for a showdown?" he echoed.

"Anna needs it."

Kevin relaxed his shoulders. His sister might be small, but she was fierce.

He called in the next patient—five more to go that day.

He was ready for the showdown.

CHAPTER TWENTY-THREE

The tap water ran over Anna's soapy fingers. Tears ran down her face. Was it the patient's fault that she had a husband by her side? Good for her. She had support during the pregnancy and would place baby Enzo in his father's arms when he was born. It was unprofessional of her to whimper over what she didn't have, over what other women had. Her baby didn't deserve a weak, pathetic mother.

Anna washed her face. She pulled paper towels from the dispenser and dried her eyes. Other patients were waiting for her. Kevin was waiting for her. Anna put on her glasses, smoothed back her hair into a ponytail, and left the restroom. She took a deep breath. At least she would have some furniture to start her new life in the condo, thanks to Kevin's help. That was an answer to her plea. She wouldn't have to leave work and go hunt for furniture. Nina had set aside the crib at the little shop. After her shift, Anna would do some shopping there. She'd seen a shelf with bed and bath linens. Maybe she'd find dishes and kitchen items. It would all work out. She didn't need much, and Nina's shop was homey. It wouldn't feel like shopping at all.

For someone who had been living on a cousin's charity, having a place of her own was a huge step forward. It really was time to leave the inn. Not that Esther was pushing her out; on the contrary, Anna felt at home there. But the move was necessary. A move to prepare her nest.

Over the next few hours, five patients came through the exam room. Anna did her work with great care. It was hard to avoid Kevin's glances. Had he been annoyed that she'd rushed out of the exam room after the ultrasound? Maybe he was just tired after a long day. The construction crew would arrive after the clinic closed to start the renovation. Kevin would have to coordinate the work so it wouldn't interrupt patient care. He was overloaded. The bills kept coming. Anna noticed his concern whenever they discussed expenses. Even so, he always tried to see the positive side of things. She wasn't going to give him more to deal with.

***

Anna locked the clinic door, leaving people's problems outside. She helped Erica straighten the waiting room. The workers had left a trail of dust coming in with muddy boots, lugging building materials. They were hammering something in the back.

"I'll mop tomorrow morning," Erica said, checking the wall clock. "I have to pick up Theo."

"Go. I'll handle the rest." Anna opened the door for her. The young woman grabbed her bag from a desk drawer and ran. She stopped beside Anna and gave her a tight hug.

"Everything looks like chaos now. But it'll end well," she said.

"Renovations end quickly," Anna agreed with a nod.

Erica squeezed the nurse's arm. "Other kinds of chaos, I mean."

"I understand." Anna tried to hold on to Erica's hopeful words.

Anna hugged her back. Erica dashed off, clattering awkwardly down the stairs, and disappeared around the corner.

With broom in hand, Anna swept up the excess dust. Trying to clean the floor would be pointless, since the crew would be there for hours and Erica planned to clean everything in the morning anyway.

Kevin came out of the office just as Anna was getting ready to leave. She wanted to catch the little shop before it closed.

"Anna, tomorrow morning I only need to take care of some paperwork here, but I'll pick up your furniture in the afternoon. Saturday's a good day, and Lola will help. I'll stop by my father's in a bit to set aside what's in good shape. If you want, I'll send you some photos."

She grasped her purse strap. She pictured her house already furnished. "All right. Thank you."

Saying goodbye to the doctor, she got in her car and headed toward downtown Grace Harbor. The store would close in an hour, which gave her little time to choose the most urgent items. The crib would have to wait. Her trunk wasn't big enough. If Lola could pick it up, that would be a great help.

Nina greeted her with a warm hug. "Have you been well?"

Anna ran her hands over her belly. "Just a bit more tired, but fine. I had tests last week and the doctor's pleased with the results. I'm entering my twentieth week."

"Good to hear. What do you need today?"

"Bed and bath linens. Some kitchen items, if you have them." Anna glanced around.

The shop bell rang. Grace came in carrying a cardboard box. Nina hurried over to help her. The two women greeted each other affectionately. Anna waved to Grace.

"Look at this, Anna," Nina said, taking the box from Grace. "Pots and some kitchen utensils."

Anna stepped up to the counter where Nina set the box down.

"Looking for kitchen stuff?" Grace asked.

"For my new house. I'm moving this weekend," Anna replied.

"Oh, God is so good! I've been hoping to find a new home for some small appliances. I'm selling my house. I bought a smaller apartment. After my Abel passed, I didn't need so much space. Actually, I've got other things if you'd like to take a look." The woman with the crooked bangs pulled out a set of pots. "My niece gave them to me, but I hardly used them. They say old pots make the best food. I didn't want to risk using new ones." Grace laughed.

Anna picked up one of the stainless-steel pots. She could see her reflection in it. "Aren't these for resale?" She looked at Nina.

Nina pushed the box toward Anna. "Those who receive much, want to give much. I learned that great lesson from Grace."

The older woman hugged Nina. "That's where abundance comes from."

Together, they helped Anna choose sheets, a blanket, a quilt and towels. The weight on the young expectant mother's shoulders eased with each item they picked and set on the counter. Other customers came and went, but Grace or Nina kept helping Anna. She wasn't alone. She had people to carry the weight with her. After an hour, three full boxes were on the counter. Anna pulled out her card and handed it to Nina, who announced:

"Today's discount day: 50%."

Anna looked around for sale signs. Nothing. "Nina, it's okay. I've barely had any expenses at the inn. Esther is priceless."

Nina smiled, glanced from Grace to Anna. "'Carry one another's burdens.' It goes beyond money, you know? Take it as a gift from me."

Anna wiped her eyes with her index fingers, maneuvering them behind her lenses. In a single day, more than a ton of weight had been lifted from her shoulders—from her very soul. "My child and I thank you."

Grace whisked the credit card out of Nina's hand and returned it to Anna. "For your mother's sake, let me cover the other half. Vanya would help her daughter and grandchild."

A sob escaped Anna. How she missed her mother! Her chest flooded with nostalgia and gratitude—an outpouring of emotion. How could she express her thanks in that moment? Her legs felt shaky.

"I don't even know what to say." Anna steadied herself on the counter.

Grace stroked the pregnant woman's hand. "You don't need to say anything. Just take care of that new life. Let the child know they're already deeply loved and awaited."

Anna's chin trembled. She placed a hand on her belly. "Thank you."

"Well then, let's load everything into your car," Grace said. "Not you, Anna. You can't lift anything heavy."

Nina and Grace carried the boxes to the Honda. Anna hoped she could count on another angel to unload and bring them into the new house.

The three women said their goodbyes. Anna drove down Main Street, along the tree-lined boulevard. She lowered the window and breathed in air that already held the faint coolness announcing the shift from summer to fall. She felt light, like a kite cutting across the sky.

The new condo wasn't far. Soon Anna was parking in front of the house with a white picket fence. She took the key to her new home from her purse and looked around. Lights were on in the neighboring houses. Dinnertime for many families. An elderly man watered his flowers and lawn with a hose. What if she asked him for help? But a woman called to him from the porch and he shut off the water and went inside.

Anna jumped in her seat at the knock on her window. She found herself face-to-face with the property manager, Martha. Anna opened the door. "Good evening."

"I hope I didn't scare you. I saw you arrive and came to welcome you. Did you bring your things?" The thin, gray-haired woman peered into the car.

"I've got a few boxes in the trunk," Anna said.

"Oh, stay put. I'll call my son-in-law to help."

"No..."

Waving off the protest, the woman crossed the street and returned with Alex, the attorney Anna had dealt with about the house. He held out his hand and offered a warm smile.

"I didn't want to be a bother." What else could Anna say? Hadn't she asked for angelic intervention?

"It's no bother," Alex said, lifting the boxes from the car.

Anna hurried ahead to open the front door. The smell of fresh paint gave her a sense of a new beginning. This would be her baby's home.

Alex set the boxes down in the kitchen and said goodbye. Anna thanked him several times as he kept repeating that helping was a pleasure. Martha helped her put the kitchen items away. She told Anna about her daughter, Shyla—married to Alex—and about her son, Noah.

"What joy Alex and his boy brought into our lives. Shyla was the child's caregiver. He's special, on the autism spectrum. Now that my daughter's finished her degree in occupational therapy, she creates all kinds of activities for Noah, but what she gives him most is love."

Anna set the empty box on the floor. She wondered about Shyla and Alex's story. Just as in Jade's case, who had a father of the heart, Noah had a mother of the heart. Inevitably—more often now—she wondered whether her own child might one day have a father of the heart. Even after all she'd been through with Dalton, Anna still believed in the family. Not everything is ideal. Many women raise their children alone, like Erica. Still, Anna had that desire in her heart: to share her child's growth with a man.

The merry widow returns, she scolded herself.

"I'd love to meet your daughter and Noah," Anna said.

"You will. They're always at my place."

Martha said goodbye after giving Anna information about the electricity and internet, leaving her by herself. The new tenant wandered from the living room back to the kitchen, then to the two bedrooms, the small office, and the bathroom. If Kevin really did pick up some furniture, Anna could move in the next day. She'd have the weekend to stock the cupboards and fill the fridge.

Her phone chimed. Kevin was on his way to his father's house and would take pictures of the furniture. Anna thanked him. She decided to order a pizza and wait for the photos right there in her new home. She wanted to daydream about the décor.

She placed the order online and sat on the step leading to the backyard. She played some music on her phone. She scanned the sky. There were the Pleiades. Maia.

Half an hour later, the pizza arrived. An hour later, her phone was still silent. Maybe Kevin had run into trouble and hadn't made it to his father's. Anna decided it was better to head back to the inn and rest. Her weekend would be busy with the move. She needed her strength. Kevin would do what he could to get the furniture, she was sure. He was a man of his word. And he had lifted two heavy burdens from her shoulders: work and the furniture.

An angel in her life.

CHAPTER TWENTY-FOUR

Theo cried, and Erica rocked him in her arms. "What are you going to do with the furniture, Dad? You don't even need it anymore."

Kevin scratched his head and looked around the double-car garage. His furniture and Erica's were piled up like junk, taking up his father's precious space, a contrast with every shelf neatly arranged, every tool in its place. Why did he insist on holding on to those stacked chairs, that table propped against the wall, those dismantled beds?

Wearing a pressed shirt and slacks, Dr. Miller stood on the third step of the staircase that led from the house to the garage. "I haven't decided yet, blah."

Kevin slapped the seat of a chair. "If you haven't decided, then it means you've got no use for them."

"Why do you even want this old furniture?" his father asked.

"If it's so old, why do *you* want it?" Erica shot back. Theo's crying grew louder.

"Can't you make that kid stop? What kind of mother are you?"

Erica marched toward him, but Kevin caught her by the arm and took Theo from her.

"I'm a mother who got kicked out by her own father," she said, fists clenched.

Kevin rested Theo's head on his shoulder, patting his back gently, rhythmically. "You're scaring your grandson. *Your* grandson—understand?"

"I didn't ask to have grandkids in this situation," the older man replied.

"What situation? Oh, you mean being a grandfather without a shred of mercy?" Erica grabbed one of the chairs. "We're taking this furniture, whether you like it or not."

"Calm down, Erica," Kevin said.

"That furniture is mine. It's in *my* house," Dr. Miller said, pointing at the beds.

Erica climbed the three steps toward him. Next to her father, she looked like a little girl again. "I just hope you never go through hard times, because when you do, you'll be alone. You and your old furniture."

"Erica, let's go," Kevin said, passing Theo back to her. "We'll find another way."

"You two are a couple of hippies anyway. Take the junk, blah." Dr. Miller turned, slammed the door, and left Kevin, Erica, and Theo stunned in the garage. The little boy stopped crying.

"Let's grab everything fast before he changes his mind and calls the police," Erica said.

Kevin grabbed the bed's headboard and carried it to Lola. Then he hauled the chairs. Erica strapped Theo into his car seat, left the door open, and ran to help her brother load the old furniture into the back of the pickup truck. Anyone watching them sprinting back and forth from the garage to the truck with furniture balanced on their heads might have thought they were thieves, given the speed with which they worked.

Theo watched from the open car door, waving a rubber elephant teether. Even he seemed eager to leave his grandfather's house and go back to the comfort of his baby-scented room.

"Let's go," Erica said, sliding behind the wheel. Kevin closed the back door of her car.

Lola and the Kia rolled down the street lined with elegant mid-century homes, their wide lawns and tall trees glowing in the late afternoon sun. Back home, Kevin parked Lola in the garage along with the rescued furniture. When he stepped into the kitchen, he found Erica laughing while she prepared a bottle for Theo.

"What's so funny? I'm boiling with indignation." Kevin tossed Lola's keys onto the table by the door.

Erica handed a cookie to Theo, who was sitting in his highchair, then shook the bottle. "This situation is ridiculous. Can you believe we just ran out of our father's house like fugitives?"

"I don't see the humor. Why is he so vindictive? Most fathers thank God when their rebellious kids finally come to their senses."

Theo threw the soggy cookie on the floor and grabbed the bottle. Erica picked up the mess and dropped it into the trash. "That's the thing—he doesn't think we have come to our senses."

Kevin sat down and propped his head on one hand. "What will it take for him to believe we've changed?"

"I don't know. Maybe if you kicked me out of here and cut your hair. Or better yet, if you sent Lola to the junkyard." Erica chuckled.

Kevin smacked the table. "Cut my hair? Not a chance. I might kick you out, though."

Erica tapped his shoulder. "Then I'll take Lola with me." She grinned, hoisted Theo onto her hip, and headed down the hallway.

Kevin glanced at the microwave clock, then pulled out his phone. He had promised to send Anna pictures of the furniture. Between the argument with his father and the chaos that followed, he had completely forgotten. She must be thinking he'd gone back on his word. But he would have gotten that furniture out of there no matter what. If his father had called the police (and he very well could have), Kevin would've found another way to furnish Anna's home. There were always people at church willing to donate. He'd talk to Pastor Wellington. He'd call every member of the congregation, whatever it took to lift that burden off Anna's shoulders.

Kevin hurried to the garage and snapped photos of the bed, the mattress, the chairs, and the round table. He sent them to Anna along with an apology for the delay. She replied almost immediately, thanking him and saying that she'd also received household items from Nina and Grace. Kevin exhaled with relief. Things were coming together for her.

If not for his strained relationship with his father—and the venom of Genise—Kevin might have said life was going pretty well. The clinic still had a long way to go before it reflected its new owner's touch, but the construction crew was working hard. Half the patient files were already digitized in the new software. Erica was proving more capable each day as a receptionist. And Anna... what could he say about her? Kevin could have interviewed a dozen nurses and still would have chosen Anna.

He went to the living room and turned on the stereo, letting the soft notes of a *bossa nova* piano calm his frayed nerves. Stretching out on the couch, he crossed his legs and laced his hands behind his head. The floor lamp cast a warm glow in the corner. Anna's face, etched in his memory, filled every quiet space in his mind.

His good sense couldn't convince his heart that she was a woman with one priority: her baby. And his heart couldn't convince his good sense that what Kevin wanted was simply to take care of her.

He hugged a pillow and closed his eyes.

A loud knock startled him awake. Kevin swung his legs off the couch and stood up. The clock on his phone showed an hour had passed since he'd dozed off. He rubbed his eyes and opened the door—then stepped back, startled.

"Dad? What's going on?"

"Since you wanted your things so badly, I brought your clothes." Dr. Miller pointed toward his car, the trunk wide open.

"Dad, what clothes? Why are you here at this hour?" Kevin wished it were just a bad dream. How far would his father's spite go?

"I need the space in my garage, blah."

Feeling like he truly was trapped in a nightmare, Kevin took the suitcases from his father's car trunk. He could hardly believe it when the man climbed back into his car and drove away.

Was it possible his father was suffering from some neurological problem? Even for him, this behavior was not normal. Kevin would talk to Erica. What if it was an illness? How would he convince his father to see a doctor?

Kevin stood on the porch, the two suitcases at his feet. A deep sadness washed over him, hollowing his chest with a familiar ache.

If only his mother were still alive.

CHAPTER TWENTY-FIVE

R elief had completed Anna's happiness the night before when she received the pictures of the furniture piled up in Lola. Now, unlocking the door of her new home with Esther, Grace, and Jade beside her, only one word filled her mind: gratitude.

Her father, who had arrived by taxi, was in the kitchen, putting away the dishes Anna had received from Nina and Grace.

Before saying goodbye to the inn that morning, Anna had received a few more gifts, this time from Jade: a nightstand, a small desk, and extra bedding that Esther had saved after renovating the guest rooms.

Jade dragged a large garbage bag stuffed with sheets, towels, and pillows across the living room floor. "Which room is yours, Anna?"

"The one next to the bathroom."

Grace wandered through the little house and returned to the living room. "What a beautiful gift from God—a brand-new house." She breathed in deeply. "Still smells like fresh paint."

The baby joined in his mother's joy, kicking hard against Anna's ribs. "Someone here is excited," she said, smiling.

"Who?" Jade asked, bouncing back into the room.

Anna rubbed her belly. "My little one."

"I used to live in my mom's belly too," Jade said brightly. "My birth dad wasn't happy when he found out I was special. But that's okay, because I got Roberto, and he's the best dad in the whole world." Completely carefree, she skipped into the kitchen, announcing she was going to see the backyard.

"Jade gives me hope to keep going," Anna said to Esther and Grace. "She's so cheerful, even after all she's been through."

"That's why we're here." Esther squeezed Anna's arm. "I know it's not easy carrying a pregnancy alone."

"I'm not alone anymore," Anna said softly.

"In Grace Harbor, no one is," Grace said, wrapping her arms around both women.

Serge returned from the kitchen. "Everything's put away in the cupboards."

Just then, the doorbell rang. Anna opened it and smiled. Lola stood out front, loaded with furniture. Erica held Theo in one arm and a bag in the other. "Special delivery for Anna!"

Kevin came through the front yard carrying a round table. Esther hurried to help him. Their neighbor, the same man who had been watering his lawn the day before, offered to help unload the truck. He introduced his wife, Celina, who was walking up the sidewalk holding a plate with a cake. Serge, unsteady but determined, carried the chairs to the kitchen.

"We came to welcome the new neighbors," Celina said cheerfully. As Kevin passed by Anna, she added, "Oh, is this your husband?"

"No," Anna said quickly.

Kevin smiled politely. "Just a friend."

"Where have I seen you before?" Celina asked, squinting.

"He's the new doctor at Grace Harbor Clinic," Grace explained.

"Oh, a new doctor? Look, hun," she said to her husband. "Now we can go back there for our checkups. The grumpy doctor left."

Erica passed by the elderly couple and stifled a laugh.

"You're very welcome," Kevin said graciously.

Anna glanced at him. Such a respectful man. He could have easily embarrassed the woman by saying the grumpy doctor was his father.

"We'll be expecting you," Anna said kindly.

Kevin added, "Anna's the new nurse at the clinic."

"How wonderful!" Celina smiled, then looked at Anna's belly. She seemed about to ask something but thought better of it.

Two hours later, Anna, her father, and their friends were gathered in the living room eating cake. The elderly couple had helped a bit more before heading to the grocery store, as they'd mentioned. That's when Anna realized she didn't have any food at home.

Kevin went to the kitchen and returned with a glass of water. "It's none of my business, but what are you going to eat?"

"You're not going hungry, are you?" Jade asked.

"No, no, Jade. I'll go to the store later."

"I can take you," Kevin offered, and all the women turned to look at him. "That is, if you'd like."

"That's a good idea," Grace said, patting his hand. "I should get going. Need a ride, Serge?"

Anna looked at her father, who quickly accepted. "I need to take my medication." He kissed his daughter's forehead. "What a blessing to have friends like these." Turning to the others, he added, "I don't have words to thank you."

"You're welcome!" Jade said brightly.

The three women left right after Grace and Serge.

"I've got to meet Daphne and the girls," Erica said, picking up Theo, who was playing with a cardboard box. They left soon after.

"Looks like it's just us now." Kevin ran a hand through his hair. "Shall we go?"

Anna could have gone alone, but she was exhausted just thinking about it: pushing the cart, checking out, carrying bags to the car, and unloading them again. After a long day of unpacking, she gave in. "I'll take you up on that offer."

They took Lola. At the market, Anna grabbed one cart and Kevin another, explaining that he needed to pick up a few things for his place, too.

They walked through the produce section. Anna picked up some apples and bananas. "I don't even know how to thank you and Erica for everything."

Kevin dropped a bag of potatoes into his cart. "It was a pleasure. The house looks so cozy now. Just missing a crib, right? I can ask Erica about that."

Anna pushed her cart toward the greens stand piled high with lettuce and kale. "Actually, I already have one."

"You do? Where?"

She pretended to check the price tag on the tomatoes. "At Nina's shop."

"Anna, I don't mind going there with Lola," Kevin said.

Anna picked up a head of lettuce. "You've already done too much."

He let go of his cart and faced her. "Please, don't ever think that. Do you think I don't know how hard all this is? I've lived through every one of Erica's tears, and her joys too. From Theo's first feedings to his fevers and bellyaches. From her postpartum depression and mood swings. She's cheerful now, but it wasn't always that way. I never saw it as a burden to walk beside her. So why would I see helping you as a burden? I do it from the heart, Anna. Believe it."

She examined the lettuce as though seeing it for the first time. "Thank you, Kevin."

"Anytime, Anna."

They filled their carts with groceries, cleaning supplies, and other household items. At the checkout, Anna paid for her things, and Kevin finished bagging his. As they walked through the automatic doors toward the parking lot, Kevin suddenly stopped. Anna followed his gaze and froze.

Genise.

"Well, well, well... the lovebirds shopping together. How romantic." Her eyes drifted from Anna's belly to their carts.

Anna kept walking, her stomach twisting.

"Good evening, Genise," Kevin said politely.

Anna heard his cart catch up with hers. Were they going to keep dodging Genise forever? What rumors would she spread now?

Kevin started loading the bags into Lola. "I didn't mean to upset you," he said quietly.

Anna lifted the last bag from the cart. "I told you—it's not your fault."

He nested the carts together, the sound of metal clanging in the still parking lot. "I just wish I knew how to fix it."

Anna touched his forearm. "After so much kindness from everyone today, I'm not going to let gossip steal my peace."

Kevin glanced down at her hand on his arm. She pulled it away. He returned the carts, then opened Lola's door for her and slid into the driver's seat. "Do you think Nina's store's still open?"

"Yes. They close in about half an hour."

Kevin turned onto Grace Harbor's main street and soon parked in front of Nina's little shop.

Fifteen minutes later, with the crib secured in the truck bed, they returned to Anna's house. Together, they carried the groceries inside, then went back for the crib.

"You shouldn't be lifting this," Kevin said, trying to manage it alone.

"I want to," Anna insisted, gripping the side rails.

"We can stop and rest halfway."

"Kevin, we're not crossing town—it's just a few steps."

At last, the crib stood proudly in the center of the baby's room after Kevin had assembled it. Anna ran her hand along the smooth white headboard, already picturing herself holding her little one there. She pushed her glasses up and rubbed her eyes.

"You okay?" Kevin asked.

"More than okay."

They stood beside the crib in comfortable silence. The baby kicked, and Anna rested her hands over the soft fabric of her maternity dress. She took in the fresh air drifting through the window, watching the birds playing hide-and-seek among the branches of a large tree already turning yellow with fall. Beyond it, the neighborhood gardens pulsed with life—children laughing, couples tending to their lawns, a young man tossing a toy for his fluffy white dog.

Next to her, Kevin stood quietly, his hands tucked in the pockets of his khaki shorts.

Anna's life was slowly finding its rhythm again, finally making sense. She looked at him.

"Thank you."

"Thank you," he said softly.

Chapter Twenty-Six

Dust rose into the stale air of the room. Kevin coughed and dropped the broom. He opened the window, scolding himself for not having done that earlier. His mind was a mess, very much a mess. It had been such a meaningful day with Anna, setting up the baby's room, grocery shopping together.

And then, Genise.

Kevin tried not to think so badly of her, but she always appeared at the worst moments. Was she stalking him? Grace Harbor wasn't that big a town, but when it came to Genise, anything was possible.

He had dropped Anna off an hour earlier. To avoid Erica's curious eyes and nosy questions, he'd decided to hide out at the clinic. He also wanted to avoid thinking about the suitcase his father had left at his house, another dart meant to wound his son.

A soft breeze began to clear the dust from the room that would soon be used for other procedures, like EKGs. The construction workers would install the new easy-to-clean flooring next week. Then came the paint. The new sink was already in place—only the counter and cabinet were missing. Kevin finished sweeping the floor and walked to his office.

This part always made him anxious. The bills were piling up, but without spending, there could be no improvement. He opened a paper folder and pulled out the week's receipts. On his computer, he opened the bookkeeping file. More expenses than income. He didn't need to be an accountant to see the numbers glowing red. Still, he hoped this was only a brief season between struggle and stability.

Kevin was lost in the numbers when the doorbell rang. He sighed, irritated. The last thing he needed was an unannounced visit from Genise. But maybe it was a delivery. He went to the door and opened it only to wish it had been anyone but his father.

Dr. Miller waved a hand in front of his face. "What a mess! If you have asthmatic patients, this dust will be a problem."

"Good evening, Dad." His father's conversations always began with criticism. "I was cleaning."

"Blah." Dr. Miller peered over Kevin's shoulder into the waiting room. "Is your nurse here?"

"Anna isn't here." *And she has a name.* Kevin could feel irritation spreading through him like heat. The numbers on his desk were waiting.

"Can we talk?" His father brushed past him, shoulder against shoulder.

Kevin gestured for him to enter, but Dr. Miller was already halfway through the waiting room. They went into the office. Kevin closed the ledger on his screen.

"I imagine money's tight with all these renovations and purchases," the older man said.

"I'm managing," Kevin replied, eyeing his father's neatly styled hair. How did he manage to play endless rounds of golf without a strand out of place? Saturdays were his sacred country club days—golf, drinks, and sauna. Same untouchable routine as always. His mother, on the other hand, had spent every Saturday with the kids when they were little. Not Dr. Miller. He'd always said he worked too hard all week and deserved to relax.

"Kevin, I have a proposal." The older man laced his long fingers, with spotless nails and all, together.

"A proposal?" Kevin didn't expect anything generous or fair.

"To cancel your debt to me."

Kevin's eyes widened. When his father had transferred ownership of the clinic to him, the contract had included a clause: ten percent of the profits would go to Dr. Miller for four years, as payment for the property. The clinic building would then be Kevin's outright. Canceling the remaining year of payments would be a huge relief. Maybe—just maybe—his father's heart was softening.

"Dad, thank you. That would help me a lot."

Dr. Miller crossed his legs and leaned back in the chair. "On one condition."

Hope deflated in Kevin's chest. "Condition?"

"Get rid of the nurse."

A sharp ringing filled Kevin's ears, pressure building in his skull. Had he heard correctly? "I'm sorry—what? What does Anna have to do with this?"

His father smoothed an invisible wrinkle from his perfectly pressed beige slacks. "I can see where this story is heading. You feel responsible for her. I've heard the gossip from that woman—what's her name?—that the baby is yours. What worries me is that your behavior toward her is the same as it was with Erica. Your responsibility is to your patients. You need to stay focused." He gestured around the office. "You can't play father to every stray child. They're distractions."

Kevin slammed his palms on the desk. The pens rattled in their holder. He stood, pushing his hair behind his ears. "Anna is an independent woman. She doesn't need me except as her employer. Why punish her? Why do you despise her?"

"I don't despise anyone. I'm trying to help you stay focused. I'll forgive your debt. Silvana is bored of retirement and could come back to work at the clinic. She was the best nurse I ever had. Never married, past the age of childbearing, no emotional drama. You're not in a position to run a daycare for other people's children, either here or at home."

Kevin thought of Silvana, the old nurse from his father's days. Stern, cold, and sporting a chin wart that had terrified him as a boy. She must have been born old and cranky.

He planted his hands on the desk and looked straight into his father's expressionless face. "No. I'll keep the debt. You're not going to manipulate me. You're not going to make me act unjustly. Anna earned her place here. I'm not the father of her child, and I'm not running a daycare. Our relationship is professional and she's an excellent nurse. End of discussion."

Dr. Miller stood, tapping his index finger on the desk. "You're a stubborn, prideful boy. You'll regret this."

Kevin clenched his jaw, heart pounding against his ribs. He took a slow breath. "I'm not a boy. I'm a man and a doctor respected by his patients."

"For how long? Until you go bankrupt?" His father raised an eyebrow. "The offer stands for seven days."

"I'm not interested."

Dr. Miller turned toward the door. "Next week, then." He left, slamming it behind him.

Kevin collapsed into his chair, pressing a hand to his chest. Was he too young for a heart attack?

He opened the ledger file again. The red numbers on the screen seemed to blur and shake.

The offer stands for seven days.

His father's voice still echoed in his ears.

CHAPTER TWENTY-SEVEN

"For the first time in a long time, I feel confident. Happy, even." Anna hugged her father's rigid shoulders. His trembling hands stroked his daughter's back. After the grocery run, she had gone back to the nursing home to pick him up, now properly medicated.

"You don't know how much that puts me at ease."

Anna stepped back and picked up the blue-and-yellow plush elephant from the crib. "I still don't know how I'm going to handle things when the baby's born. I need to find a daycare. Erica gave me a list. I just need the courage to go visit them." She set the elephant back in the crib. "Lots of mothers do this. I can't let myself feel guilty."

Serge sat in the rocking chair with yellow cushions. He laced his trembling fingers together. "I wish I could help. I'm a carpenter who can't saw." He looked down at his hands. "I didn't count on this forced retirement."

Anna knelt beside him and held his arm. "Dad, I'm fine. My salary is enough to support us." She ran a hand over her belly.

"I don't need the therapy sessions. You know very well my illness is progressive. I think it's a waste of money. I want to bless you and my grandchild."

"We've talked about this. The therapies are important to strengthen your muscles and improve your balance." Anna braced a hand on the arm of the rocking chair and stood. "Dr. Kevin has been generous and understanding. He's renovating the clinic, and we'll be able to see more patients."

The evening breeze fluttered the white curtain. Anna drew in the air tinged with a faint smell of the sea. She peeked at the starry sky and thought of Lola. Yes. It had been a long time since she'd felt as relaxed as she did now in Grace Harbor. She was happy there; she had a good job; her father supported her. Esther and

Erica were good friends. Her neighbor and landlord, Martha, always waved from the window or front yard when she saw her. She wasn't going to let Genise ruin any of that.

"Dr. Kevin seems like a decent man. When will I get the chance to talk with him? On moving day we exchanged just a few words, but I liked him already."

Anna pulled her phone from the front pocket of her denim dress. "How about now?" She sent Kevin a message asking if they could swing by his house on the way back to the nursing home. She waited. He'd seen the message, but the reply didn't come right away. Maybe he was busy or out with Lola.

"How about some tea while we wait?" Serge stood with difficulty from the chair. It took him a moment to settle into his short steps before heading to the kitchen. What must it feel like not to be able to coordinate his feet? Anna watched her father place one foot slowly in front of the other until he finally moved in a straight line.

Her heart, both as daughter and as nurse, wanted to help him, but Serge preferred his independence. The day would come when he wouldn't walk unaided anymore. He wouldn't dress himself or handle a fork. Simple everyday tasks would become risky maneuvers. One wrong step could send him to the floor.

Anna made the tea and poured a cup for her father. She checked her phone again. At last, the reply arrived.
With pleasure. We'll be waiting.

With a sigh, Anna read the response to her father. They finished their tea and headed to Kevin's house. He was waiting for them on the porch and greeted them with a smile. Kevin started to help Serge up the steps, but the older man raised a hand to say he'd go up on his own.

"Anna talks about you all the time." Kevin sat in the armchair after his guests settled onto the sofa.

"And she about you. My daughter is very happy working at your clinic," Serge said.

Anna noticed the worried look on Kevin's face. Was he still upset about running into Genise at the store earlier? "I was telling my father I haven't felt this at ease in ages." The corner of Kevin's mouth twitched before he smiled. Anna shifted on the sofa. Maybe they'd caught Kevin at a bad moment. "Well, we just came for a quick visit. Nurse's orders, in this case." She tried to smile and stood.

Theo's sweet little giggle filled the room. Erica and her son were coming in from outside. "Oh, callers. How nice!"

Erica shook Serge's hand while balancing Theo on her hip.

"Na-na." The boy reached his arms toward Anna.

"You little rascal," Erica said, squeezing her son's chubby arm. "Since when do you know how to talk? What happened to just 'mama'?"

Anna went over to the boy and picked him up. "Theo." Her heart swelled like a balloon. "I'm Anna. Anna."

"Na-na." Drool trickled down his chin.

Anna wiped it away with her hand. She handed Theo back to Erica, but he grabbed a fistful of her hair. "We're just stopping by. We'll head out." She tried to untangle her hair from Theo's fingers.

"Stay." Kevin stepped closer to her. "Let's have something to eat." He glanced at Serge to second the invitation.

"Yes, stay," Erica said. "I'll pop a pizza in the oven." She dashed to the kitchen.

Kevin held out his arms for his nephew. "This one needs a bath."

Anna hugged the boy. "Can I? If you don't mind."

"Sure. I'll chat with your father." Kevin sat on the sofa next to Serge.

Anna passed through the kitchen and told Erica she'd take care of Theo's bath.

"Wonderful." The young mother closed the oven door. "You can grab pajamas from the top drawer of the dresser. Everything else is in the bathroom."

What had gotten into Anna to take such liberties? The warmth she felt from Kevin and Erica. Her current vulnerability. The scent of a baby. The life inside her.

In the hallway, Anna heard her father laughing, followed by Kevin. What were they talking about? It didn't matter, as long as her father was happy.

"Na-na." Theo pointed toward the bathroom.

"We'll take a bath, yes. Pajamas first." She entered the boy's room. She stopped in the doorway and took it in: the dark-wood crib, the mobile of stars and planets (but of course), toys strewn across the rug, the dresser with two drawers half open, showing colorful clothes.

Theo squirmed this way and that in Anna's arms, pointing at the toys on the floor. He made a sound like a car engine, spraying a mist of spit, and stretched his body, trying to wriggle free.

"Bath," Anna said, opening one of the drawers and picking out a blue pajama set she thought would be cool enough for the night.

In the bathroom, she balanced Theo on her hip while filling the tub. Soon he was slapping at the water, splashing Anna, who had knelt beside him. She narrated what she'd do next: wash his hair, rinse, wash his bottom, his feet. Theo tried to mimic some of her sounds while he played with a rubber duck and a dinosaur.

Minutes later, she was dressing him in his room. She wrestled to keep Theo still long enough to get the diaper on, but won the battle. Anna combed his fine hair. Sleep was already weighing on his bright little eyes. When Anna returned to the kitchen with Theo resting on her shoulder, Erica was shaking a bottle.

"It was a busy day for him. Want to feed him?"

Anna took the warm bottle. "Where's my father?"

"He and Kevin are in the garage. Men and their garages." Erica grabbed plates from the counter.

Back in the bedroom, Anna sat in the armchair and fed Theo, who rubbed his eyes with pudgy fists. After he burped, she laid him in the crib. She switched off the light and slipped out, not without first breathing in the cozy scent of the room.

The men returned from the garage. Erica pulled the pizza from the oven and the four of them sat down.

"Kevin is a woodworker too," Serge said, struggling a little with the knife and fork.

"It's a hobby," Kevin said.

"He bought a complicated power saw and doesn't even know how to use it." Erica cut a slice of the pepperoni pizza and popped it into her mouth.

"He does now." Serge smiled.

Anna hadn't seen her father this happy since her mother died. He loved feeling useful. At the nursing home, there were few chances to show his skills. With trembling hands, even hitting a nail square-on was a challenge, let alone more complex tasks.

The evening would have been perfect if not for the nagging feeling Anna had, seeing Kevin's heavy eyes and furrowed brow. Was the work at the clinic taking more out of him than he'd expected? The construction, the new patients, the new hours, the bills. He was a young doctor on his first solo run. He certainly needed Anna's help. Despite the fatigue she'd been feeling, she had to help him. After all, Kevin had given her the job knowing her situation and what it would mean in the near future.

Anna owed him a great debt of gratitude.

CHAPTER TWENTY-EIGHT

"One week?" Erica paced the kitchen, a wet knife in her hand.

"Calm down." Kevin took the knife from her, dried it, and slipped it back into the drawer.

"He must be losing his mind. Dad's tough, but this time he's gone too far. Does he really want to destroy his own son?" She scrubbed the pizza pan so hard that soap suds splashed onto her blue apron.

"Not destroy," Kevin said quietly. "Just... make things harder for me. He wants to turn me into a man, I guess. This must be his way of teaching a lesson." He took the pan from her hands and set it aside. "Let me do this. You're making a bigger mess than you're cleaning up."

Erica dried her hands on the apron and sat on one of the stools by the island. "So, what are you going to do about Anna?"

Kevin turned off the faucet and placed the pan on the drying rack. "What do you think? She stays. I'll make it work. Reduce the renovation work. Slow it down. Maybe take out a loan. The clinic will pull through and so will we."

Erica let out a long sigh. "I wish I could help."

Kevin tossed the dish towel at her. "You already do. What other receptionist would let her boss underpay her and still smile about it?"

She wrapped the towel around her hand. "And what other boss would give a home and food to a single mother and her child?"

Kevin pulled out another stool and sat beside her. "I'm going to call Alex."

"Are you going to sue Dad?"

"No, but I need to get our agreement in writing. What if he's getting sick?" Kevin ran a hand over the cool granite countertop. "I can't lose the clinic. Starting over somewhere else would break both my legs."

"Then call him." Erica slid off the stool. "Where are the suitcases?"

"Why?"

"Did you open them?"

"No. Why?"

She traced a line on the counter with her fingernail. "There must be a reason he brought them. Depending on what's inside, it could be a sign."

"What kind of sign?" Kevin stood up.

"Let's go find out." Erica headed toward the hallway, Kevin right behind her.

In his bedroom, they dragged the suitcases out and opened them on the floor. Erica sat cross-legged on the rug; Kevin sat on the edge of the bed. He saw nothing unusual, just his clothes. Erica sifted through dark shirts and pants, running her hands along the linings.

"I never did drugs," he joked, laughing at her thoroughness.

She lifted a bundle of clothes. "Your only drugs were those dark books you used to read. Thank goodness your taste changed."

"Foolish, naive kid," he said softly. "I let myself fall in with the wrong crowd. Renewed mind—thank God." The foolish, naive kid was long gone, even if his father still didn't believe it.

"Aha!" Erica pulled out a brown envelope.

Kevin dropped to the floor beside her. "What's that?"

Erica opened the envelope and dumped the contents onto the pile of clothes. Two smaller envelopes fell out. "Letters?"

Kevin picked them up and saw his name written in delicate, familiar handwriting. "They're from Mom."

"You knew about them?"

"No. This is news to me." He pulled one letter from its envelope. The date was from his hardest year, right before college. "Why didn't I ever get these?"

Erica rested her head on his shoulder. "Either she changed her mind about sending them, or Dad took them."

Kevin opened the first letter, his palms damp. His chin trembled as his eyes scanned the page. They were Bible verses. He noticed a theme throughout: *prayers*. Psalms. Apostolic blessings. Each one a plea for God's miraculous intervention.

It was just like her to pray using Scripture. Her way of blessing her children. Since he was little, Kevin had heard those prayers, the same ones he now whispered over Theo and Erica. His sister did the same each night when she laid Theo in his crib.

A tear fell onto the page, blurring the words *"I pray for them."* Kevin wiped his nose with his fist. From the sniffle beside him, Erica was reading and recognizing the verses too. The second letter held similar passages, different words, same spirit.

"Why would Dad put these here?" she asked.

"I don't know. I'd rather believe he found them among Mom's things," Kevin said. The words entered through his eyes and sank deep into his heart. Before she died, his mother had told him her prayers had been answered. Why couldn't his father see that? Why did he still call him irresponsible?

Kevin knew he wasn't perfect. The hurt he carried proved that. But he wasn't the depressed, lost young man he used to be. Life had flavor again. Even with the bills piling up and his father's threats hanging over him, his spirit was lighter.

The visit from Anna and Serge that evening had been a balm, even if the weight of responsibility still pressed on his chest. In the garage, Kevin had felt compassion for Anna's father—his trembling hands trying to show Kevin how to use the power tool. Yet they'd talked about woodwork and shared old stories. Serge had made furniture to live; Kevin just tinkered for joy.

Erica began folding the clothes back into the suitcase. "So, what are you going to do?"

Kevin returned the letters to their envelopes. "First, I'll do what Mom did and start writing out Scriptures and pray them. I need to exercise my faith. I'll talk to Alex next week and stop by the bank. Prayer and action."

"Have I told you lately how proud I am of you?" Erica knelt and kissed his cheek.

"No," he said, smiling. "At least someone believes in me."

"Not just me."

"Who else?" He frowned. "Theo?"

"Him too, but he doesn't know it yet. I mean Anna."

"Anna." Kevin ran a hand through his hair. "If she only knew how weak I feel when it comes to Dad."

"I never said you were Superman. Anna believes in you because she believes in your vision for the clinic. The other day she told me she's sure it'll grow more than you imagine because of your competence."

Kevin pressed a hand to his chest. "She said that?"

Erica sprang to her feet. "What's that goofy smile for?"

He glanced toward the mirror above the dresser. "There's no goofy smile. But it's nice to know I'm useful."

A baby's whimper came from the hallway.

"You're very useful," Erica said. "Now go check on your nephew so I can have a long bath." She left the room.

Kevin stood and went to soothe Theo. Erica had lifted a heavy weight off his shoulders. It felt good knowing Anna believed in him. He cradled Theo and whispered one of the verses from his mother's letters.

His decision was made, not that he'd had doubts. He'd straighten out his finances, meet with Alex, and talk to the bank manager. The renovation would go on. Anna believed the clinic would grow. Grace Harbor was growing, so naturally the need for medical services would grow too.

He even began to dream bigger. Perhaps someday opening a day hospital, offering urgent care, expanding his staff. Maybe even partnering with other health professionals.

Then he remembered—Alex's wife, Shyla, was an occupational therapist. Alex had once mentioned she wanted to leave the hospital and start her own practice. She could be his partner.

Excited, Kevin laid Theo back in the crib and hurried to his room. He opened his laptop and researched occupational therapy services in the area. Almost none. Then he checked Shyla's professional profile—she specialized in working with children with special needs. The demand was high. Kevin could give her one of the clinic's rooms. Eventually, he'd build more. His father's property (note to myself: settle ownership soon!) was large enough.

He sent Alex an email explaining the situation with the clinic and floated the idea of expanding services to include occupational therapy.

Action. Now he needed prayer.

Kevin had moved several steps back on his game board. Now it was time to move forward again. Too many people depended on him: his patients, the people of Grace Harbor, Erica, Theo, and Anna.

More than anything, he wanted to be living proof that even the most hopeless case, like himself, could be transformed.

His mother hadn't prayed in vain.

Chapter Twenty-Nine

The Kevin from the previous Saturday had given way to Monday Kevin. Despite his determination, Anna found it hard to keep up with the doctor's pace as the week began. He seemed to have downed several bottles of energy drink. By midafternoon, they'd handled several minor emergencies, examined two patients with gallstones, referred another to the hospital, and wrangled with an insurance company. From Anna's perspective, Erica must have drunk the same thing as her brother. Her whole attitude had shifted from "the doctor's sister helping out" to fully professional. What had happened to the siblings to spark such a change? Before taking her father back to the care home after their visit to Kevin and Erica, Anna had told him she was worried about her boss. Serge replied that he didn't know the young doctor well, but that their chat in the garage had been pleasant and he'd liked him quite a bit.

"Anna, prep the ultrasound," Erica said, hanging up the phone. "I managed to squeeze in the patient who canceled last week."

Anna looked at the five patients waiting in the chairs. An ultrasound would push appointments back. She decided to take the gentleman with a cane into one of the rooms and get a head start on charting his symptoms. She opened his file on the laptop and went through the usual questions.

"Please wait—the doctor will be right in," she said.

The man hung his cane on the chair and picked up a pamphlet about diabetes.

Anna readied the ultrasound room. She opened the patient's file on the computer and left the information on-screen.

When Kevin walked in, she said,

"Mr. Bastos' case is straightforward. Better to see him now."

Kevin took the suggestion and stepped out. Anna went to receive the patient for the scan. Half an hour later, the exam was done.

The clinic kept buzzing until closing. Erica dashed out to pick up her son, and Kevin called Anna into his office.

The pile of papers on the desk had vanished. The books were organized on the shelves. Anna remembered her job interview. Almost two months had passed, but it felt as if she had always worked there. She felt a responsibility for the clinic she had never felt at the hospital.

She adjusted her glasses and rested her elbows on the chair arms.

"How are you feeling?" Kevin asked.

Was this a medical consult? Anna straightened her back. "Fine. Why?"

"Just concerned sometimes." Kevin pulled the cap off a pen and rolled it between his fingers.

Anna's heart sped up. Was he disappointed with her performance? "I'm fine. Don't worry."

He clicked the pen shut and set it aside. "I'm going to expand the clinic."

Anna tilted her head. "I thought you were already doing that—the remodel and everything."

"More. I just need to take care of a few loose ends. I'm meeting with Alex later."

"How can I help?" Anna needed to face the challenge, even though the baby kicking her belly reminded her time was moving on.

"How would you feel about training a newly graduated nurse?"

He's going to replace me? "Of course."

"It's not to take your place. I can't afford someone experienced yet, but I know I can count on you until—"

"You can count on me until the baby's born, and after." How she'd manage it was still an open question.

"And Anna, if you get too tired, tell me."

"Okay." She started to rise.

"And your father—how is he?"

"He enjoyed the visit. Said you've got a knack for woodworking." She let her tired body relax into the chair.

"I don't have much time for it, but it does me good. A boyhood hobby I set aside when life got complicated."

Anna laced her fingers. She had the impression Kevin wanted to say something specific. "Teenage crises?"

He pushed his hair back. "Plenty. I disappointed a lot of people."

"People change. You did, I imagine."

"My father doesn't think so." He looked down, then back at Anna.

"I don't know much about your dad, but he should feel proud of his son. Look at the clinic growing, the patients satisfied. Your sister must see it differently, right? She speaks of you with pride. She's very grateful." She shifted in the chair. "I'm grateful too, if that helps." Anna noticed the faint smile on his face. Was that relief she saw there?

"The gratitude is mine."

A calm silence settled over the room. Fatigue washed over Anna. If she could have sat there until morning, she wouldn't have had to spend more energy getting home, making dinner, getting ready for bed. Kevin's phone broke the silence. Anna stood.

"If you want help interviewing candidates, just say the word. I'll get going."

Kevin thanked her and took the call. Anna said goodbye and left. In the car, her phone buzzed. The message lifted her spirits: Esther inviting her to dinner. It was worth a detour for good company and a meal—one less task in the kitchen.

As always, Esther met her with a warm hug and a basin of warm, salted water.

"You take Jesus' example of washing friends' feet seriously." Anna leaned back in the armchair and loosened the drawstring of her blue uniform pants.

"I know what it's like to work all day with a belly." Esther set Anna's feet in the water and sat on the sofa.

"Did your pregnancy go to forty weeks?" Anna wiped her lenses with the hem of her scrub top.

"Thirty-eight. Jade stayed in the incubator for low birth weight."

A chill ran up Anna's legs despite the warm water. She hadn't factored in the possibility of a premature birth and the many other risks of pregnancy. If that happened, she'd be leaving Kevin in the lurch. "What was hardest about caring for Jade?"

"The first months. The first years," Esther said, then smiled. "Hardest of all was hearing so many hopeless words. The doctors suggested ending the pregnancy. It felt like they were telling me to pull out an ingrown toenail."

Anna rubbed one foot against the other. "Our society is contradictory: it talks about inclusion and special-needs children, but the ones in the womb are disposable."

"Exactly. I never considered my Jade disposable. Was I scared when I saw the ultrasound result and the diagnosis at birth? Yes, very scared. Especially because my daughter's biological father agreed with the doctors." Esther sighed. "Every day Jade proves she isn't disposable."

As if on cue, the young woman came in carrying a laptop. She greeted Anna and asked if she'd hurt her feet. "My mom uses this salt basin when my feet hurt. They're really small, you know?"

Anna smiled. "I like small feet. And I love your sneakers."

Jade looked down at the rainbow-laced shoes. "My dad gave them to me for my birthday. You know I'm not a teenager anymore? Teenagers are annoying, my classmate's mom said. I'm not annoying anymore because I'm mature."

"Jade, did you finish the work?" Esther cut in.

"I did. I deleted all the old photos from the file you sent," Jade said, pointing at the laptop. "Can I eat now?"

"As soon as your dad gets here."

Jade nodded solemnly. "Anna, your belly is get— Your baby is growing. Is it a boy or a girl?" She turned to her mother. "Can I ask that?"

Esther answered, "You can."

Anna ran a hand over her belly. "I don't know yet. I'd like to, to get the layette ready."

Jade plopped down beside her mother. "Lay—what?"

Esther explained. Anna smiled at the girl's excited face.

"How do we find out if it's a boy or a girl?" Jade asked.

"With an exam called an ultrasound," Anna said.

"Oh, I know. I had one on my belly when I threw up green goop."

"Jade," her mother scolded.

"It's okay. I'm used to it," Anna said.

"Why don't you do the exam?" Jade swung her chubby legs.

"Dr. Kevin has a new machine, doesn't he?" Esther asked.

"Oh, I wouldn't do it with him. I can ask my OB. I have an appointment in two weeks." Anna lifted her feet from the water and dried them with the towel beside the basin.

"I think it's easier if he does it. Then you don't have to wait," Esther said, picking up the basin.

It wasn't a bad idea. Anna was curious about her baby. "I'll talk to him."

"We could throw a gender-reveal party," Esther suggested.

A party. Anna hardly thought about parties, though her baby deserved a celebration. She'd discovered the pregnancy in a season of mourning and bitterness. In the days after Dalton's death, she'd spent her time visiting lawyers, talking to the insurance people, paying bill after bill. Losing her house to the bank. "Would you come with me to the exam? Then Kevin can tell you the baby's sex. I want to be surprised—for the party."

"Paaarty," Jade sang, doing a happy dance in the living room. "I can blow up the balloons."

The three of them planned the party. Anna would include Erica; she could liven up any room.

Esther drafted a guest list, including Nina, Grace, and other family members. "My backyard has space to spare."

Anna reread the notes Esther had made while mother and daughter set the table. Roberto arrived soon after, and the four of them ate chicken fricassée, laughing at Jade's décor ideas. In moments like this, Anna forgot the doubts and worries that weighed on her heart. How good it was to have friends who not only distracted her but gave her a new perspective on life—proof that hope insists on surviving in the most barren ground. Watching Jade talk about balloons, sweets, and music, Anna surrendered to the joyful mood of the dinner, which would, soon enough, come to an end.

Two hours later, Anna was getting ready for bed. She doubted she'd fall asleep quickly. The day had been intense—the siblings' newfound drive, the clinic plans, and prepping for the gender-reveal party. Anna hoped Kevin wouldn't mind doing the exam.

Sleep didn't come for hours. Anna felt a moral debt to Kevin. Her baby would arrive in four months—or less. Even if everything went as expected, Anna's routine would change completely, and with that change, the clinic would inevitably take second place.

CHAPTER THIRTY

"Gender-reveal party?" Erica stepped out from behind the clinic's front desk, dashed to the door, and locked it. Just as fast, she hurried over to Anna and clapped her hands. "Count me in. And when's your appointment?"

"In two weeks." How was she supposed to bring up Esther's suggestion, asking Kevin to do the ultrasound? Given the hectic day at the clinic and the exhausted look on his face after that brief meeting with Alex right there in the clinic, Anna didn't have the courage to ask.

"Two weeks? Then why do we have an ultrasound machine?" Erica took a few steps toward her brother's office.

Anna caught her by the arm. "Kevin's overwhelmed."

Right then the doctor opened the door and ran his fingers through his messy hair. He looked as if he'd just come out of a bar fight. His shirt was half untucked, sleeves rolled up. The stubble on his chin was a couple days old. No. It wouldn't be fair to pile more work onto him.

"What is it?" He came over to the women.

"Nothing important." Anna winked at Erica.

"Anna wants to throw a gender-reveal party, but her appointment isn't for two weeks." Erica smiled and took her brother by the arm. "Little brother, how about putting us out of our misery?"

"Honestly, Kevin, I can wait." Anna wiped her damp fingers on her top. She should be taking weight off Kevin's shoulders, not adding more. But his smile disarmed her.

"You have no idea how happy that request makes me. We can do it now." He tucked his shirt back in.

Anna frowned. "I planned with Esther that she'd come with me. I don't want to know the sex now, only at the party."

"How exciting! I'll call Esther and see if she can come." Erica lifted the front-desk phone from the cradle and punched in the numbers.

Anna turned toward her, tempted to say no. Esther was busy too. But when she saw Erica hang up with a smile, her doubts faded.

"I need to pick up my Theo. I'll call Esther later to plan the party. Love ya." The young woman shot out the door and slammed it behind her.

"I'll get the room ready." Anna pressed her lips together to hold back a sob that would unleash a flood of tears.

Kevin smiled. "Let me know as soon as Esther gets here."

Fifteen minutes later, Esther was holding Anna's sweat-damp hand. Lying on the exam table in the dim light, she listened to Kevin typing the usual details. With every click-clack of the keys, her anxiety rose. Finally, she lifted the exam gown and felt the cold gel spread across her belly. Her heart felt like it was splitting her chest open—love for her child and gratitude to Kevin and Esther. And to Erica, of course.

When she heard her baby's heartbeat thrum, echoing through the amniotic fluid and through the dark room, Anna let the tears run freely.

"Strong heartbeat." Kevin moved the transducer over the right side of the patient's abdomen and pressed, sliding it slowly. "Ah!"

"What?" Anna looked at the screen, afraid he'd found something wrong.

"Everything's fine. In fact, the sex is crystal clear."

Anna took her eyes off the monitor and rested her head back. She squeezed Esther's hand. "Go on—look. I really do want the surprise at the party."

Esther went over to the doctor, who whispered a few words to her.

"Oh, how lovely! Not that it would matter either way." Esther returned to Anna's side. "The real problem will be keeping this from Jade. She saw me leaving and said she'd be waiting at the door."

Anna laughed with joy. Tears ran down her face and neck.

"Measurements are right on track, and the pregnancy is going very, very well." Kevin stripped off his gloves and tossed them in the bin. "I'll leave you two alone. I'll be in my office."

With the door closed, Anna sat up and took the paper towels Esther handed her. She wiped the gel from her rounded belly, took off the gown, tied the drawstring of her scrub pants, and pulled on her scrubs top. "Thank you. Erica jumped the gun when she heard the idea. I know you're busy."

Esther nodded toward the ultrasound machine. "I wouldn't miss this for anything. Now I just have to manage Jade's curiosity."

Anna saw Esther out and locked the door, then stopped in the middle of the waiting room. This place hadn't even existed in her life almost two months ago. Kevin hadn't, nor Erica, nor the friends in Grace Harbor. Dalton was the distant, sorrowful past. Still, Anna couldn't erase him. Her child had the right to know about the father, the good things about him. Anna didn't quite know what those good things were, since she'd believed in a Dalton who never existed. She'd cling to the ordinary things he used to do: fixing what broke at home, grocery shopping, grilling meat on the barbecue. Maybe time would show her more once the crust of resentment thinned.

She went to the office door and knocked softly.

The answer came at once. "Come in."

Anna eased the door open, as if she didn't want to interrupt something important he might be doing. "Thank you."

Kevin set the pen in his hand down on the desk. "Thank you."

She tilted her head. "For what?"

He stood and came around the desk to face her. "For giving me the privilege of meeting your child."

Anna's face crumpled, and she couldn't stop the emotional tears. Kevin drew her in by the arms and rested her head on his shoulder. There she stayed, sobbing, wiping her eyes and nose on her sleeve. Her glasses ended up in her top pocket. She felt his breath rise and fall against his chest, the warmth of his skin under the rumpled shirt. It felt good to rest her head on a solid man, one solid in character.

"Shhh, it's going to be all right. I promise," Kevin whispered, patting her back the way he did with Theo.

Realizing how unprofessional she was being, she pulled away and tugged tissues from the pocket of her scrub pants. "I'm sorry. I didn't mean to fall apart like that." She put her glasses back on.

Kevin pulled up a chair and gestured for her to sit. He leaned against the desk facing her. "Never apologize to me. Anna, I'm not just your boss. That word actually scrapes my throat on the way out. We're past formalities. I'd rather believe we're friends, that you and your dad are friends of my family."

What kind of man is this, God, standing in front of me? Anna thought that under other circumstances she'd never let a boss or any colleague get this close. But everything with Kevin was different, starting with the unconventional hire, the closeness between their two families, their mutual confessions, and the stargazing rides with Lola.

Anna pressed the crumpled tissue to her nose. She studied his serious face, the unshaven jaw. For Kevin, she'd stretch herself to share his burdens, even while feeling so tired and heavy herself.

For the next few ticks of the second hand on the wall clock, Anna and Kevin stayed quiet, each leaning back in their chairs. They looked at each other, looked away, then met each other's eyes again. Anna had so much to say to her boss—to her friend. So much to thank him for. At that moment, he knew who her baby was. He had seen the little face, the arms and legs. He had heard the tiny heart drum. He knew whether it was a boy or a girl. Maia. The name came to her naturally. But if it was a boy, she'd ask Kevin for a star's name for her son. Among thousands and thousands (or millions and millions?) of stars in God's firmament, a beautiful masculine name would fit perfectly for Anna's child.

She smiled.

"What?" He smiled too.

"I was wondering if you'd know a boy's name, a star. Maia's already on the list."

"Orion, Draco, Hercules." The dimple reappeared.

Anna's tear-bright eyes widened. "Draco? I'm not feeling very convinced by those."

He let out an easy, pleasant laugh. "There's Pegasus, but that's a horse's name. I'll think of a good one. I promise."

Anna shifted on the vinyl chair. "You make a lot of promises, Dr. Kevin."

His face grew serious. "I make them out of conviction. I keep them all though not in my own strength. God enables me."

The flood threatened again. "I don't doubt it." Anna rose. She needed to get out of there. Her thoughts were racing in a reckless direction. The warmth of his chest and the rise and fall of his breathing, she still felt them as if they were pressed together. Her face felt magnetized back toward Kevin's shoulder.

She stood too fast; her head went hollow and little stars speckled her vision. She took a deep breath, said goodbye, and hurried out of the clinic, leaving the doctor wearing a puzzled expression.

Heart pounding, she got in the car and shut the door. She lowered her head to the steering wheel so the blood would circulate properly and wipe away the little stars. Minutes later, she started the engine and pulled out of the lot, nearly clipping the curbside pole.

Kevin's scent had seeped into her clothes. She scolded herself, asked God's forgiveness, and blamed her hormones. What kind of mother was she, anyway? A merry widow wouldn't be fit to care for a baby.

"Get a grip," Anna shouted at herself, looking into the rearview mirror at her wild hair and puffy face.

CHAPTER THIRTY-ONE

"What's wrong? Is Anna's baby okay?" Erica set Theo's plate on the tray of his high chair.

Kevin dropped his car keys on the kitchen counter. He scratched his head, making his hair even messier. "The baby's fine. Anna too." He filled a glass with lemonade from the pitcher on the table and gulped it down.

"Was it Dad? Genise? You look like you just came out of a meat grinder." Erica took him by the arms. "Did the clinic catch fire? Spit it out—you're killing me."

Theo flung his spoon to the floor, splattering yellow soup everywhere. Kevin grabbed a paper towel and crouched down. Erica crouched too, snatched the towel from his hand, and looked him in the eyes.

"You're making me nervous. Did someone steal Lola?"

Kevin stood and leaned against the counter. "I'm losing my mind."

Erica ignored her son smearing soup on his face with his hands. "Now you're scaring me. Come on, sit." She tugged him to a chair at the table and sat beside him.

"I did something I shouldn't have." Kevin could still feel Anna's breath on his neck, warm and damp, and the clean scent of her hair.

"What, for heaven's sake?"

"Anna."

"You fired her because of Dad? Are you insane? That's exactly what he wanted. What will happen to Anna? She'll never find another job with that belly." Erica sprang up so fast the chair almost toppled. Theo looked at his mother and wiped his hands through his own hair, streaking it with bits of carrot.

Kevin braced his elbows on his knees and dropped his head into his hands. "I'm in love with her." He saw his sister's feet move closer. He felt her hand stroke his hair.

Erica crouched and took his hands, forcing him to lift his head. "I suspected as much."

If Erica suspected, would Anna suspect too? "How?"

"The way you look at her when she walks by. Worse than when you thought you were in love with Carol in eighth grade—only now it's with a man's intensity, not a teenager's."

Kevin's eyes went wide with genuine horror. "I'm a monster. She's a widow. She's pregnant. She's my employee. Everything—everything—about this is wrong. No wonder Dad calls me irresponsible, a hippie. I'm weak, detestable. A freak."

"Mah-mah," Theo babbled.

Kevin and Erica glanced at the soup-smeared boy. Erica opened the cupboard, pulled out a pack of crackers, and handed him the entire thing. She sat again.

"Listen, Kevin. You're not a monster or a freak. I know you. A pregnant woman is still a woman. We have longings, desires. You think I didn't want a real man to show up in my life when I was pregnant?"

"Thanks for the implied compliment," Kevin half-smiled.

Erica smacked his leg. "You know what I mean. A man. A husband. A father figure for my son. I don't even know if a man like that exists, other than you. Even pregnant, I thought about it. Now," she shrugged, "this is my reality: Theo, covered in soup and cracker crumbs."

"I didn't know that. That you thought about it." He tugged his shirt from his waistband and slumped against the chair.

"You think I was going to confess this sin or secret to my brother, who was bending over backward to give me a roof, that I had a woman's desires?"

"You're taking a weight off me. But I don't want to scare Anna. What now?"

Erica plucked a soggy cracker chunk that Theo had tossed into her hair. "Nothing. Keep supporting her like you do. Give her time to get settled, to find her footing when the baby comes." She lifted Theo from the high chair. His sticky little fingers went straight to her face, and she licked them one by one. Theo giggled.

The doorbell rang. Brother and sister traded a look. Kevin knew what Erica was thinking: their father, probably, for another round of accusations.

"Stay there, clean up the mess, I'll get it." With firm strides, Erica crossed the living room, her sticky toddler on her hip.

Kevin wiped down the high chair and watched her open the door. To his horror, it wasn't their father but Alex's law partner. Erica exchanged a few words with the man, dark-skinned, clean-shaven, and shifted Theo to her other hip, then invited him in. Kevin raked a hand through his hair. What a contrast between his own disheveled and pitiful state beside the man's impeccable suit.

He went to the living room and greeted Felipe Cruz, whom he'd met on a visit to the firm. He introduced his sister and nephew. "Sorry about the mess."

Felipe smiled. "I've got nephews too. I get it."

Erica excused herself and left with the boy. Kevin and Felipe chatted briefly, and Kevin promised to return the signed documents the next day after reading everything.

"Call if you have any questions. My card's in the envelope. Good night." Felipe took a few steps toward the porch, then turned back. "Tell your sister the answer is pumpkin." He chuckled, waved, and descended the porch steps toward his silver Mercedes.

Kevin closed the door and shook his head. What kind of answer was that? He found Erica sitting on the blue bath mat, playing with her son as he splashed in the tub and gnawed on a yellow rubber duck.

Erica turned to him. "How embarrassing! Dad's curse. Me, all smeared, face to face with an ebony Adonis."

Kevin burst out laughing. "Ebony Adonis? Where did you get that image?"

Erica grinned. "From mass-market paperback with Fabio on the cover, naked chest. My favorite back in my rebel days."

"Get it, get it. Felipe is very good-looking, though. No naked chest imagery of Fabio, please."

Erica flopped onto the bathroom mat and doubled over laughing. When she caught her breath, she sat up, lifted her son from the tub, and wrapped him in a yellow towel on her lap. "Why is it so hard for men to say other men are fab-u-lous?" She stood with Theo.

"And do you have to talk like that? By the way, your ebony Adonis said the answer is pumpkin. I have no idea why."

"Oh, an Adonis with a sense of humor." She tousled her son's damp hair. "I was so flustered running into him that the first thing I said was, 'Do you know what this soup in my hair is?' Can you believe it? I'm pathetic!"

"Well, he nailed it. It is pumpkin even with the bits of carrot in Theo's hair."

"Next time warn me so I look more presentable and crumb-free." Erica glanced at herself in the mirror and made a face.

Kevin kissed his sister and nephew and went to his room. Sitting on the edge of the bed, he looked at the two suitcases. Leaning forward, he pulled out the envelope their mother had left and took one of the letters. How he needed his mother's prayers right then! His chest felt like pure turmoil, a storm on the open sea of emotions. The talk with Erica in the kitchen had given him a new perspective on women, which didn't mean Anna was looking for a man.

Maia. When Kevin saw the baby's sex, he rejoiced for Anna. The star from the Pleiades already seemed chosen by the mother with her little passenger aboard. He couldn't wait for the party that weekend. Esther had sent an invite hours after the exam. Until then, Kevin would have to protect Anna's emotions. He needed to tuck his urge to hold her again deep into a corner of his heart.

And for the next two days, Kevin and Anna made a silent pact to focus only on work.

Two potential nursing candidates were interviewed by Anna. She passed her notes to Kevin, who gave her full freedom to choose. On Friday, at the end of the day, Anna told him that the quick-footed, easy-smiling Asian young woman would join the medical team. Kevin spoke briefly with Siyin Li and agreed with Anna's choice. He forwarded the info to the accountant to process the hire. The following week would start a little lighter for Anna.

And a little tighter financially for Kevin.

Chapter Thirty-Two

T he dish of scrambled eggs took its place on the table beside a plate stacked with pancakes in Anna's airy kitchen. She filled her mug and her father's with fresh coffee. Her appetite had grown considerably in recent days, and she tried to keep her cravings for junk in check. But on weekends, she allowed herself the pleasure of eating whatever she wanted. She would resist devouring the pancakes because, late in the afternoon, she'd be having cake and other treats that Esther, Nina, Grace, Erica, and Jade were preparing for her baby's gender-reveal party.

"Yesterday I talked to Shyla Romano, the occupational therapist. She said there are new mobility strategies that help people with Parkinson's. I'd read about them, but never dug in." Anna sat down and put two pancakes on her plate. She spread them with butter, which melted on contact, and drizzled honey. Her mouth watered.

Serge sipped his coffee, the mug trembling. "It doesn't make sense for me to live with you and be one more burden."

"You're not a burden. I need your emotional support. Shyla can help." Anna remembered her conversation with the daughter of the woman who managed her son-in-law's properties. She had learned that Shyla was adopted from an orphanage in India at age five. A hard worker, she had always dreamed of helping others as her adoptive parents had helped her. When hired to take care of Alex Romano's autistic boy, her dream became a reality. A widower, Alex fell in love with sweet Shyla and soon they got married. She later graduated as an occupational therapist and started practicing in Grace Harbor.

Shyla had assured Anna the new strategies gave Parkinson's patients greater mobility and independence. The truth was that Anna was afraid of caring for the baby alone, not because she doubted her abilities, but because she felt more fragile with each week closer to the birth. She needed her father's support.

"You're putting me in a tough spot. What if I end up giving you more trouble than helping?"

"We'll figure something out. With you here, I feel calmer."

Father and daughter ate breakfast in silence. With the plates empty, they started tidying the kitchen.

"I have a plan," Serge said, setting the dishes in the sink. "I'll stay with you a year. Then we reassess. Your life could change a lot in that time. We don't know what God has prepared for you."

Anna set the frying pan in the sink and hugged him. "Thank you. I don't have the gift of seeing the future, but we'll talk if things change." Anna hoped nothing would. Leaving Grace Harbor would be the last thing she wanted. Her circle of friends was growing, which tied her even more to the place. If Kevin kept expanding the clinic, her professional life would progress.

Kevin. How would his life change in a year? He was a handsome man, a man of character. What if someone showed up in his life? Anna shook her head, trying to chase away the improper thoughts of a cheerful widow with a child in her belly.

Father and daughter spent a peaceful morning making plans for his move into the house. The third bedroom, still empty, would be Serge's for a year. They decided he would move in a couple of months to allow Anna time to settle down in her own place.

In the late afternoon, Anna and her father drove to the inn for the party. Esther hadn't let her help with the preparations, determined not to spoil the surprise. And what a surprise it was! Kites of every color and size adorned the gazebo in the inn's garden, fluttering like a burst of joy in the afternoon breeze.

Jade greeted Anna and her father. "My mom didn't tell me if it's a boy or a girl. She said I can't keep my mouth shut." She pressed her lips together for a few seconds. "See? I can keep it shut! But what she means is that I can't keep secrets. And I think she's right."

"So it'll be a surprise for me, for you, for my dad, and a bunch of people. That'll make it even better." Anna gave Jade a hug and laughed. The place was cheerful and perfect.

Anna greeted the women who had prepared the party and was introduced to Daphne Olson, the famous cozy-mystery writer, her husband, Andrei, and the other guests. To her great delight, she met Parker, Esther's brother and Nina's husband. How many stories had she heard about him from his proud sister? In many ways, Parker resembled Kevin in character. Both had cared for their nephew and niece and given of themselves for their sisters' sake. The true meaning of sacrificial love.

Parker pointed to the kites and said to Anna, "They're part of our story with Jade. She can tell you more later."

Anna smiled at him and at Nina. "I can only imagine. Jade flies like kites."

A pile of gifts formed a pyramid beside a panel shaped like a giant kite.

Esther came over and hooked her arm through Anna's. "Kites have an important meaning for our family. I hope you liked the decorations. It was Jade's idea."

"I thought it was cheerful and original. Parker was just telling me about kites." Anna smiled.

Esther went to greet other guests. Nina and Parker rushed to rescue the kite panel that the children were threatening to topple.

The arriving autumn breeze swirled under Anna's navy dress, cooling her legs. She scanned the guests, who were chatting. She waved to Erica. With Theo on her hip, Erica was talking to a young, clean-shaven man with a shaved head. He laughed at something Erica had said. A little bird seemed to whisper in Anna's ear what might be going on between Erica and the guy.

"Anna."

She jumped at the sound of the voice. She turned and looked at Kevin. His face carried the same unreadable expression that had appeared the day they'd embraced. Her insides churned. Something was wrong.

"Kevin."

"Curious about the gender, I suppose." He adjusted the collar of his dark shirt. His smile didn't reach his eyes. Didn't even hint at the dimple she liked.

"Dyingto know." The words came out lighter than she felt. Inside, a ripple of worry tightened her chest.

Esther called Anna and the guests to the center of the gazebo. Kevin vanished among them.

"I know how curious Anna is, so let's reveal the baby's gender right away and celebrate the arrival of another Grace Harbor resident," Esther said.

The guests cheered, many shouting their predictions. Jade appeared from behind the house with a beige gift box topped with a silver bow. She set the box on the table beside the presents. "Come, Anna."

Anna stepped forward with her hands clasped tightly together. Esther came to her side and said:

"Inside the box there's a kite. It will reveal the baby's gender."

"And then we're going to the beach to fly the kite," Jade shouted.

The guests offered their guesses again.

"I think it's a girl." Jade clapped when Anna took hold of the box lid.

Esther said:

"We'll count down from ten, and you lift the lid."

Anna's heart pounded. This would be the first thing she'd know about her baby's identity. She counted with the others:

"Ten, nine, eight..."

Her heart sped up.

"Three, two, one!"

Anna lifted the lid and pulled out a pink kite. She pressed it to her chest. The guests tossed confetti of the same color into the air, covering the lawn and heads.

"Maia, Maia," Anna whispered, hugging the kite.

"I knew it!" Jade threw confetti over Anna. "Let's go to the beach."

"Pebble," Roberto set a hand on her shoulder, "after food and cake. We can't go without having cake, right?"

"Cake, woohoo!" Jade started scooping confetti off the grass and tossing it back up.

Anna hugged Esther, and a line formed to congratulate the young mother. Erica handed Theo to Daphne and pulled Anna into a long embrace.

"I'm so happy for you. I'd be happy either way."

When the guests were distracted by the food and her father had gotten into an animated conversation with Roberto, Anna filled a small plate with savories and wandered across the lawn. Instrumental music floated on the cool, salty air.

Kevin was sitting alone on a park-style bench on the far side of the inn. Anna crossed the lawn and approached.

"If you'd rather be alone, I'll head back." She pointed to the cluster of cheerful guests.

He patted the bench, and Anna sat down.

"Maia," he said.

Anna set the plate on the seat. "So that's why you wouldn't give me a decent boy's name."

"I was very happy with what I saw. I'm happy for you."

Anna studied his face, still unable to decipher his expression. "I'm glad you were the first to know. Maia."

He sighed. "You're remarkable and courageous. You'll be an amazing mother, Anna."

She felt her cheeks grow warm and her heart flutter. "So courageous that I've asked my dad to come live with me."

Kevin smiled. "That's really good. And I think a good mother seeks help."

"I'm afraid I won't be able to handle it." She looked down.

"You're very strong. And God will be by your side."

Anna tilted her head and looked at Kevin. "I need a miracle."

Kevin found himself telling Anna about his mother's letters with Scripture prayers. "Erica and I do that for Theo. I'll add you and Maia to the list."

Anna nodded, feeling somehow special. "I really need it." She stood with the small plate in hand. "I'll head back. After all, they threw this party for me."

"Of course."

Anna fixed her gaze on him. "Come too. Without you, I wouldn't have a party, wouldn't have all this support. You weren't just opening a job opportunity for me that day. You were opening a door to a new life for me and Maia."

"Anna, the credit is yours, for your determination." He stood up.

She shook her head vigorously. "Determination without this job at the clinic wouldn't have opened these doors. Even my father, Kevin, is more upbeat. He's made friends. He had lost almost all of his old friends because of Parkinson's. People drift away, you know?"

"I'm glad to be part of this new beginning."

"Thank you."

"Thank you."

She smiled. "Why do you always answer like that, with another thank-you?"

Kevin tucked his hair behind his ears. "Because I'm grateful for you, Anna."

"Any other nurse would do the same, work just as hard or harder." She brought her hand to her belly.

"You've influenced Erica. She admires you a lot. That makes my life lighter. You make my life lighter."

The flush returned to her face. "I think I brought more weight."

"No, Anna. Lightness."

In the garden, encircled by trees and twinkling Christmas lights, Anna and Kevin looked at each other for a while. The instrumental *bossa nova* drifted over to them, and Anna felt herself float.

Lightness. Beside Kevin, in Grace Harbor, the hard moments were woven with lightness.

A voice called Anna. It was Jade. "Let's sing happy birthday to your baby."

Anna followed the girl, fully aware Kevin was coming with her. Around the cake, the guests wished Anna well, and she revealed her daughter's name. Grace prayed, and Jade insisted they sing "Happy Birthday." When the song ended, Esther and Nina cut the cake, which quickly began to shrink. Finally, Roberto announced they would go to the beach to fly Maia's kite before sunset.

Everyone walked to the beach. Anna carried the kite. Kevin walked at her side. On the sand, she slipped off her sandals and tossed them onto the growing shoe pile.

"I don't know how to fly a kite," she confessed.

Jade took the kite from Anna, let the line play out, and the kite rose. "See how easy it is?" She handed the kite to Anna, who laughed with delight as the pink triangle climbed into the sky. The smile lingered for a long time when Anna saw Kevin arriving with her father, who was walking in slow, careful steps.

After the sun went down, the guests started saying their goodbyes. Anna and her father thanked each one enthusiastically.

Back home, in pajamas and under the covers, Anna laid a hand on her belly. Nothing could have been more perfect than that party. The pink kite was fixed to the wall above the crib's headboard. The pyramid of gifts sat in the living room. After church the next day, she would open each one with her father.

Anna turned on her side and closed her heavy eyes. Her phone buzzed on the nightstand. She pulled it over and read the message:

Thank you.

She replied to Kevin's message with a smiling-face emoji.

CHAPTER THIRTY-THREE

I t was like the blade of a guillotine. Kevin's father had left a voicemail, reminding his son of the deadline to accept the offer to wipe out the debt in exchange for letting Anna go from the clinic. Kevin had already made his decision and wouldn't change his mind. Even in front of the computer in his office, with the ledger open and smeared with red, he would keep his promise to Anna.

Kevin deleted the message.

He treated patients that day under the threat of the guillotine. His father wouldn't accept defeat. He might go so far as to take the property back from Kevin. Alex had prepared the agreement Kevin would present to his father, but his fear of triggering an outburst kept him from taking the document over.

At the end of the day, Erica closed the clinic and left to pick up Theo. Anna and Siyin went to the exam rooms to set them up for the next day. Kevin was pleased with the choice of the new nurse. She did her work quietly but with great skill. Kevin could relax, knowing Anna would have backup if she had an emergency.

The two nurses and the doctor said goodbye in the clinic parking lot, and each went their own way. On the drive home, Kevin wanted to call Anna and invite her for a ride in Lola. But the idea of sharing Lola's cab and bed with Anna made him restless. It was too risky to have her so close, to smell her perfume and hear her melodious voice when she talked about Maia.

So he went home to take care of his responsibilities with Theo and Erica. His sister had her head in the clouds. She would have her first date with Felipe. Kevin had talked with him at church the previous Sunday and learned the young lawyer volunteered in a prison. "A lot of young men are in there just for keeping bad company. I want to help them redirect their lives," he had explained.

Kevin worried for Theo. It was far too early to know whether Felipe would be good company for Erica, given her current situation.

The siblings ate one of Erica's new recipes: chicken with creamed corn. Kevin smacked his lips.

"Where were you hiding those culinary skills?"

Erica gave Theo another spoonful. "I have my secrets."

The doorbell rang. Kevin went to the door and opened it. The guillotine threatened again. "Dad."

Dr. Miller came in. "I came for your answer. You should've answered my message."

Kevin closed the door and headed for the kitchen. His father followed but barely greeted his daughter. He ignored his grandson.

"I already gave you my answer that day. Anna stays. I'll pay what I owe you." Kevin stood in the middle of the kitchen.

"Having another nurse must be costing you." Dr. Miller lifted his chin.

"The clinic is growing."

"So are the debts."

"Dad," Erica shouted. "It's none of your business." She stood up with her fists clenched.

Theo threw the spoon on the floor and cried.

"Take care of your fatherless child."

Erica charged at her father with her fists raised. Kevin grabbed her around the waist, lifting her off the floor. "Take Theo to your room. He doesn't need to witness his grandfather's cruelty. He doesn't need that memory."

Erica picked up Theo, but stayed in the kitchen.

"Please leave," Kevin said to his father.

"Blah. Don't you learn anything in church about respecting your elders?"

Kevin clenched his teeth before saying, "I respect you. Otherwise I'd shove you out of here."

"Brat."

Kevin pressed his hands to his forehead. "Why do you take pleasure in tormenting us? What do you want from me? Is it the hair? Is that it?" He yanked open a kitchen drawer with a bang. He rummaged through it, the clatter of utensils filling the room. He pulled out a pair of scissors.

"Kevin!" Erica set the loudly crying Theo back in the high chair. She ran to her brother. "Don't do this. Nothing we do will ever be enough for Dad." She tried to pull the scissors from Kevin's hand.

He stepped away. He lifted a lock of hair. Light strands fell to the floor. Erica cried and begged him to stop, but Kevin kept grabbing fistfuls and cutting.

Theo banged his spoon on the tray and cried, as if asking his uncle to stop. When Kevin's hair covered the floor around him, he set the scissors down on the counter with a thud. He spread his arms. "There. Was that it? The hippie hair is gone. Do I deserve your regard now? Your respect?" Kevin opened the kitchen door.

Dr. Miller, his gaze icy, said,

"I came in through the front door. I'll leave through the front door." He turned and headed for the living room. The door opened and shut in seconds.

Erica scooped Theo up and covered him with kisses. Then she ran to Kevin and hugged him. The boy was squashed between mother and uncle, but stopped crying.

They stood still in the sea of hair on the floor. A knock at the kitchen door made Kevin break the embrace. Had his father come back for more torment?

Kevin opened the door and found Anna and Serge staring at him, alarmed. She came in without a word. She studied Kevin's face, then looked at the hair on the floor.

"My father was here," Erica announced.

Anna drew a breath and moved toward the young mother. "Take Theo to the other room. I'll take care of this."

Kevin watched her from where he stood. His legs felt so heavy he couldn't move. She went to him and guided him to the table. "Sit."

He obeyed. She filled a glass with water. Serge opened the pantry and took out a broom. He began sweeping the hair into a corner, his trembling hands maneuvering the handle with difficulty.

Too stunned to speak, Kevin drank the water. He scratched at his neck, prickling with cut hairs.

"Can we talk outside?" Anna asked, and he nodded.

"I'll handle things here." Serge squeezed his daughter's hand as she and Kevin passed him on their way to the door.

Anna followed Kevin out to the garage. He opened Lola's door for her to get in. He walked around the Chevy and sat in front of the steering wheel, where he rested his forehead. "I lost my temper." He looked at her. "Nothing I do pleases my father. Nothing. I'm starting to think he's sick."

"I'm sorry."

Kevin turned to Anna. "That's why I need to be a good father figure for Theo. My father picked a fight with us in front of him. Erica went berserk. Theo got scared." He hit the steering wheel. "If I'm Theo's father figure, I have to protect him, even from my own father."

"And you do, Kevin. Erica looks up to you. Theo looks at you with eyes full of joy. What woman wouldn't want that father figure for her child?" Anna put a hand to her belly and gasped, shocked at her own comment.

Kevin squeezed his eyes shut; they burned. He wanted to shout that he would protect Maia. Inside, he did shout. But the only sensible thing he found to say was, "I'm here for you two, Anna."

"I know."

"Your father must have been shocked by what he saw in my kitchen." Kevin ran his fingers through his hair.

Anna shook her head. "My father has dealt with difficult people in the past. My grandfather was a sadist. He forbade my aunt from playing the guitar. One day he said he was going on a trip but hid in the garage. My aunt took the guitar and used the time to practice. My grandfather appeared at the window, tore the guitar from her hands, and set it on fire. My father knows the difference between a psychopath and an anguished person. Because of Parkinson's, my father has grown gentler. He's seen how life plays tricks. He admires you, Kevin."

"I still need to apologize."

"Don't worry about that now. Rest. Why don't you put some music on?" She pointed to the stereo on Lola's dash.

Kevin turned the key just enough to switch on the stereo. Soft musical notes danced in the air, composing a message of calm and hope. Kevin let his head fall back against the seat.

What if I pull Anna to rest her head on my shoulder? Kevin closed his eyes with that thought.

CHAPTER THIRTY-FOUR

The musical notes floated inside Lola and blended with Kevin's soft snoring. He sank into a deep sleep. Anna studied his face—serene, yet sad. The fine lines at the corners of his mouth curled like tiny quotation marks.

She lifted a hand toward his now much shorter hair, a lump in her throat threatening to spill into tears. The kitchen scissors had done a very poor job on his light brown hair: too short in places and riddled with holes. A barber could tidy the mess, but wouldn't bring back the beauty of the longer locks. Anna swallowed hard. Her chest ached over Kevin's conflict with his father.

She drew her hand back the moment her fingers brushed his head. Gently, Anna opened Lola's door and climbed out. She leaned over the truck bed and pulled one of the blankets from the metal toolbox. Back in the Chevy's cab, she draped the blanket over Kevin, tucking the ends around his neck like an oversized bib.

Leaving the garage, she turned out the light. Kevin needed rest. Lola would embrace him in her place.

When she stepped back into the house, the kitchen floor was clean and the dishes washed. Only the spotlights over the island were on. The house was quiet. Where was her father?

On tiptoe, Anna walked to the living room. Her father sat by the window under a lamp, reading. Seeing his daughter, he set the book on his lap.

"How's Kevin?"

"Sleeping in the car." Anna took a seat beside him on the sofa.

Serge squeezed her hand. "Theo took a while to calm down. I think he and Erica are asleep. I told her I'd take care of the kitchen."

"Thank you, Dad. Kevin's feeling embarrassed." Anna slipped off her glasses and rubbed her tired eyes.

"He doesn't have to worry about me."

"I told him that. Kevin is a good man, Dad." She put her glasses back on.

"It shows." He cleared his throat. "You like him, don't you?"

"Who doesn't? He treats patients with respect and care." Anna gestured around the room. "And the way he took in Erica and Theo."

"Patients, sister, and nephew like him. And you?"

Anna set her hands over her belly. "He's a good friend. A dear friend."

"A friendship worth nurturing," Serge said, stroking his daughter's cheek.

"No doubt about it."

He stood with effort and slid the book back on the shelf. "We'd better go. It's past ten, and you still have to drive me back."

Father and daughter left the house and closed the door. Anna texted Kevin and Erica to say the door was unlocked.

After dropping her father at the home, she drove slowly through Grace Harbor to her condo. The houses were mostly dark now, save for a light here and there. Maia would grow up in this beautiful town. She would know these special people, and they would know her. Nothing would be lacking, because she would have the love and respect of her mother's new friends.

"Everything's going to be alright." Anna stroked her belly as she pulled into her garage.

***

Sun bled into the sky in shades of orange. Anna pushed open the kitchen window and breathed in the new day. Dressed in her work uniform, she ate some yogurt and a banana, then hurried to the bathroom to finish getting ready. She wanted to reach the clinic well before Kevin, Erica, and Siyin. When the first rays of sun woke her, Anna decided she would knock down every professional obstacle that day for Kevin and Erica's sake. She felt energized, despite the fitful sleep after the scene at the doctor's house the night before.

Unlocking the clinic door half an hour later, she said a quick prayer. She wanted to be an instrument of peace and calm for the Miller siblings. Her admiration for them grew by the day. The more she understood their struggles, the more she took it upon herself to support them.

She sat at Erica's desk and booted up the computer. She pulled the charts for the day's patients, then jotted down the messages from the phone's voicemail. Over the next half hour, she prepped the exam rooms with everything Kevin would need. In the kitchen, she started the coffee maker.

By the time Siyin arrived, the clinic was ready for the first patients.

"At this rate you'll put me out of a job," the young woman with sleek black hair joked. She slung a stethoscope around her neck and clipped a pen to the pocket of her purple scrubs.

"Don't worry. With today's appointment list, the two of us will be busy enough."

Erica came in next, eyes hollow and sad. She dropped her bag on the counter and hugged Anna. Discreetly, Siyin slipped into the back.

"I don't know whether to apologize or to thank you. Maybe both," she said, voice thick with tears.

Anna smoothed a hand over the young mother's curls. "Neither. We're friends, aren't we?"

"A very good friend," Erica said, wiping her eyes and nose with tissue paper.

"How's Theo?"

"He slept well. Woke up in a good mood." Erica stepped behind the counter. "You open the charts? Thank you."

"I came early."

The door opened and Kevin walked in. His hair was slicked back with gel. Unprofessionally, Anna felt the impulse to run to him and hug him, as she had Erica. She held back. "Good morning. Want some coffee?"

He came closer. The clean scent of soap reached her, but the bath hadn't washed away the fatigue and sadness from his face.

"I woke up at three in Lola with a blanket."

"I didn't want to wake you and thought you'd be cold."

He gave her a faint smile. "Could you come to my office?"

"What about the coffee?" she asked.

"Later. I need to talk to you." He crossed the waiting room toward the office.

Anna's heart kicked. Had she done something wrong? It didn't sound like good news.

She sat across from Kevin in the tidy, orderly office. He set his satchel on the floor, picked up a pen, tapped it on the desk, then set it aside.

"I don't know if I should apologize or thank you," he said.

Anna let out a breath of relief. "Erica said the same thing. My answer: neither." She scooted to the edge of the chair. "Family isn't always the way we want."

"Your grandfather, right?"

"My grandfather, my brother. Did you know my brother doesn't speak to me? I don't even know why. My father doesn't understand it. I admire your friendship with Erica." Anna let her shoulders drop.

"And I admire yours with your father. Nothing is the way we want. One day, if I have my own family—wife and kids—I'll do everything I can for us to be close."

"That's what I want, too." Anna laced her fingers together.

Their eyes held. A knock on the door broke the moment. Erica came in.

"Timmy's burning up. His mom says he coughed till he couldn't breathe."

The urgency in Erica's voice sent doctor and nurse into the exam room. The day took the expected turn of hard work and distraction from personal troubles.

That week passed, and another began at the same pace. Anna spent the weekend organizing the baby-shower gifts into Maia's drawers and closets. She had received several gift cards in varying amounts, all anonymous. One held an exorbitant sum—enough for three months' rent. Her father said God made it rain blessings in times of drought, and that those tokens of care translated to love.

Anna didn't hear from Genise or from Kevin's father for a while. When she entered the third trimester, Kevin's hair had grown long enough to tuck behind his ears. Theo took his first steps and always ran to Anna when she visited the family. He enjoyed the outings in Lola more and even hummed a few of his uncle's favorite songs.

Serge began bringing some of his things to his daughter's house and setting up his room. Shyla visited him twice a week to teach exercises and mobility strategies. Anna noticed he held utensils and cups with greater steadiness, despite the tremors.

Her prenatal appointments were uneventful. Maia grew and filled out. Anna felt it in her own legs and hips. By day's end, her back screamed for a massage. The shower took the edge off the pain.

It was that night, stepping out of the shower and toweling off, that Anna saw the stain. A wave of dizziness washed over her and she had to brace herself on the towel rack. Head bowed, she sat on the toilet. Her heart hammered. Her phone was in the bedroom.

Anna pulled some toilet paper and wiped. The paper came away with blood. She tried to recall every pregnant patient who had come to her care and how their bleeding had turned out. It wasn't necessarily cause for alarm, especially at twenty-eight weeks. Anna ran through the possibilities as she breathed slowly. There were no cramps. Or were the back pains actually cramps? She opened the vanity drawer and took out a pad. She slipped on her underwear and her robe.

Kevin. She needed to call him. She needed him.

Slowly, she settled onto the bed, wet hair dripped down her face and neck. So did the tears. She wanted to curse Dalton for all this, but she thought of her daughter.

Anna reached for her phone on the nightstand. She tapped Kevin's contact. One ring. Two. Four.

"Anna?"

"I need your help."

Chapter Thirty-Five

K evin slipped on the bathroom floor as he hung up and caught himself on the sink. He stared at his soapy body and wet hair in the mirror. He'd been ignoring the phone buzzing; after the persistent rings, he'd peeked at the screen from the shower and seen Anna's name.

And this couldn't be anything but serious.

He toweled off haphazardly, ran the towel through his hair, grabbed the crumpled jeans off the floor and sprinted to the closet. He yanked a T-shirt from a drawer, shot through the kitchen while snatching his car keys, and shouted to Erica what was happening.

"Keep me posted," she yelled as he slammed the door.

The blocks seemed to stretch out forever. Kevin ran two red lights before reaching Anna's house. She was waiting with the door open, lying on the sofa. Her belly showed where her robe gaped.

"Kevin."

"Easy, Anna. Don't panic. You know this can happen. I'm taking you to the clinic."

"My clothes?"

Kevin scratched his head. "I can grab a dress from your closet."

"The navy one. Second door."

He nodded and went to her room. Her floral perfume lingered everywhere. He opened the closet and pulled the dress from a hanger, then returned to the living room.

"I need some water," he said, ducking into the kitchen. He braced both hands on the sink. Anna had been working too hard. She was going to need a rest.

"Kevin, I'm ready."

He went back to the living room and helped her into the car.

At the clinic, he brought her to the ultrasound room. Anna lay down and lifted the dress. Kevin did all the prep.

"I'm going to check that Maia's okay. First thing tomorrow morning, call your OB. She'll tell you the cause of the bleeding."

The transducer traveled over Anna's belly. She let out a long breath when Maia's heartbeat filled the room. "Everything's fine, within the parameters. That's a big relief. Tomorrow we'll see what caused the bleeding."

Anna wiped her belly with the paper sheets Kevin handed her. "What about work?" She pulled her skirt down and pushed the sheet aside.

Kevin helped her sit up. "Rest until we know the cause and what you need to do. We hired Siyin for this very reason."

"You hired me for this," Anna said, crumpling the paper in her hand, the crackle echoing through the exam room.

He pulled the rolling stool over and sat, scratching the back of his neck. He scooted closer to Anna. "True. I hired you for this. A lot has changed."

"What? The workload's up, the expenses are up. Doesn't that worry you?"

Worried? The red in the ledger gave him nightmares. "Of course it does." Kevin rubbed his neck. "But I don't see you as a means to fix my professional problems. I didn't hire you on a timer. This stretch—your rest and all—will mean very little when we look back a few years from now." He took her hand. It was cold and sweaty. "Right now not much looks promising, but I know the clinic will grow. I'm in talks with Alex and Shyla. She wants to set up an occupational therapy clinic and, who knows, a rehab wing."

Anna glanced around the room. "We don't have the space."

"Not here, but somewhere else."

"And your father? What will he say?"

Kevin let go of her hand and stood. He ran a hand through his hair. "Nothing I do will convince my father I'm not a kid. I'm doing this for myself, for Erica and Theo. For you, Anna."

"For me?" She touched her chest. "Why?"

"Because you're capable. Because I trust you. Because I need you." He felt a chill in his gut before finishing, "I need you to help me expand the clinic."

Anna held her belly. "I'm kind of useless right now."

"You're never useless. Right now, you're carrying a life. Nothing nobler or more worthy. When Maia arrives and things settle, we'll talk."

"Do you think I can do it?"

Kevin smiled. "That and more."

That night he persuaded Anna to stay at the inn under Esther's care. Esther, however, took the young mother to her own home. Early in the morning she would take Anna to her doctor.

When Kevin finally lay down, two feelings wrestled in his heart: one, worry for Anna and Maia's well-being. The other, a sweet hope that Anna would always be part of his life. He longed to be an influence in Maia's life, as he was in Theo's.

The next day's news lifted the worry: Anna would be fine, according to her doctor. She needed a few days of rest, but would be back at work soon. Kevin handed more responsibilities to Siyin, who gladly took on the extra load. He had plans for the young nurse as well if the clinic's expansion panned out.

Fueled by hope and resolve, Kevin ended his workday with one mission: go to his father's house with the agreement Alex had drafted. Kevin had suggested some bold changes, but backing down was not an option. He needed to grow with or without his father's approval.

He said goodbye to Erica at the front desk. She hugged him tightly. "I'm with you no matter what. Me and Theo."

Parking in front of Dr. Miller's house, Kevin stayed in the car a moment to run through his speech. The house on the raised lot was lit, but there wasn't much life inside. He stepped out with the envelope under his arm and climbed the stone path that cut across the immaculate lawn. How many times had he, Erica, and their friends slid down that lawn on pieces of cardboard? His mother would follow with little bags of buttery popcorn. Times that wouldn't return.

With a sweaty hand, Kevin pressed the doorbell. Dr. Miller opened. No smile. No apology. No word about his disappearance since the scene in Kevin's kitchen.

"Come in."

Kevin felt like an unwelcome door-to-door salesman hawking vacuum cleaners or old-school encyclopedias.

In the tastefully furnished living room, whose contents could easily cover all of Kevin's, Erica's, and Theo's bills, Kevin sat facing his father. The older doctor settled into his leather armchair, a throne given the man's posture.

Kevin set the brown envelope on the coffee table. "It's unlikely we'll resolve our differences."

"Blah."

"That's why I'm returning the deed to the house. I'm not interested in it anymore."

"And this paper?" Dr. Miller pointed his long finger at the envelope.

"The terms of the arrangement. I want everything clear."

"You really have no sense. Who in their right mind gives back a valuable property?" The man gave a caustic laugh. "All because of the nurse?"

"All because I don't want to owe you anything. I'm only asking for a month to find a new place for the clinic."

Dr. Miller leaned forward and slapped the envelope. "And why would I sign this?"

Kevin pushed his hair behind his ear. "Because serious men handle their business properly."

"Serious men?" Dr. Miller leaned back, folded his arms, and eyed the envelope. "And why would I give you a month?"

Kevin leaned in and fixed his gaze on his father. "Because serious men negotiate what benefits both sides."

"Leave the paper. I'll consult my lawyer."

How did we get to the point where my father and I need mediators? It used to be my mother who stepped in when he got angry at me and Erica. Now, lawyers. Kevin stood. "I won't take up your time."

"And where are you moving?"

"I'm looking."

"You're going to dig yourself in deeper."

Kevin headed for the door. "And do you care?"

His father let out a sound of disdain.

Back in the car, Kevin's legs shook. Cold fear crawled over his skin. With or without a signature, he had to sever things with his father once and for all. His father only understood the language of contracts and signed agreements. Only the desperate or the mad would give a property back. As long as he was bound to his father by any reason or favor, the man would torment him. Kevin needed to follow his own path. He'd given up proving to his father that he'd grown up. Only distance would give him the peace to make plans without constant criticism.

Kevin felt like mythological Atlas, carrying the world on his shoulders. He could not let down the people he loved most in life—two of them, defenseless babies.

Chapter Thirty-Six

"I'm worried about Kevin." Anna cut a piece of the chicken breast Esther had just taken out of the oven. The aroma of garlic and lemon spread through the kitchen.

"I understand your concern, but he's not the kind of man who runs from problems." The innkeeper poured a glass of pineapple juice for Anna and sat down on the other side of the table.

Esther's cozy kitchen exuded the aromas of her delicious cooking. Whenever Roberto and Jade went out for their father–daughter date, Anna had supper with Esther. Their own time to strengthen the friendship.

Anna swallowed the piece of chicken and wiped her lips with a cloth napkin. "What are men of grit made of?"

Esther smiled. "When I think of Parker and Roberto, I see similarities with Dr. Kevin: humility, faith, perseverance, love. So many virtues. I think that's how they strengthen their true, God-given masculinity. They need to go through the trials by fire. Purified gold, right?"

Kevin's face danced in Anna's mind. "It makes me angry I can't help more. He and Erica deserve so much!" She smiled. "I wish I could give them the stars."

"I'm sure they already have the stars when they go out with Lola. Isn't that the pickup's name?" Esther squeezed Anna's hand. "You're a gift in their lives. In ours. Grace Harbor is better with you. It's so good to meet people who arrive to add to our lives. I hear people talking about your work, your care. Keep it up and you'll help Dr. Kevin and Erica."

"Your words are precious. You've been an example to me."

"I'm nothing without my brother, my Jade, and Roberto. They're my north, my safe harbor. God couldn't have given me a better family. When I was abandoned by Jade's biological father, I thought that would be the end. But it was just my beginning. Some things have to die for new ones to grow. Some die without needing to, but die anyway. Those bad, foul-smelling experiences can serve as fertilizer for good things. It's the good that comes from evil."

Anna dabbed a tear with the napkin. "Thank you, Esther. You're very wise."

"That wisdom isn't mine. Mine is rags." She pointed upward. "Don't be afraid. God love you. And so do we."

Jade burst in like a whirlwind. She said she'd eaten a lot but still had room for the chocolates Roberto gave them. Anna took the cue, thanked the family, and said goodbye. In the car, she drove the opposite way from home. She stopped at Beth's bistro and bought dulce de leche and strawberry cake. Minutes later, she pulled up in front of the house with the navy-blue door. Never had her heart been so abundantly full of love for Kevin's family. Anna felt as if her heart might burst at any moment. She needed to show that love and her gratitude. A cake was a trivial token in return, but it was the only thing she could think of at the moment, since she couldn't give them the stars.

Anna rang the bell and adjusted her denim overalls, which were already tight at the waist. Balancing the cake box in her hand, she waited. Kevin opened the door, his wet hair from a shower dripping onto his white T-shirt, and looked curiously at the white box.

"Some surprise in there?" He motioned for Anna to come in.

"A little gift to brighten your and Erica's evening."

"I like unexpected gifts." He followed Anna to the kitchen.

Erica came down the hallway behind Theo, who was toddling along.

"Nana," the boy shouted and ran to Anna.

Anna leaned down, kissed Theo's head, and held his hands. "Nana brought a present."

"Present." Erica came up to the box and clapped like a little girl.

Anna lifted the lid. "I thought you'd like it."

"Like it? Sugar? Who doesn't like it?" Erica ran to get a knife.

Kevin raised a hand. "Wait. And Lola?"

Erica waved the knife and put her other hand on her hip. "Does Lola eat cake?"

Anna laughed, loving the light banter.

Kevin tapped his sister's head as if knocking on a door. "Hello, hello, my little sister. Why don't we eat the cake under the stars?"

I wanted to give them the stars. Cake under the stars. Anna smiled and readily agreed.

"I'll get Theo ready." Erica went down the hallway, pulling her son by the hand.

With the navy-blue sky pierced by celestial diamonds, the four of them stopped in their clearing. Kevin jumped up into the truck bed and spread out two thick quilts. Anna came up with the cake.

"New quilts," she said.

Kevin opened a cloth bag and pulled out three pillows. "It was time to redecorate Lola."

Erica arrived carrying Theo. The boy squirmed to get out of his mother's arms. "Lo-lo," he babbled.

"That's right. Lola." Erica set the boy down in the truck bed and fetched a basket of toys from the car. The young mother plopped onto the soft comforter and took her place with Theo in one corner of the pickup.

Kevin held out a hand to Anna, who scooted to the other corner. She opened the box and served slices of the delicious cake on the disposable plates Erica had brought. Under the velvet mantle of the night, they savored the light crumb and creamy frosting of Beth's cake. Theo got a little piece, but soon demanded more. Erica gave in to the fussing, justifying that a little sugar wouldn't hurt her son.

With their palates satisfied, the three friends leaned back on the pillows and admired the sky. Theo amused himself with a little flashlight and a toy telescope.

An hour of quiet conversation passed when Erica announced she would head home. "You two enjoy your stargazing because my daily expiration time has hit. And with all that sugar circulating in my baby's veins, I'll have a hard time putting this one to bed." She packed up the toys and climbed down from Lola.

"We should go too," Anna said.

"Good night, you two." Erica took her son and drove off into the dark road.

Anna stretched her arms and legs. She grabbed a pillow and hugged it. The pine-scented breeze brushed her face. Remembering her conversation with Esther, Anna was overcome by a great sense of peace, as if she were levitating off the comforter toward the sky. Kevin was, in fact, an admirable man.

"A slice of cake for your thoughts." He crossed his legs and sat facing Anna.

Her face warmed. "Thinking about the conversation I had with Esther earlier."

"Girly secrets?" The dimple appeared in the moon-lit gloom.

Anna hugged the pillow tighter. Why was she trembling? Maybe it was the breeze. "So to speak."

"So it was a serious talk." He tucked his hair behind his ear.

Anna adjusted her glasses. "Clarifying. Inspiring."

"And mysterious. Does the cake have something to do with it?" He pointed at the white box.

"The cake is a thank-you."

"Why, Anna? You've thanked so much already." He took her index finger and wagged it.

The trembling returned. "It feels like it's never enough."

Kevin scooted closer. "You don't thank for lo… for friendship." He lowered his hand to hers.

She looked at his finger entwining with hers. Then she raised her eyes to him. Kevin's pupils caught the moon's glow. "True. It's just a way to express my affection. For you all."

"And we have great affection for you, Anna. And for Maia. Can we consider ourselves a family?"

Anna's heart pounded. Maia did a somersault in her belly. What did it mean to be part of Kevin's family? Some families were more than blood relation. Her own brother hadn't even sent a message asking about Anna and Maia. Surely her father had told him about her recent bleeding. Blood, in this case, meant nothing.

Anna looked at the moon reflected in Kevin's pupils. "I'd very much like us to consider ourselves family." She ran a hand over her belly. "I know Maia would too. After all, it was Uncle Kevin who gave her the name."

He kept his gaze on Anna for a moment. "Uncle Kevin can't wait to hold Maia in his arms."

Anna's chin trembled. She took off her glasses and rubbed her eyes. "Dr. Kevin, you can't do that to an emotional pregnant woman."

He smiled. "Dr. Kevin is a big softy who melts for babies."

On impulse, Anna took Kevin's warm, soft hand and set it on her belly. "I think Maia is listening to our conversation."

He brought his face close to her belly. "Hi, Maia. It's your Uncle Kevin. I'm waiting for you. I'm going to show you the stars, the moon, the planets. You're a star, you know? I'll tell you all about the other Maia and her sisters."

Anna wiped away more tears as she listened to Kevin talking to her daughter. In that moment, breathing in the scent of shampoo from Kevin's hair, she dared to wish he would be more than an uncle to Maia.

Chapter Thirty-Seven

"Anna, Anna, Anna." Kevin pulled the pillow over his head.

If there were a way to bottle a moment, it would've been the one in Lola's truck bed an hour earlier. He'd felt Maia's tiny kicks. Breathed in Anna's perfume. Was he losing his mind? Yes. He had been for a while, ever since he first saw Anna.

Then he'd learned about the pregnancy and forced himself to step back. He was mad. The madness haunted him the way a ghost train ride did a child, jerking, twisting, revealing skeletons and witches at each turn.

Only this time, Kevin wasn't a boy, and that was no ghost train ride.

Anna was real. Maia was real.

But Kevin's feelings were uncharted territory. He had never faced a moment when every sense conspired to make one woman, and her voice, her face, her scent, fill his whole being, invading every cell of his body and soul.

He heard Theo whimper down the hallway, but soon the dark house fell silent again. Kevin tossed and turned on the firm mattress—on his stomach, on his side, on his back. Nothing helped.

The phone pinged, and a blue light cut through the darkness. Kevin kicked the quilt aside and grabbed the device, fingers trembling, eyes searching for Anna's name. But the message was from his father.

Kevin sat up against the wooden headboard and read the sentence that hit like a hammer:

Return the property, but you have two weeks to vacate. My lawyer will contact yours.

Nausea rose in his throat. Two weeks? How could he possibly find another place and move everything that fast?

He glanced at the corner of the room, where the two suitcases still sat.

What could explain such hatred, such bitterness? His father had an endless well of vengeance against his own children.

Sweat dripping down his armpits, Kevin read the message one more time. He didn't reply. Instead, he sent an email to Alex, asking for help and guidance.

Sleep, already disturbed by thoughts of Anna, vanished completely. Kevin sat alert, as if a new day had already dawned, one terrifying, dark day.

He got up, walked to the kitchen in the dark, filled a glass of water, and sat on the island stool. Pressing his palms to his temples, he tried to squeeze an idea from his overworked brain. He jumped when he felt a hand on his shoulder.

"Kevin, what is it?" Erica slid onto the stool beside him.

"Dad's giving us two weeks to move out of the house."

She slammed a fist on the countertop. "He wants to destroy us. Why?"

Kevin pressed his temples. "He must be sick."

"He just wants attention. Always the center of everything, always in control. I don't get it." Erica switched on the light and paced the kitchen. "This isn't normal, not even for the arrogant Dr. Miller. What are we doing now?"

Kevin rested an elbow on the counter. "I emailed Alex for advice."

She threw her hands up. "And all that money you've been putting into this house? Doesn't Dad have any mercy? Two weeks! He's a monster." She growled in frustration.

"Shh. You'll wake Theo. Tomorrow's going to be one of those days. Honestly, I can't even remember the last time I slept through the night." Kevin gulped the water and hiccupped. His throat was bone dry, his eyes burned, his chest felt tight.

Erica sat back down, laying her head on her folded arm. "His grudge got worse after you brought me here." She lifted her head. "What if I find a place for me and Theo?"

Kevin waved a hand. "No! Absolutely not. Even if that solved anything, I wouldn't allow it. You think I'd turn my back on my sister and my nephew? What kind of jerk do you think I am?"

Erica hugged him. "You're not a jerk. I didn't mean it that way. I just want to help somehow, even if it means stepping out of your way."

"No one's leaving. You two will go when the time's right."

What kind of mess was their father creating now? Kevin felt like a cornered mouse facing a cat in the kitchen. *God, I really, really need some direction here.*

Theo's cry reached the kitchen. Erica sighed, kissed her brother's cheek, and left.

Kevin switched off the light and went to the dark living room. He turned on a soft *bossa nova* tune and lay down on the sofa, staring at the ceiling.
No stars there—only Anna's face.

He dozed, woke, dozed again. Finally the first rays of sun pierced his eyelids, waking the ache of another difficult day.

Kevin took a cold shower and wrapped himself in a towel. In his bedroom, he opened the two suitcases and pulled out a T-shirt with a heavy-metal band logo on it. That had been a crazy, crazy phase. Not that he was against rock, but those sounds carried bad memories now. *Bossa nova* calmed him. He went to the kitchen, grabbed two large trash bags, and began sorting piles of clothes—one for the dump, one for donation.

At the bottom of the suitcase were some heavy metal magazines featuring long-haired rockers. Maybe that was why his father hated his long hair—he'd always associated rock and heavy metal with drugs and rebellion. But Kevin had cut his hair right there in the kitchen, and the resentment had stayed.

His clothes were classic now, his appearance completely different from everything his father had despised. But the real change was inside. God was at the center, and Kevin leaned on His grace to keep growing.

His earthly father demanded more than his Heavenly Father ever would. God was patient, loving, merciful. Dr. Vincent Miller demanded unattainable perfection.

Kevin and Erica ran in circles like a carousel spinning out of control, never moving forward, always back where they started. They demanded impossible sacrifices, stripping away the very blessings God had given. Because Erica, Theo, and Anna were blessings. And Dr. Miller wanted to erase them from his son's life.

As Kevin shoved the magazines into the trash bag, a notebook fell to the floor. He picked it up, not remembering ever owning a leather-bound one. Flipping through, he recognized his mother's handwriting again. On one page, a recipe. On others, prayers for her children.

Sitting on the floor, Kevin leaned against the bed, listening to Erica and Theo moving around in the house.

Near the end of the notebook, he found a prayer for his father. His mother's tone was different, tired, almost defeated. The prayer didn't follow her usual pattern with Scriptures; it was more of a confession.

No sacrifice is too great for family. I feel fulfilled serving each of them. Vincent has his reasons that go beyond work. It's not my place to judge or tell him how to deal with his conscience. Your grace is sufficient. No one brings a child into the world to turn their back on them. Kevin and Erica are safe in this regard.

Kevin reread the last two sentences. Turn their back on a child? What had she meant? His father had never been close to his children, but Kevin and Erica had never felt abandoned. Pressured, yes. But not abandoned.

"Kevin, I'm taking Theo to Daphne's," Erica called from the hallway.

He checked the time on his phone. "I'm heading out too."

Placing the notebook in the nightstand drawer, Kevin got dressed for another long day of work, his mind spinning, his eyes burning.

Chapter Thirty-Eight

I t wasn't her job to diagnose people's health issues, but Anna's gut told her Kevin was sick. Maybe a 24-hour virus. The night before, when he'd been talking to Maia, there'd been no sign of illness; yet as soon as he walked into the clinic, Anna noticed the pale lips, the slumped shoulders, the shuffling feet as he crossed the waiting room to his office. She glanced at Erica, who was on the phone with a patient while typing information into the computer. Siyin was checking in new arrivals, sending some straight to the exam rooms.

"You can change Mr. Suarez's dressing," Anna told Siyin, trying to keep her voice steady. Worry for Kevin had left her rattled. She imagined the doctor bedridden, patients waiting, she, Erica, and Siyin scrambling to keep up. She turned to the office's closed door. Her heart thudded. Resolute, Anna went to the door, knocked softly, and stepped in.

Kevin had his back to her. His spine was curved, head bowed, the posture of a man carrying the weight of the world or sapped by a nasty bug. Anna closed the door and hurried to him, circling the chair.

She laid a hand on his shoulder. Kevin was trembling. She couldn't see his face; it was buried in his large, clean hands.

"Kevin, what happened?" She crouched as far as her belly allowed and took his wrists. "Look at me." Anna slipped into nurse mode.

He lowered his hands. His eyes were bloodshot, tiny vessels webbing the whites. "I'm fine. I didn't sleep well."

Anna knew it was more than a bad night. She'd seen Kevin tired before, but nothing like this, reddened skin mottled with pale patches. She grabbed a water bottle from the mini-fridge in the corner, opened it, and handed it to him.

"Are you sick? Did you take your temperature? Nauseous?" The questions tumbled out of order.

Kevin took a few swigs and stood. "I'm not sick." He stopped in the middle of the office and looked at her. "My father gave us two weeks to get out."

Anna steadied herself on the desk. How would they find a place, move everything, and notify the patients in two weeks? She pictured the waiting room, now full. This week's appointments and next. The renovation nearing completion. Payroll, now including Siyin. Anna drew a long breath.

"It isn't much time. But we'll manage," she said.

Kevin stepped closer. "This isn't your burden."

Anna looked at his hands hanging at his sides and, not very professionally, took them in hers. Kevin dropped his gaze to their fingers.

"We'll find a solution together," she said.

A knock broke the moment of encouragement, of tenderness. Siyin's round face appeared in the cracked door.

"Mr. Suarez's all set. I've brought the others into the exam rooms," she said professionally.

"I'm coming," Kevin answered. Siyin closed the door.

Anna turned to go, duty calling. Kevin called her back. She looked back, hand on the knob.

"Thank you."

"Thank you." She gave a weak smile and left.

The hectic day gave Anna no time to dwell on the Herculean task ahead of her and Kevin. It wasn't her place to judge Kevin's father or meddle in family conflicts. Still, she couldn't fathom her own father abandoning her, and on top of that, actively making life harder. In her work and life, Anna had learned people acted strangely when at war with themselves. Maybe Dr. Miller was ill, or hiding more skeletons than anyone knew. But none of that was her business.

What was her business was easing Kevin's load: she cared for that day's patients, spoke with the medical supply vendors, helped Erica reschedule appointments, and used her break to scout new locations for the clinic. She found one on the edge of Grace Harbor, apparently in a new commercial area, not far from downtown and accessible by public transit.

Between comings and goings, the Grace Harbor Clinic team treated everyone with professionalism and compassion. Anna wasn't surprised by the doctor's resolve to care for each person despite his own troubles.

Mrs. Newton, the last patient, tucked a prescription for a new cream for her leg rash into her leather purse. Anna was washing her hands as Kevin opened the door for the elderly lady, whose gray hair was set in perfect curls as if she'd spent all day in rollers.

"Thank you, son. Grace Harbor couldn't ask for a more dedicated doctor." She turned to Anna, who dried her hands with a paper towel. "And such attentive nurses." She squeezed Kevin's hand. "Your work is not in vain."

Kevin smiled his thanks. He walked the patient halfway down the hall and returned. Anna dabbed her eyes with a damp tissue.

"Anna." He closed the door. "I'm sorry about this morning. You must think I'm weak."

She tossed the crumpled towels in the trash. "When we're weak, God is strong." Maia seemed to agree, landing a kick to Anna's ribs. Her daughter was hinting: those words were for the young mother too.

Kevin smiled. His mother would have said the same.

Anna pulled her phone from the pocket of her light-blue scrubs. "Look what I found."

Kevin took the phone and scrolled. "This must have been listed just now. What do you think?"

"I took the liberty of booking a showing. In half an hour." She wondered if she was overstepping as nurse, employee or even as friend. But Kevin's face said she wasn't.

"What are we waiting for? We'll take my car."

They stepped into the waiting room. Erica had already left, and Siyin was straightening the magazines on the coffee table.

"Thank you for today and for everything," Kevin said to the nurse.

"You're welcome, doctor." The young woman flushed slightly. "I never imagined I'd get to work with you. People say such good things around town. I'm the one who should thank you." She grabbed her bag, said goodbye, and left with a broad smile.

"I don't think it's a coincidence getting two compliments in a row," Anna said.

"One more reason to fix this situation."

Minutes later, Anna and Kevin were driving toward the edge of Grace Harbor. After a few miles on a newly paved avenue, they reached a commercial area dotted with modern buildings under construction. The sun was setting. Between cranes and new facades, Anna glimpsed a sliver of ocean.

"Alex's office is around here," Kevin said, following the GPS. Soon he pulled up to a steel-and-glass building. "This is it."

He parked in a yellow-striped spot. He and Anna met the realtor in the lobby, where a uniformed guard manned the marble-topped desk.

Kevin introduced himself and then Anna to the realtor. Stanley, a gray-haired man with a leather briefcase, pointed to the elevator.

"Second floor," he said.

When the doors slid open, Alex appeared with his partner, Felipe.

"Kevin, what a coincidence. I just emailed you. I was in a hearing and couldn't reply earlier."

Kevin introduced Anna to both men. "We're here to see the suites for lease."

Alex loosened his tie. "Great. Shyla told me about this place this morning. Why don't we take a look together?"

Felipe said his goodbyes and left. Stanley led the way when the elevator opened on the second floor.

Anna stepped out first. Her feelings were a seesaw: happy at the prospect of a new space, sad to leave the house that meant so much to Kevin and to her. While the realtor rattled off details, Anna remembered the day she'd sat in her car looking at the Grace Harbor Clinic sign, wondering what her future held. She vividly remembered her anxiety as she considered telling a lie or omitting a truth to secure the job. She had no idea what awaited her behind the door of that charming old house. On the other side stood Dr. Kevin Miller. Kevin. His story with Erica and Theo. Rides in Lola under starry skies, lively chats at the siblings' home. Behind that door, flung wide for her, grace had been waiting in the person of Kevin. Her chest tightened as she looked at the floor-to-ceiling glass doors and windows of the office suite. A shiver ran through her despite the pleasant, air-conditioned cool.

"Twenty-four-hour security," Stanley said.

Anna walked to the big window and looked out. The last light of day reflected off neighboring glass towers, blocking the view of the sea. She looked at Kevin and saw a glint of hope soften his features. She had no right to cling to the house, however important it was to her story. They needed to move forward. What mattered was that patients held Kevin in high esteem. And Anna would be at his side to help with the transition.

"Shyla's excited about having her Occupational Therapy office," Alex said.

It sounded, Anna thought, as if the arrangement with the lawyer's wife was already in motion. It was what Kevin wanted: better care for patients. The place would do. If he could detach from the family house, then so could she. Nostalgia was a poor guide for decisions.

Back in the car, Kevin took the coastal road, detouring around construction. Anna lowered her window and breathed the salty air.

"What do you think?" Kevin asked.

She looked at him. The emotional seesaw continue. "Great place and location."

He slowed for a red light and turned to her. "What do you *really* think?"

Anna sighed. "It can't be easy letting go of the house."

Kevin hesitated when the light changed, then drove under the speed limit. "Not easy."

Anna squeezed his forearm. "Don't do anything rash."

"My father gave me two weeks. And I have to give Stanley an answer by tomorrow afternoon. Plus, Alex and Shyla are excited about joining forces with our clinic."

They passed new homes with manicured lawns and wide, lit windows. Anna wished for the right words. "Kevin, whatever you decide, I know it'll be for the best even if it isn't what you want right now."

He glanced at her and smiled. "We'll make it. God is with us."

"Yes, Kevin." Anna let her tired body sink into the leather seat. Maia somersaulted, as if to agree.

CHAPTER THIRTY-NINE

The knot in his stomach didn't loosen after a night of deep sleep. Kevin brushed his teeth and combed his hair, which now brushed his nape. He finished buttoning his light shirt and slipped out before Erica and Theo woke up. He needed that Saturday morning to put into action a plan that had taken shape in his mind as soon as the first rays of sun slipped through the blinds in his bedroom.

Kevin left the house on foot, taking the tree-lined lane. He passed other craftsman-style homes. With each block, his conviction grew. After he'd left behind his rebellious phase of dark, ripped clothes and dim rooms that smelled of cigarettes and other substances he'd never touched, Kevin had promised himself he would seek whatever offered light and air. Thinking back to the suites he'd seen the night before with Anna and Alex, the knot in his stomach tightened. Light those rooms had plenty but not air. Not the air that drifted in through windows of a place on a leafy street where he could watch the seasons change. Steel and glass wouldn't convey what he wanted for his new clinic. He needed to see spring blossoms, summer green, autumn's falling gold, and winter's bare branches. Confined to a glass box, Kevin would wilt.

Crossing the street, he took Main Street with its vintage-style shops, like Love at Second Sight, still closed at that hour. Beth's Bistro was already welcoming the first customers hungry for caffeine and carbs fresh from the oven.

Kevin pulled the door open and held it for an older gentleman in a hat, who greeted him by name. At the counter he ordered an espresso and a croissant. He scanned the full café and found a small round table for two by the restrooms. Setting down his cup and the plate with the croissant, he sat and pulled out his phone to start searching. His conviction dimmed as his options shrank to three or four. He ruled out the first house, not far from his own. The listing showed it needed renovations. The money he had for renovations was already sunk into the house he'd have to vacate in two weeks.

The knot in his stomach kept him from eating the croissant, fragrant as it was. The second rental was a storefront at the end of the street. He'd noticed the "for rent" sign the day before. No. His patients deserved a welcoming place, not a warehouse.

Kevin opened the last link. His heart leapt and the knot came undone. He read the details and downed the rest of his coffee. On impulse, he sent a message to the realty office, which was probably still closed. He left the croissant untouched and texted Anna, hoping she was already up. Drumming his fingers on the wooden tabletop, he watched for the delivered/read indicators, then for a reply. Long, dragging minutes. Nothing. Kevin stood, said goodbye to Beth, and stepped back onto the street. Nina's little shop was now open. A detour wouldn't hurt. He went in and greeted Nina and Grace.

"Dr. Kevin, you don't rest on Saturdays?" the lady with the crooked bangs asked.

"I've got a few things to sort out." He glanced around.

"What are you looking for?" Nina came out from behind the counter, smiling.

He turned toward the book shelves. "I'd like a gift for Anna's baby. I was thinking one or two books."

"We've got a whole shelf of children's books." Nina led him to the right side of the shop. "Take a look." She left him to browse.

Kevin checked his phone. No reply from Anna yet, but an encouraging message from the realtor. He ran his fingers along the spines. He pulled out a book about the universe. Flipping through, he spotted the Pleiades constellation. He tucked the book under his arm and kept looking. He smiled when he drew out a pink Bible: The Girls' Bible.

He paid, and Nina assured him Anna would love the gifts. His phone buzzed as he left the shop with the paper bag.

"Anna. Sorry to bother you so early," he said.

"Is it an emergency?"

"I need your opinion." He pictured her face. Was she rolling her eyes? Not like Anna. She always listened carefully.

"Of course."

He let out a small breath at her calm answer. "I found it."

"Found what?" Anna asked.

"The house. Near Esther's inn. I'd really like you to see it with me. I just got a message from the realtor, and he'll be there in fifteen minutes. I understand if you can't."

"Send me the address. I'll meet you there."

Kevin said goodbye and hung up. He texted the address to Anna and picked up his pace. He wanted to see the house from the outside, alone first to feel whether it was the place.

Passing Tranquility-by-the-Sea Inn, Kevin admired the surrounding homes. The knot kept loosening and his conviction grew. When he stopped in front of the house, his sigh confirmed it: this was the place. In two weeks or less, the ties to his father would be cut. The emotional bonds had already frayed over years of strife between Dr. Miller and his children. The family home, which Kevin had longed to own, would no longer be a source of fights. What would his father do next?

Kevin took in the façade of the yellow house with white windows. The wide porch could seat some patients on warm days. The listing said five bedrooms. One could be for Shyla and her patients. Pleased with the exterior, Kevin leaned against the white fence and checked whether Anna had texted back. The realtor would arrive any minute.

"Well, look who's up early."

Kevin turned, and his excitement deflated. "Good morning, Genise."

Dressed in black workout shorts and a tiny white crop top, she sauntered over. Every one of Kevin's internal alarms went off.

She glanced from the sign to Kevin. "Thinking of shacking up with your pregnant nurse?"

Kevin's chest burned. In the distance, he saw Anna turn the corner. She stopped.

"Business matters. And if you'll excuse me, I'm waiting for the agent." He fixed his gaze on her, hoping she'd catch the seriousness of the moment.

"Leaving your daddy's clinic? Family drama?"

Kevin was saved by the realtor, who pulled up to the curb and got out of a black Honda.

"Happy deal-making." Adjusting the thin strap of her top, Genise added, "Since you denied me care, I'm seeing a new psychologist who just got to Grace Harbor. He understands my problems." She bent to retie her already perfectly tied laces, waved, and jogged off. She brushed past Anna and bumped her in a pathetic attempt to make the nurse lose her balance.

Anna caught herself on the fence. Kevin went to her.

"You okay?" He glanced toward Genise, now sprinting like a gazelle in an open field.

"Interesting woman," Anna said.

"Very troubled. She found a male therapist."

Anna stifled a laugh. "Poor guy."

Inside, Kevin confirmed yet again: this was the place. Anna agreed.

"It's written all over your face," she said.

A quick chat with Stanley made it clear Kevin had to act fast.

"I'm showing it to two other parties today. You know how it is, Grace Harbor's drawing professionals from Providence," the agent said.

Kevin asked for a few hours to decide and said goodbye to Stanley.

On the sidewalk, he and Anna quickly weighed the two options. Practicality or charm? Modern or homey?

"I know you'll adapt to either." Anna looked from the house to Kevin. "But your eyes light up here. Why not talk to Erica first?"

Erica. If she knew about their mother's notebook entry, she'd confront their father on the spot. Maybe Kevin should keep that to himself until the move was settled. The last thing he wanted was another blowup with his dad. If his father was hiding something from his children, this wasn't the time to lift the rug and stir up the dust.

"I'll do that." Kevin looked at the house once more and sighed.

They walked back along Grace Harbor's Main Street. Shopkeepers and pedestrians greeted them as they passed. In front of Nina's little store, Anna stopped. "I'm going to peek at a few things for Maia."

"I'll call you as soon as I decide." Kevin said goodbye and headed home.

By the time he turned onto his street, his decision was already made. He'd talk to Erica out of courtesy, but that was that.

In better spirits, he hurried the last few yards and climbed the porch steps into the living room.

In the kitchen, he saw Erica pacing. She turned as he entered and waved a notebook in the air.

"What does this mean?" Her tone was sharp.

Before Kevin could answer, she lifted Theo from the high chair, handed him to his uncle, and said:

"I'm going to ask Dad about this. What children he turned his back on?"

"Erica, I don't think that's a good idea," Kevin said.

Without replying, she stormed out the kitchen door, slamming it behind her.

CHAPTER FORTY

"And that's why we'll have to move next week," Kevin said.
Anna ran a hand over her belly, which itched a little, wondering where she'd find the strength to organize the move from the clinic to the new house in just a few days. The schedule for the coming week was already full. Erica would have to reschedule appointments. They'd need to deal with Internet installation, clean the new place, hire a moving truck and crew, and inform all the patients. The list of tasks scrolled through Anna's mind like one of those flashing signs on a busy city street.

Erica bounced Theo in her arms as she paced the living room. "This is my fault. I shouldn't have poked the bear. What else could I expect from Dad?" She pressed her fingers against her eyelids. Theo squirmed, wanting down. Erica set him on the floor, and the little boy ran straight to Anna, who gathered him close beside her on the couch.

Sitting on the edge of the armchair, Kevin scratched his head. "It's not your fault. He's lost his mind." He waved the brown envelope in his hand. "At least, with this signed, the threats end here. We'll leave the house and cut the ties for good."

Anna didn't know the exact contents of the document, but she remembered it was an agreement between father and son to nullify the previous deal regarding the house where the clinic operated. Maybe this break was for the best. Dr. Miller had been using the property as leverage, keeping his son bound by the contract. As exhausting as a rushed move would be, starting fresh elsewhere might finally give Kevin some peace.

"I already called the realtor. I'll sign the lease on Monday," Kevin said.

At the start of the week, with the contract signed and keys in hand, Kevin and his team gathered to plan the move while still caring for their patients. That afternoon, Siyin stepped into Kevin's office, where he and Anna were discussing which patients would need priority once the relocation was complete.

"Sorry to interrupt, Dr. Kevin. Mrs. Mildred just told me there's a rumor going around town that the clinic is closing permanently. I heard something similar while having coffee at the bakery."

Anna glanced from Siyin to Kevin. How quickly people could fan the flames.

"Explain that we're not closing and share our moving plans. We'll send an email to all patients by the end of the day," Kevin said.

Siyin nodded and closed the door.

"Anything done in a rush invites speculation," Anna said.

By the end of the day, the rumors were contained with an email to all patients. Then Anna, Kevin, Erica, and Siyin threw themselves into tackling Kevin's long to-do list. The four of them were in his office when Kevin's phone rang. He looked at the screen.

"The hospital. What now?" He answered.

Anna saw his expression change as he listened to a woman's voice on the other end.

"What happened?" Erica asked, rising from her chair.

Kevin ended the call. "Dad had a heart attack."

***

Lying in bed, Anna drifted in and out of sleep. The soft light of the bedside lamp cut through the darkness. Two hours had passed since Kevin's last message, saying his father was going into surgery at Providence Hospital.

Another prayer. Anna felt too helpless even to pray. How was Kevin handling yet another blow? What if Dr. Miller didn't make it? How would Kevin and Erica face the harsh reality of never having made peace with their father?

Anna knew about unresolved matters. Dalton had died, leaving her with grief, anger at his betrayal, unpaid bills, and a daughter without a father. She had tucked all the bitterness away into a hidden corner of her soul. But it was still there: hot, foul, acidic. Who was she fooling? Maybe herself but not God. One day, she'd have to open that compartment and clean it out, like draining old oil from an engine. She had promised herself her daughter would not grow up with only a negative image of her father. But before that, Anna would have to make peace with her past, or what she'd pass on to Maia would be her own poison.

Adjusting her white nightgown on her round middle, Anna rested her cheek on her palm on the pillow. She stared at the dark phone screen on her nightstand. The sounds of the night floated in through the half-open window, crickets, barking, a distant meow.

Then the soft blue light of the phone lit up: Kevin. She reached out and answered.

"Kevin."

"Anna." His voice was heavy, slow. "The surgery's over. He's in the ICU. The first few hours are the most critical, as you know."

"Were you able to talk to him before?"

A pause.

"Yes. Anna, there won't be any move."

Anna switched the phone to the other ear. Maybe she hadn't heard right. "What do you mean?"

"Before the surgery, I think he was afraid. Erica and I spent a little time with him. He said the house is mine, and if he makes it through, he'll transfer everything to me and Erica."

Hot tears spilled down Anna's cheeks. What an irony. The father might not survive, and the house would go to the children anyway. "That's good news, Kevin."

A pause.

"Anna, there's still so much I need to make right with my dad. I don't want him to go. He doesn't understand that Erica, Theo, and I—we still need him. I hope one day he knows that. It's not supposed to be like this."

Anna wiped her face with the corner of the sheet. "No, it's not, Kevin. But I believe there's a purpose in all of this." Just like there's a purpose in my circumstances, she thought.

"Try to get some rest, Anna. Don't come to the clinic too early. I've asked Siyin to send another email to the patients. A colleague of mine will handle tomorrow's appointments. Dr. Cristina Lu. I'll stay here at the hospital."

"Do that, Kevin. Your father needs you, even if he doesn't show it."

A pause.

"Anna?"

"Yes, Kevin."

Another pause.

"I don't know what I'd do without you."

Without hesitation, she replied, "And I don't know what I'd do without you."

"Good night, Anna."

"Good night, Kevin."

Anna turned off her phone and the lamp. She closed her eyes and pulled the blanket up to her chin.

"We don't know what we'd do without you, Kevin." She placed her hand over her belly, and Maia answered with a gentle kick.

Chapter Forty-One

D r. Miller was discharged from the hospital. He hired a nurse, but Erica took over running her father's household. She handled the grocery shopping, hired a housekeeper, and even cooked for her father, who was convalescing in his king-size bed with a long scar on his chest beneath his silk pajama top.

Theo went along on a few visits and, according to what Erica told Anna, the old man let his guard down and even told his grandson a story.

Anna was cheered by the good news. She herself had wonderful things to share with the siblings about her father moving into her home. Maia would arrive in a few weeks. The latest ultrasound showed a healthy baby. Esther had gone to the appointment with Anna and was already on standby for when Maia announced it was time to come into the world. The two friends were cementing their bond with beach walks (good for the baby's health, according to Esther), visits to the other women in the family, including Grace, and long talks about single motherhood, a term Anna was starting to dispense with, since she was never truly alone.

Serge had adjusted well to life in his daughter's home. With Shyla's guidance, he changed some strategies so he could do things without help. On some nights of the week, he'd slip away to Kevin's house, and the two would spend a long time in the garage. Anna couldn't get either of them to say what they were up to. Erica said she heard the sound of a saw.

And it was on a beautiful Saturday afternoon that Maia came into the world. Esther was ready when Anna called to say her water had broken and the contractions were intensifying. Serge went along in Esther's car, while Kevin and Erica followed right behind. Theo stayed with Roberto and Jade.

Perhaps out of self-consciousness, Anna preferred that Kevin not enter the delivery room until Maia was born. Esther was the one who held her hand and wiped the sweat from her brow.

When Maia let out her first wail (so loud the doctor laughed), and the nurse had seen to Anna, Kevin and his father came in first. Esther excused herself and said she'd grab a coffee with Erica.

With hair plastered to her forehead and neck, Anna took her daughter in her arms. She breathed in her warm little bundle, wrapped in the hospital sheet. She didn't mind the tears mingling with her sweat.

Her father and Kevin stepped up to the bed. Anna wished she could snap a photo of their goofy grins. Serge moved closer, kissed his daughter's forehead, and spoke words of welcome to his granddaughter. He sat in the chair beside the bed and sighed.

Then it was Kevin's turn. Anna hadn't expected him to kiss her forehead, but she liked it when he leaned in so that his face was very close to hers.

"Anna, she's beautiful. Like her mother."

"Thank you, Kevin."

He went on, "Little Maia, may the God who made you and the stars watch over your every step."

"Amen," Anna and her father said.

Esther came back into the room with Erica. Anna closed her eyes, grateful to God for her big family.

Maia had arrived in the right place at the right time. No other spot on Earth could have been more perfect to welcome her beloved daughter.

In the weeks that followed, Anna settled into her new routine. Kevin gave her four months' leave—"nonnegotiable," as he told Anna when she insisted on returning to work. "You come back gradually as you arrange childcare. No pressure. Doctors orders," he had said. Dr. Cristina Lu, who had helped Kevin when his father had surgery, joined the clinic's medical staff. The experienced physician, who had retired the year before, told Kevin she couldn't stand being idle. So she offered to work a few hours a week to "keep busy and help Kevin." Meanwhile, Shyla and Alex took care of the addition to the clinic, to include a big room for occupational therapy.

Anna accepted Kevin's decision and took the opportunity to get to know her daughter better. The two would wake early and go outside to sit in the sun in the backyard. Autumn had arrived, but the sun still bathed Grace Harbor with its warmth. In the afternoons, mother and daughter napped while Serge went for walks with two friends from the condo. Between sleepless nights and more peaceful ones, mother and daughter found their rhythm.

For Maia's one-month birthday, Erica threw a little party at her house—really just an excuse to gather friends. Maia watched the bustle with her dark eyes wide open. Jade declared herself aunt to both Maia and Theo, and everyone agreed the title fit.

After Esther's family said their goodbyes to the tiny birthday girl, Erica made an announcement while putting the leftover cake into a container in the kitchen. Anna, seated at the table with Maia asleep in her arms, looked over at Kevin. He shrugged and mouthed, "No idea."

"Felipe invited me to dinner at his parents' house," Erica said, placing the container in the fridge.

Kevin wiped Theo's face with a napkin. "That's good, isn't it?"

"I can watch Theo for you," Anna offered.

Erica leaned against the sink. "That's the thing. He said he wants his parents to meet Theo. I'm thinking this visit is kind of serious." She gave a shy smile.

Kevin stepped closer to his sister. "It's not the visit that's serious. The man is serious. Inviting Theo means something very important."

"We've only gone out a few times," Erica said.

"And, as you just said, Felipe is wonderful," Anna added with a wink.

"That he is," Erica said, smiling.

"Then it's good that it's serious." Kevin ruffled his sister's hair.

"Then stop treating me like a child." Erica gave his arm a playful tap.

Kevin pulled her in and kissed the top of her head. "You'll always be my little sister. But you're a woman, a strong and beautiful woman."

"Ugh, you're such a sap." Erica kissed her brother's cheek, grabbed Theo by the hand, and the two disappeared down the hallway toward the bedroom.

Maia fussed in Anna's arms. Dressed in a yellow onesie, she puckered up as if she might cry, but then changed her mind.

Kevin sat down beside Anna. "You know what this celebration is missing?"

Anna looked at that familiar face she'd come to respect. She and her daughter were safe. Kevin had made that possible. God cared for them through him. "I don't think it's missing anything. I wasn't even expecting a party."

He stood. "That's where you're wrong. And what about Lola? She's jealous."

"You mean... a drive?" Anna's heart leapt with joy.

"Exactly." Kevin glanced toward the living room. "Let's take advantage of your dad being absorbed in that never-ending war movie and sneak out."

"Who am I to disappoint Lola?" Anna settled Maia into the car seat and fastened the three-point harness.

Kevin grabbed Maia's diaper bag and headed for the garage, Anna right behind.

"And the surprises don't end there," he said with a smile.

Anna secured the car seat in the middle and sat down. "Hmm, what are you plotting?"

"Just wait." He closed her door, walked around Lola, and climbed into the driver's seat.

Soon they were on the tree-lined road. Dry leaves danced in the wind, lit by Lola's headlights. Kevin turned on the music. Anna's favorite kind of outing was complete, with a soundtrack and everything.

"Ta-ta-ta-ra-ra," Kevin hummed.

"Ta-ta," Anna chimed in. In those moments, the world felt so much easier to face. It was more than a drive along Grace Harbor's road; it was a space voyage away from worries. It didn't solve any of her problems, but it gave Anna a way to recharge her batteries after a stressful day. Even so, this had been a good week—professionally and personally. Ending the night with Kevin and Maia under the starry sky was the cherry on a multi-layered cake that had been baking ever since she moved to Grace Harbor.

"Ta-ta-ta." Kevin turned the wheel and pulled into the clearing. He looked at Anna. "Stay here while I set things up." He hopped out and shut the door.

Anna twisted around to look through the rear window. Kevin tapped the glass and motioned for her to face forward again.

Maia whimpered. Anna checked the time on her phone. Not feeding time yet. "Shh, shh. First let's look at the starry sky and your sisters in the Pleiades."

"All set," Kevin said as he opened the door for Anna.

They settled onto the soft duvet in Lola's bed. A white cloth covered something in the corner.

Anna placed Maia's car seat beside her and tucked a little yellow blanket around it. "I'm curious. Is it a telescope?"

Kevin sat cross-legged and whisked the cloth away. "Congratulations to Maia."

Anna knelt and reached out to the wooden rocking horse. She ran her fingers over the caramel varnish. "It's beautiful, Kevin! When did you make it?"

"We made it. Your dad and I, but he doesn't want any credit. He said the gift is just from me. It isn't."

Anna inhaled the scent of wood. It brought back the memory of her father's garage, where he used to craft his pieces. She looked at Kevin. "Was it very hard for him?"

"On the contrary. He only needed my help with the power saw. Otherwise, he sanded and varnished it himself."

Anna threw her arms around Kevin's neck. "Thank you, thank you for everything." She felt his hesitant hands circle her waist. She pulled back. "You never stop surprising me."

His face grew serious in the moonlight. A tingling spread across Anna's shoulders and chin. She tried to pull her gaze from Kevin's, but couldn't. He drew her into his dilated pupils. Her soul seemed to float toward the two black holes in Kevin's eyes. She wanted to go in, search, understand his soul, pull it out and, joining it with hers, rise to the stars, orbit the moon, on a celestial journey.

"Anna," he whispered.

She came back to earth. "Kevin."

Maia shattered the spell with a heartfelt cry. Perhaps it wasn't the right time for heavenly journeys.

CHAPTER FORTY-TWO

Anna adjusted the blanket on her shoulder, making sure to cover both Maia's head and her own breast. Kevin, lying on his back in the truck bed, aimed the small vintage telescope toward the stars, giving Anna privacy to nurse her daughter.

"I have another gift," he said, without taking his eyes off the sky.

"You're spoiling Maia," Anna teased, pulling her red sweater back up and resting Maia on her shoulder, patting her gently on the back.

Kevin set the telescope aside and pulled a gift box from beneath the white cloth. He slid it toward Anna and motioned for her to hand Maia over. "I'm an expert at getting babies to burp."

Still under the lingering spell of their intergalactic journey, Anna smiled and passed Maia to him. She opened the box and found two books inside. Turning on her phone's flashlight, she said, "They're beautiful! Maia's first books."

Supporting the baby's head so it wouldn't tilt back, Kevin said,

"I thought she might like to learn about her sisters, the Pleiades. And may the Bible always be the light that guides her path."

Anna turned off the flashlight and hugged the books to her chest. Kevin had a way of drawing out every tender emotion she possessed. Watching him cradle her daughter on his shoulder moved her to tears. She took a deep breath.

"God won't let me go on holding this resentment toward Dalton," she said softly.

Maia burped, and Kevin laid her gently in his arms, covering her with the little blanket. He rocked her tenderly. "It's hard, isn't it?"

"Very. But I've decided not to paint a negative picture of Dalton for Maia. I'm sure he would've loved her unconditionally." Anna wiped her eyes with the back of her hand.

"Then tell her that love story," Kevin said, gazing at Maia. "Your healing will come through that. Children have this power to pass on love through their innocence. That's why Jesus said we must become like them."

Anna watched him hold Maia close to his chest, his dark sweater soft against her tiny form. Maia would be surrounded by love from every side, but she also needed to understand her earthly father's love. "How have things been with your dad?"

"The crusts are falling away," Kevin said quietly. "Mine, Erica's, and his. Theo has had a lot to do with it. My father confessed that he had a child before marrying my mother when Erica confronted him with Mom's notebook entry I told you about. He never acknowledged the boy, who later died of lymphoma as a teenager. All his anger toward me and Erica, really, it was his own guilt for never making peace with the child's mother. He actually looked her up recently, but she tore into him. I don't know exactly what she said, but he told me it was painful to hear the truth. He said he always felt accused by the way I helped Erica, that it reminded him of his own sin."

"But you and Erica didn't know. How could you accuse him?" Anna smoothed the pillows behind her back.

"The shoe still fits, even if you don't know you're wearing it," Kevin said. "Conscience accuses, and without forgiveness, the soul gets sick. Erica and I thought he was ill, and he was, just not in body. In his soul. Now he'll have to seek forgiveness from God and from himself. If my half-brother's mother never forgives him, he'll have to live with that too."

"Forgiveness should be simpler, don't you think?" Anna asked.

Kevin sighed, looking from the sky back to her. "If it were easy, I don't think we'd ever understand the forgiveness we've received from God for all our own sins."

Anna took off her glasses and rubbed her eyes. "I have a confession too, something I need forgiveness for."

"You?"

"When I came for the first interview, I thought about hiding my pregnancy."

Kevin rocked Maia gently. "But you didn't."

"No, but I considered deceiving you."

He scooted closer, Maia still in his arms, the quilt bunching beneath them in Lola's truck bed. "You don't need my forgiveness, Ana, only my eternal gratitude." He handed Maia back to her and lifted his eyes to the heavens. "It was all written in the stars."

CHAPTER FORTY-THREE

The bride entered triumphantly, walking down the aisle lined with white satin-covered chairs. The flower girl scattered red rose petals along the path toward the groom. Holding her father's arm, the bride smiled at the guests dressed elegantly while the musicians played the wedding march.

Anna held Maia's little hand as the girl stood on the chair, bouncing with excitement, her curls bobbing like springs.

"Erica looks so beautiful and radiant," Anna whispered to Kevin.

"She does," he replied, "but you're the most beautiful guest here."

Anna suddenly became aware of how her emerald-green gown hugged her figure. The pregnancy weight was gone, and she was finally beginning to enjoy her own body again—no more swollen feet, no more aching breasts, no more wild hormones. Correction: her emotions *were* running wild at that very moment, sitting beside Kevin in a navy-blue suit and crisp white shirt, front row, in the magnificent Grace Harbor Country Club ballroom.

"Elca!" Maia called out, and several guests smiled. Erica waved to the little girl, then turned her gaze back to her groom, Felipe, who waited for her beneath a canopy of white flowers.

When Dr. Vincent Miller handed his daughter to the groom, the guests took their seats. The pastor began to speak, but Anna couldn't focus on his words about love. Ever since that moonlit drive with Lola, when she'd opened her heart about forgiveness, Kevin had changed. He often looked at her at work or during family gatherings, as if he wanted to say something but always hesitated and turned away.

Those thoughts kept Anna awake many nights. If she confessed her feelings, would it ruin their friendship or their professional relationship?

The pastor's voice brought her back. "A man shall leave his father and mother..."

Kevin brushed his hair back behind his ear and rubbed his hands together. Anna pretended to smooth an invisible wrinkle on her long skirt, but her eyes couldn't leave his.

"Love is patient, it always trusts..."

The musicians drew a soft melody from the violins.

"These rings symbolize commitment..."

Violins again.

"...you may now kiss the bride."

The hall erupted in applause, and the sound of *bossa nova* filled the air.

Maia tugged on Anna's arm. "Mama, cake."

Anna blinked, waking from her daze. Kevin jumped up and scooped Theo into his arms. The guests began filing out behind the bride and groom and their wedding party.

Anna was immediately surrounded by her friends. Esther, Nina, and Jade gushed over her dress.

"You look like a celeb—cerebri..." Jade struggled for the word and looked to her mother for help.

"Celebrity," Esther helped with a smile.

Grace approached with Anna's father at her side. "Jade's right. You look like a celebrity."

Anna pressed her silver clutch. She wished for her glasses; her contacts were starting to burn her eyes. Too hard, looking like a celebrity. She missed her scrubs.

"Mama, cake," Maia tugged again.

Esther scooped the little girl up. "Let's go get some cake."

The women drifted out with the other guests, leaving Anna alone with her father.

"You look beautiful. Always will," he said softly.

Anna looked at his face, lined with time. Serge looked handsome in his dark suit, though his hands trembled a little more these days. "And you look so handsome!"

He smiled. "It's time to move forward. You're still so young."

What did he mean, move forward? Look for another job? Another town? "I'm happy in Grace Harbor, Dad."

Serge squeezed her hand and shook his head. "I'm talking about Kevin."

Her eyes widened. "What about him?"

"That man is hopelessly in love with you."

Anna's hands turned icy, as if she'd plunged them into a bucket of ice water. Her heart pounded, her knees went weak. "What are you saying?"

"You two are the only ones who don't see it. The whole town of Grace Harbor knows. I wouldn't be surprised if even Maia has noticed." He patted her shoulder and walked off down the aisle, leaving Anna alone in the empty hall.

She looked around at the lilies, the satin, the candles. Erica had just walked out of here a married woman. Theo now had a father in his life. Maia already had a father figure—two, actually: her grandfather and Kevin. That didn't mean he was in love with her.

Anna shook her arms and marched down the hall. Her father didn't know what he was talking about.

***

Kevin scanned the ballroom impatiently, weaving between guests balancing plates of hors d'oeuvres. He couldn't spot her among the sea of people gathered around the long banquet table.

Blue dresses, red, yellow—no green. He couldn't wait any longer. He needed to see Anna. Maia was being passed from arm to arm among Anna's friends. Was Anna not feeling well? Her face had looked pale during the ceremony. Had he made her uncomfortable with his staring? He hadn't been prepared for the jolt he felt when she walked in wearing that green gown. After months of seeing her in scrubs or maternity clothes, he was used to her casual style. But tonight, with her hair pinned up (what did women call that style?), she seemed taller, graceful, breathtaking. And yet, her eyes, those gentle, thoughtful eyes, were still the same.

The same Anna who'd charmed him at their first meeting, when her skirt button popped off and she tried to hide it under her shoe. The same Anna who'd fought through morning sickness with paper tissues in hand. The same one who'd taken him to Lola after he'd cut his hair in defiance of his father. Anna, who could talk about deep things with kindness in her gaze, who sought forgiveness despite betrayal, who wanted to teach her daughter that everyone had some good in them.

The *bossa nova* song Erica had chosen for the reception floated through the air. The musicians Kevin had hired as a wedding gift were playing, their fingers flying over piano and guitar strings, the soft percussion tapping out the unmistakable rhythm of Tom Jobim and João Gilberto.

Kevin loosened his tie. He caught his breath the moment he spotted the green dress. Weaving through the crowd, he reached Anna and gently took her wrist.

"May I have this dance?" he asked, pulling her close.

Anna molded against him, cheek to cheek.

"Ta-ta-ra-ta," he whispered, his heart racing like a galloping horse.

Kevin guided Anna away from the crowd, their faces touching, swaying in time with the music.

"Anna."

"Kevin," she breathed near his ear.

He drew back slightly and brushed her cheek with his hand. "Come with me."

They crossed the glowing mezzanine. Kevin opened the French doors and led her onto the terrace.

Music pulsed from the ballroom, wrapping around them. The terrace overlooked a lawn with a fountain in the center. Kevin took her hand.

"Kevin?" Anna stepped closer.

He ran a hand through his hair. "I can't wait any longer, Anna."

"Wait for what?"

He pressed his fingers to his forehead. "To tell you that you're the most extraordinary woman I've ever known. The day of your interview, I fell for you. Then I had to fall *out* of love because you were pregnant, and then I fell right back in. Again, and again, and again. Do you know the chaos you've caused in my head, in my heart?" He dropped her hand. What had he done? Why did Anna's face look so serious?

Slowly, she took his hands in hers. "You confuse me too," she said with a soft, trembling smile.

Kevin stepped closer. "I've lived recklessly before, without thinking of consequences. I'm wiser now." He gave a nervous laugh. "Anna, I've thought about this a lot—"

She tilted her head. "Thought about what?"

"That I want to be your husband and Maia's father."

Anna took another step forward until they were face-to-face. "Kevin, I loved you first for your kindness to me and my baby. I then loved you for your wisdom and the way you cared for Erica and Theo. I also loved you as a friend and as a partner at work. But now, I love you as a man—the man of my life."

Kevin swept her into his arms and kissed her. All the kisses he'd held back over the past year and a half poured out now, sealing the truth of his love. Anna returned his kisses with the same depth and devotion. When their lips finally parted, Kevin held her close and began to dance with her to the melody drifting from the ballroom.

"Ta-ta-ta," she whispered in his ear.

"*Bossa nova* will never mean the same thing to me again," he murmured. "It's *our* rhythm now." He kissed her cheek as they swayed together.

She stopped for a moment and looked up at him. "You're the man God put in my path so He could bless me and Maia."

"You're the woman God placed in my life to give me balance. Whatever we build together will stand on the rock."

Just then, Jade appeared at the door and tapped on the glass. Kevin opened it.

"Erica and Felipe are looking for you two! Enough with the hugging—come on!"

Kevin laughed, and he and Anna followed Jade back inside. Hand in hand, they entered the ballroom. Erica spotted them and ran through the crowd, leaping into her brother's arms.

"You two are finally together! I knew it, I *knew* it! You couldn't stand the suspense anymore, could you?" She threw her arms in the air and twirled toward her new husband, who was dancing with Theo. "Love is patient—but you two pushed it to the limit!"

Kevin drew Anna onto the dance floor among the other guests. "Guess we'd better fix that mistake."

"About waiting?" she laughed, her cheek against his.

"How about a wedding on the next full moon?" he whispered.

Anna laughed. "Erica warned me you were a werewolf. When's the next full moon?"

He looked into her eyes. "Two weeks."

Anna ran her fingers through his curls. "I'm already counting the days and the stars."

The music swelled around them. Wrapped in each other's arms, Anna and Kevin floated across the floor—two hearts on a journey written in the universe.